In the Family Way

In the Family Way

A Novel

Laney Katz Becker

HARPER

AN IMPRINT OF HARPERCOLLINS*PUBLISHERS*

IN THE FAMILY WAY. Copyright © 2025 by Laney Katz Becker. All rights reserved. Printed in the United States of America. No part of this book may be used or reproduced in any manner whatsoever without written permission except in the case of brief quotations embodied in critical articles and reviews. For information, address HarperCollins Publishers, 195 Broadway, New York, NY 10007.

HarperCollins books may be purchased for educational, business, or sales promotional use. For information, please email the Special Markets Department at SPsales@harpercollins.com.

FIRST EDITION

Designed by Michele Cameron
Interior art © venimo/Shutterstock

Library of Congress Cataloging-in-Publication Data
Names: Becker, Laney Katz, author.
Title: In the family way: a novel / Laney Katz Becker.
Description: First edition. | New York, NY: HarperCollins Publishers, 2025.
Identifiers: LCCN 2024033445 (print) | LCCN 2024033446 (ebook) | ISBN 9780063423244 (hardcover) | ISBN 9780063423268 (trade paperback) | ISBN 9780063423251 (ebook)
Subjects: LCGFT: Novels.
Classification: LCC PS3552.E25616 I58 2025 (print) | LCC PS3552.E25616 (ebook) | DDC 813/.54—dc23/eng/20240724
LC record available at https://lccn.loc.gov/2024033445
LC ebook record available at https://lccn.loc.gov/2024033446

25 26 27 28 29 LBC 5 4 3 2 1

Dedicated to my sisters
Sheila Rothstein & Marci Ungar

When we were young and used to bicker with one another, our dad, of blessed memory, always told us to be nice to each other because "how many sisters do you have? One day, they will be your best friends."

He was right.

(Can't you just hear him now? "Of course I was right. I'm your father!")

Women's progress has been a collective effort.

—GLORIA STEINEM

Well-behaved women rarely make history.

—LAUREL THATCHER ULRICH

You are a light. You are the light. Never let anyone—any person or any force—dampen, dim or diminish your light. Study the path of others to make your way easier and more abundant.

—JOHN LEWIS, *ACROSS THAT BRIDGE: A VISION FOR CHANGE AND THE FUTURE OF AMERICA*

Mid-November
1965

Miss Betsy Ann Eubanks

The housemother from Raven House is already backing out of the driveway by the time I reach the front door. I'm here to babysit and to help with some light housekeeping. In exchange, I get food and a place to live for the next four months, assuming all goes as planned.

I'm unsure whether to knock or ring the bell, but the door swings open before I have to decide. The woman standing in front of me is much younger than I imagined. And way prettier. When the house-mother said Dr. and Mrs. Berg have a seventeen-month-old little girl, I got the idea that a doctor's wife would look like a fuddy-duddy schoolteacher. Man, was I wrong. Mrs. Berg looks like she just stepped out of a fashion magazine. She has a hairdo that's high on top, and wears a blue velvety headband that disappears behind her ears. Her headband matches her shift dress, and both of those match her pale blue eyes. She's so glamorous, like a movie star.

"Hello there. You must be Betsy. I'm Lily. Uh, Mrs. Berg, uh, Lily Berg. Please come in."

Everything about Mrs. Berg is the opposite of my mom. Mrs. Berg is obviously younger than my mom, and she's wearing makeup, which my mom only does on special occasions. She's also tall and looks thin, but it's hard to tell because her dress is pretty full. My mom is not much taller than me—meaning she's probably five foot two—and not to be mean, but my mom is sort of roly-poly.

When I step through the front door, my first thought is that the Bergs must be rich. Their house is bigger than mine in Michigan, and a quick glance around reveals furniture that doesn't have any rips or tears.

Mrs. Berg interrupts what my mom calls "nosying around."

"Let me show you to your room so you can put down your things." She gestures at the trash bag I'm grasping.

"Groovy." The bag isn't heavy; it's just bulky, mostly because I'm holding it from the bottom so it doesn't split and dump all my stuff all over the floor.

Mrs. Berg leads me through the small entry hall, pausing in front of a closet. She takes my jacket and hangs it alongside the other coats. Over the coming days, I learn the terms "entry hall," "utility room," and "front hall closet" when Mrs. Berg takes me through the house, showing me around. "The house is a split-level," she says now, gesturing to let me know I should follow her down the stairs. As we near the last step, she points to her right. "That's the family room." Then she turns left. "And this is the utility room and where you'll stay." It doesn't even have a door.

There is a twin-sized, roll-away cot, which is already set up and made with a pillow, sheets, and a blanket. It's next to the washing machine. On the other side of the cot is a three-drawer dresser. An alarm clock, which is on top of the dresser, shows the time but also has a built-in radio. Mrs. Berg makes a big deal about it, mentioning the radio is both AM and FM. There's also a contraption that looks like a portable closet, only it's on wheels. There are two dresses hanging on the bar. "Those are from our last unwed mother," Mrs. Berg says. "Her water broke a couple days before she was supposed to go back to Raven House, so everything was rush-rush and she left these behind."

She pauses and looks at me. I feel like I'm supposed to say something, but I don't know what, so I just nod.

"When I called Raven House, the housemother told me that Kathy didn't want them back. She was our previous unwed mother. Kathy."

Man, Mrs. Berg sure talks a lot.

"Groovy." I don't know anything about broken water, but I'm happy to have the dresses since some of my clothes already don't fit me.

Mrs. Berg puts her hand on the rack, and it slides—and just keeps going until it's stopped by a thing that looks like a fire hydrant. "The floor isn't quite level." She rolls the dresses back toward the cot and then uses her foot to press a doohickey down by one of the wheels that locks it into place.

"What's that?" I point to the hydrant.

"Oh, it's just a sump pump. When we get a lot of rain, it keeps the basement from flooding."

Dr. and Mrs. Berg might have a house that's bigger than mine, but at least we don't have floors that go downhill or a basement that floods.

"I'm sorry we can't give you a real room," Mrs. Berg says, spreading open her arms. "But it's only a three-bedroom house."

Mrs. Berg goes on to explain the setup. Obviously she and Dr. Berg require one bedroom, and their baby, Jo-Jo, needs another. Why couldn't I have the third? As if reading my mind, Mrs. Berg says, "We're turning the empty room into a big-girl room for Jo-Jo. That way, when the baby comes, we can move Jo-Jo into that room and put the new baby into Jo-Jo's nursery." "Nursery" is yet another uncommon word that will soon worm its way into my everyday vocabulary.

Mrs. Berg pats her stomach. "Yep. I'm expecting. *Sur-prise, sur-prise, sur-prise.*" Her imitation of Gomer Pyle is good, and I laugh.

"Don't mind me," she says. "I watch too much television. But isn't it exciting? We're both going to be expecting at the same time. I'm only a little over a month behind you."

Mrs. David Berg

(Lily)

Today is my turn to host canasta. Our group consists of me and three other women who live in the neighborhood. I could describe them in no special order, except why not put my best friend first? That's Rebecca Hudson, who goes by Becca. The others are Sarah Bloom and Robin Thompson. We meet every week for girl talk and to play cards.

We're all housewives, and about a year ago, someone had the great idea to get together on a regular basis. We wanted to do something that didn't involve all the household chores we're already responsible for. That meant nothing even tangentially related to grocery shopping, vacuuming, dusting, mopping, laundry, ironing, making the beds, doing the dishes, or tidying up after our husbands and children. It also meant nothing related to baking or cooking, like recipe swaps. Becca said she would only agree if we did something where she could get off her feet, so that meant window-shopping was also out. I suggested cards, and since Sarah and I both already knew how to play canasta and the other two agreed that it sounded fun, we taught them how to play. Now, between cutting, shuffling, and taking our talons, we catch up with each other, and exchange neighborhood gossip, along with anything else that might be of interest.

My husband, David, calls the canasta group my "cast of characters," and he's not wrong, especially when it comes to Becca. She lives three doors down, on the opposite side of the street from us. She's a few years older than me, but when we met, we just clicked. She's full of energy and has the best sense of humor. Becca has the most flexible schedule, since her three boys are all in elementary school until 3:30 p.m. every day, to which she says, "Hallelujah!" Becca's lived in the neighborhood the longest, and was a great resource when we first moved in. She, like me, got married right after high school, but that's where the similarities between us end.

Becca married her high school sweetheart; David was already in medical school by the time we met. Becca started her family right away; David had his hands full with his medical training, and money was tight, so we waited a couple years before having Jo-Jo.

Though she always wears a wristwatch, Becca is never on time; I'm always punctual. She always wears a bunch of bangle bracelets, mostly metal, but sometimes she'll add a plastic one to match her outfit. I love accessories, especially jewelry, but I don't stop with just bracelets and a wristwatch. Becca always looks disheveled, even after she's just been at the beauty shop, whereas I take great pride in my appearance and always make sure I'm in clean clothes by the time David comes home from the hospital, no matter how many times Jo-Jo has spit up on me that day. Perhaps the most distinctive thing about Becca, however, is how often she mentions her certainty that at least one of her boys will wind up in juvie. Becca claims she's got very good reasons for her habitual tardiness and her unkempt appearance . . . It's because she's trying to keep her boys out of juvie! Like I said, she's got a great sense of humor. But she's not wrong—her boys are a handful. I've often joked with her that between all their shenanigans, which more often than once have resulted in stitches and broken bones, it's possible she spends more time at the hospital than my husband.

But Becca is the woman to ask if you need something. She's the one who told me about the grocery stores and filling stations that give out S&H green stamps, which I'm collecting for a free set of new drinking glasses and a matching pitcher. She also told me about a beauty shop that's nearby where they can do a wash and set and have me on my way without taking up the whole day. Becca is just someone who knows things.

Sarah Bloom and her husband, Joel, moved in roughly two years ago, and live immediately next door to us. You can learn a lot about a couple if you catch enough glimpses of what comes out of their moving truck. I wasn't snooping, no matter what Becca says. But as the van pulled away, I already knew they didn't have any children and that the lady of the house was roughly my age, but I had no idea that they'd moved from Indianapolis to Akron because her husband, who's an engineer, took a job with Goodyear. "I don't know a soul here," she said as I handed her a plate of freshly baked peanut butter cookies. I thought I detected a tremble in her lower lip. She was pretty, with large green eyes lined in black liner that tipped up at the corners. I didn't want to be too forward, but I knew it wouldn't be long before I'd ask her to show me how she did it; my eyeliner always looks so shaky. Sarah had curtain bangs and her dark brown hair fell a couple inches past her shoulders. It was back-combed just a bit to give her some height on top. Very pretty indeed. And stylish. "I love your outfit," I said. Sarah was wearing culottes with a matching headband. Both were made from the same floral print.

"Thank you. I made it."

"Really? You could have fooled me; it looks store-bought," I said. "You're really good. When did you learn to sew?"

"I started at school in home ec, but I didn't get serious about it until close to two years ago, a little after Joel and I got married." She bit her lower lip, something I'd later learn was something Sarah often did when she was debating about how much she wanted to say about something or another. "We don't have kids, as you probably noticed, so sewing gives me something to do after I've finished my housekeeping chores."

Of course I was dying to ask whether she was planning to have children, but I'd only just met her and didn't want her to think I was pushy. "Well, I can't sew at all," I said, steering the conversation away from kids. "When a button falls off my husband's shirt, I have to take it to the tailor." I smiled, wondering why I was confessing to something that even my husband didn't know.

She arched her perfectly penciled brow, as if she thought I was joking.

"I'm serious."

"Well, I like creating things," she said.

I removed the Saran Wrap covering the cookies that I'd baked while the movers unloaded the truck. "Does this count as *creating things*?"

She gave me the most heartfelt smile, looked down at the cookies, and promptly started crying. "I'm sorry." She balanced the plate in one hand and swiped at her tears with the other. "It's just sort of scary, you know?" I watched as her perfect eyeliner melted away and started its voyage down her cheeks. "It's so hard, starting over in a brand-new place."

I put an arm around Sarah's shoulder and assured her that it would all be fine. That the neighborhood was filled with some lovely housewives, and it would be my pleasure to introduce her around. "You're so sweet," she said, wiping away the last of her tears. "And in exchange, I'll teach you how to sew on a button. And after a lesson with me, if you still can't do it, I'll sew on the button myself. How's that sound?"

It sounded like I was going to adore my new neighbor.

Our foursome for canasta is completed by Robin Thompson. Technically, she's not a neighbor. She and her husband own the house behind ours, on an entirely different street. But our backyards adjoin one another, and she has five-year-old twins, a boy and a girl, who often play on the swing set in our backyard, left over from the people David bought the house from. I sometimes think Robin is really a hippie who's dressed up and disguised to look like a housewife. She likes to talk about current events and whatever protest marches are going on around Akron or Cleveland. One way to get her really fired up is to ask her about the Vietnam War or civil rights. I truly don't understand how she finds time to read the newspaper and watch the news and stay on top of such things when she's a housewife and a mother, but she does. A while ago, she stopped asking us if we wanted to go with her to the marches and rallies. Now she just tells us she's going and waits to see if anyone asks to go with her. We never do.

Roughly a quarter mile behind the Thompsons are the railroad tracks. About four or five times a day, freight trains pass through. The contents are a mystery, except for the coal—we can see the black mounds in the open cars. When we initially moved in, I found the blasting horn of the trains loud and disruptive. Becca assured me I'd get used to it, and I offered the same assurances to Sarah when she arrived. Now I hardly even notice. Robin says her kids, however, are completely tuned in to the train whistle, and as soon as they hear the first blast, they each yell out their guesses about whether the caboose will be red or green. "One of the older kids in the neighborhood told the twins that when you hear the horn you're supposed to guess the color of the caboose. Then, while the train is passing through, you make a silent wish. By the time the caboose arrives, if you guessed the right color, your wish will come true."

"Does it work?" I asked Robin, only part joking.

Robin is twenty-six. She met her husband, Harry, when they were both in college, and soon after, she dropped out to get married. Harry finished school, and they moved into a dormitory housing for married students. He went on to law school and got his JD, while Robin got her PhT (Putting Husband Through) by working as a secretary. Of course, when she got pregnant, she was fired, but it was okay because by then Harry had a job. The other thing to know about Robin is that she's a natural blonde, unlike Becca, who has to dye her hair. I, like Sarah, am a natural brunette, but sometimes, when I see the Clairol commercial on TV that says "Blondes have more fun," I'm tempted to find out whether it's true. But David says he likes my dark hair because it makes my eyes look so blue, and he's the one who counts.

WE PLAY CANASTA EVERY TUESDAY, and meet at noon, except for Becca, who is always at least a few minutes late. Even though we meet at lunchtime, we decided that whoever is hosting only has to provide snacks, not a full meal, because we all spend enough time in the kitchen as it is. So, everyone knows to have an early lunch on Tuesdays. It was my turn to have the girls over two weeks ago, but I swapped with Becca since I couldn't get a sitter. "Our new unwed mother comes in a couple days," I told them. "So, if you give me just two more weeks, I'll be the hostess with the most-est."

I wonder if this qualifies as "the most-est" as I scurry around, unfolding collapsible tray tables and setting down snacks of peanuts and bridge mix, along with an ashtray for Becca and Sarah, since they both smoke.

I don't want to ask Betsy for help, because right now, I want her sole focus on Jo-Jo. I'm trying to be sympathetic and remind myself that it took a couple weeks for our last unwed mother from Raven House to settle in, but Betsy is so green. Unlike Kathy, our previous girl, who was the oldest of four kids and did a lot of babysitting before coming to us, Betsy is an only child and, from what I can tell, never changed a diaper before last week. I had to show her how to put her hand between the cloth and Jo-Jo's skin so she didn't prick my little angel with the diaper pin. Sadly for Jo-Jo, I only realized that Betsy needed teaching after the damage was done. Once Jo-Jo stopped screaming and was ensconced in a new, clean, dry diaper, covered by a pair of rubber pants, I brought Betsy up to speed on the diaper service. "They drop off clean diapers and take away the dirty ones every Wednesday."

"Groovy."

"So, when you change Jo-Jo, put the wet diapers directly into the diaper pail." I pointed across the nursery. "If it's dirty, it needs to be washed out first." I gathered up the soiled diaper and told Betsy to follow me into the bathroom. Standing over the toilet, I unfolded the diaper as pieces of poo fell into the bowl. "I typically dunk it into the toilet a couple times, just for good measure," I said as I demonstrated. "Finally, wring it out and take it back to the diaper pail in Jo-Jo's room." Then I pushed Betsy aside and vomited into the toilet. "Sorry. Morning sickness. It sometimes just sneaks up on me," I said before thoroughly washing my hands so I could cup them under the faucet to rinse out my mouth.

"I don't miss that," Betsy said. "My sickness was all gone by the time I got to Raven House."

I know it's crazy, but it wasn't until that moment that it struck me: Even though Betsy and I are in the same boat and will be going through our pregnancies together, we are rowing in completely different directions.

Mrs. Marty Seigel

(Rose)

I want to meet my sister's new unwed mother, and I haven't seen my niece, Jo-Jo, since last week, so I decide to drop by Lily's house after school. I drive a little over the speed limit, hoping to get there before her canasta game ends so I can say hello to her friends, who, slowly but surely, are becoming my friends, too. In fact, since I got married last year, they've started inviting me and Marty to their neighborhood parties.

When I arrive, I don't bother to knock; I just announce myself with a loud hello. As I squirm out of my coat, I bypass the front hall closet and head immediately into the living room, where I toss my jacket over the couch, being careful not to dislodge the clear plastic slipcover. Lily's neighbor and best friend, Becca—her best friend who is not her sister, that is—is offering to help with cleanup.

"Absolutely not," Lily says. "Go home and rest. I've got everything under control."

"I can help with dishes and stuff," I say as Sarah, Becca, and Lily offer me hellos. "Why are you so tired, Becca? Are the boys acting up again?"

"Not any more than usual," she says.

Sarah then points to Becca. "She should rest because . . . she's got a bun in the oven! Isn't that exciting?" Sarah's smile is wide, but there's something about it that seems like she could go from smiling to weeping any second. It makes me think that maybe Lily was right when she speculated that Sarah and Joel were having troubles getting pregnant. Except my sister didn't say that. She avoids using the P-word and says things like "I think they're having difficulty starting their family," or "She's not expecting yet, and I think they're trying." This is because my sister *is* the P-word, if that word is "prim" or "proper" or "prudish" or "prissy."

Lily is not just my sister, she is also my best friend, so I don't point out her prudishness to be mean, or even to be critical. It's just part—a big part—of who she is. Mom named Lily and me after flowers, but we're different in many ways. She's two years older, but she seems much more. Maybe it's because she's already a mother. Or perhaps it's because our mom died when I was twelve, and Lily assumed the grown-up role and stepped into her shoes. Or it's possible it's because Lily got married right after high school and I went to college, which opened my eyes to a lot of different types of people who weren't like me and didn't grow up like me. But whatever the reason, if there even is a reason, I lost that sense of being all prim and proper, if I ever had it at all, and Lily? Lily is just Lily. Dependable, loving, kind, sweet, but oh so prudish.

Sarah and Joel moved next door to David and Lily the year before I got married, so if Lily's correct, that means they've been trying to get pregnant for at least two years, but maybe even as far back as when they lived in Indianapolis.

When month after month passed and there was no announcement that they were going to be a family of three, Lily began to wonder. "They've been married almost four years already, and he's got a good job. What are they waiting for?" She once asked me if I thought she should mention that her husband, David, might be able to help, since he's an OB-GYN, but before I even had a chance to answer, Lily decided it wasn't a good idea. "It would be too weird having him examine one of my friend's private parts, don't you think?"

I almost said that having my sister, who at the time was almost twenty-five, call a woman's vagina her "private parts" was what was so weird, but I refrained.

"I can't exactly ask her outright if they're trying, can I?" Lily asked.

Knowing how much I hate it when Lily bugs me about when Marty and I are going to start our family, I didn't hesitate. "No, Lily. You cannot ask her! If she wants to talk about it with you, she will. She knows where to find you. She is also well aware of what David does for a living, and if she wants his help, she knows where to find him, too." Fortunately, that put the kibosh on Lily's wondering.

Now I look at Sarah. *Is* she happy about Becca's pregnancy? I can't get a good read on her. However, a quick look at Becca tells me she is not at all happy about it. "Becca?"

She offers a long, audible exhale. "It's true. I've got an oops baby." She puts her hands on her belly, causing her army of bracelets to jingle.

"That's it," Sarah says, seemingly unaware that the mother-to-be is as miserable as I've ever seen Becca. "I have a great idea of a name for your baby. If it's a girl, you can name her Daisy. You know. Because of her being an oopsie-*daisy* baby. Isn't that cute?"

Becca offers a tight-lipped smile, and I try to telepathically tell Sarah to stop talking or at least change the subject.

I walk over to give Becca a hug, which is less congratulatory and more sympathetic. It doesn't matter. She's clearly a woman in need of a hug. I don't feel the slightest roundness to her waist, so she must be early on. That's when a visibly pregnant girl emerges from upstairs.

"Peace," I say, flashing my fingers into a V. "You must be Betsy. I'm Lily's sister, Rose."

She returns the peace sign and smiles.

Sarah turns toward Betsy. "We all just learned that Mrs. Hudson is pregnant. It'll be her fourth!" Maybe Sarah is genuinely happy;

her excitement seems real, but still, how can she be so oblivious to Becca's mood?

"Groovy," Betsy says. "Four is a lot of babies, Mrs. Hudson."

"Every baby is a blessing," Sarah says, placing her hands, one over the other, just beneath her clavicle bones.

"Yes, it is indeed a lot of babies," Becca says. "Though it's certainly not something I planned on. Betsy, you, of all people, understand that, don't you, dear?"

There's a sudden silence, even from Sarah, whose effervescence over Becca's pregnancy seems to have finally quelled.

Becca's face is pale. "I'm sorry, Betsy. That was unkind, and I have no right to take it out on you. It's just all still so new and it wasn't something I was expecting." Becca gives a wry laugh. "No pun intended."

"No sweat," Betsy says and turns toward my sister. "Mrs. Berg, I was wondering if you wanted help cleaning up. Jo-Jo is still napping."

"Darn it," I say. "I was hoping to see the little munchkin."

"Betsy, it's very kind of you to offer to help," Lily says. "But you need your rest, too. In fact, whenever Jo-Jo is napping, you should do the same. I insist."

Betsy doesn't need to be told twice, and disappears down the stairs into the basement, once again uttering that it's nice to meet me.

I wait for Sarah and Becca to leave. "I guess I missed Robin. She's not pregnant, too, is she?" I don't give my sister a chance to answer. "I mean, between you and Becca and Betsy all . . ." I use a sweeping gesture in front of my stomach to indicate a pregnancy.

My sister laughs. "No. Robin is without child, at least as far as I know. Speaking of, when do you plan on joining the mothers-to-be sorority?"

I knew we'd get around to this, because somehow we always do. But I finally got smart and prepared a response. "Last time we talked about it, Marty said he was due for a promotion, and if we wanted our baby sleeping in a crib and not inside a dresser drawer, we should probably wait a while longer."

"That husband of yours is a barrel of laughs," she says. "But I can't argue with his logic. Having a baby is expensive, and you'd have to leave your teaching job once you start showing, so he's got to make enough to support both of you and, of course, the baby."

"Exactly. And you know I love my job. In the meantime, Marty and I are having lots of fun practicing."

"Rose!"

I watch Lily's neck turn pale and then pink and then red. Soon the colors move into her face. "What? Is my sister mortified to talk about sex, or is my sister mortified to talk about sex being fun? No. No way. My sister is mortified to hear me even say the word." And just because I know it's true, I repeat it multiple times. "Sex. Sex. Sex. Sex." I watch the hues in my sister's face fluctuate all over again.

"You're having too much fun, Rose. You should be nicer to your only sister."

I ignore her attempt to make me stop. "Oh man, Lily. We are living through a sexual revolution, or haven't you heard?"

"Oh, I've heard." Her color still hasn't returned to normal. "Just promise me you won't wait too long to have a baby. I mean, you're going to want more than one and . . ."

"Yes, I know. You want your kids to have cousins who are close in age," I say, doing my best imitation of my sister. "So, not to change the subject, but to change the subject, tell me about Betsy."

Lily replaces the last of her snack tables into the holder and rolls it into the corner. "Betsy is not exactly what I was expecting, but I'm not sure what exactly I was expecting, if that makes sense. I can't tell if she's shy, or whether she's just not really talkative, or maybe she simply needs more time, but she's pretty quiet. When she does speak, she loves the word 'groovy.'"

I laugh. "I noticed."

"So far, I've learned she's an only child, and she seems to have grown up in a very conservative home. One thing I found out the hard way is that she doesn't have a clue about how to care for a baby."

"*Oy vey.*"

"*Oy vey iz mir!* Also, from what I've been able to suss out, I'm not entirely sure she understands how her body works."

"Well, obviously she figured it out." I shimmy my shoulders. "Hubba-hubba."

"Rose!" My sister laughs hard and cradles the paunch of her pregnant belly, which is actually more than a paunch, even though she's only a few months along. "But seriously. Betsy asked me if it was okay if she kept her monthly supplies in the bathroom or if I preferred that she keep them in her bedroom. I really don't think she understands that she won't be needing them."

"That is so sad. It's 1965, for God's sake. How does she not know?"

"Just remember, dearest one, not everyone is as lucky as you to have a perfectly wonderful older sister who could tell you all about the birds and the bees. When Mom explained it all to me, I thought she was going to have a heart attack, the way she kept hemming and hawing, trying to find the right words. There was a lot of talk about 'private parts' and where 'supplies' were kept. I don't know who was more relieved when it was over, but I figured it had to be her because when she stopped talking, she said something like 'I'm glad that's over. Now when it's time, you can tell your sister!'"

"She did not."

Lily crosses her heart using her index finger. "Swear."

"I'm not gonna lie. You really are the best big sister."

Lily rolls her eyes. "Okay. What do you want?"

"Nothing." My turn to use my index finger to cross my heart. "I swear. I just dropped by to see the munchkin and to meet Betsy. I can return to my childless abode feeling secure in the fact that the munchkin is getting her beauty rest and I've now met Betsy."

"I didn't mean to complain about her, really, I didn't." Lily smooths the front of her freshly pressed dress. Without question, there's definitely a roundness to her that wasn't there last month. "I appreciate the help, and even though she needs to be trained, she's got a really gentle nature, and Jo-Jo can sense it, too. She already adores Betsy, I can tell."

"She's lucky to have you," I say.

"Who? Betsy or Jo-Jo?" Lily smiles and offers a wink.

Betsy isn't the only one with a gentle nature. For as long as I can remember, whenever I've felt alone or scared, I've turned to Lily, who has a knack for making me feel better. I'm fairly sure it's not just me, either. It's evident to me that, even though Becca's older and clearly more experienced on the childcare front, she and my sister are close. Even Sarah, who's the newest one in the neighborhood, admires Lily; I can just tell. Of the canasta group, I know Robin the least well, but it seems my sister is the linchpin of a nice little clique of girlfriends.

Lily is not just kind, either; she's also incredibly resourceful. Once, when I got a D on my report card, I went crying to Lily, and she fixed it by turning my almost-failing grade into a B before I showed it to our parents. Lily did it using a special pen that she bought from the drugstore with her babysitting money. Of course she made me pay her back, but she also gave me the pep talk I needed to start paying attention in school, no matter how bored I was or how stupid I found the homework—otherwise, she said, she'd tell our parents about my real grade. Then she checked up on me to make sure I was fulfilling my part of the bargain. Mom and Dad had no idea. *Lord, what fools these mortals be*, which I only know comes from Shakespeare's *A Midsummer Night's Dream* thanks to Lily, because without her, I wouldn't have made it to Kent State, where I not only discovered but also fell in love with Shakespeare. The bottom line is that Lily encouraged me to follow my dreams. She reminded me that from the time I was in kindergarten, I used to line up my dolls and play school with them, with me always assuming the role of teacher.

It was Lily who convinced me that I'm capable and smart. And when Mom died, Lily became both my sister and my mother. Of course, at the time, I didn't always like her telling me what to do, but now I'm so grateful that she looked out for me.

"Well, let's get this place cleaned up before your husband comes home," I say. We clear the game table of the cards, score sheet, and card holder and load all the dirty dishes into the sink. "You want to wash or dry?"

When Lily picks up the dishcloth, I have my answer and slip my hands into the yellow rubber gloves, plug the sink, squeeze a few drops of Joy into the water and wait for the sink to fill with suds.

Miss Betsy Ann Eubanks

I was living at Raven House for nearly two weeks when the house-mother asked to see me and said she had found me a family. *I already have a family* was my first thought, but I knew better than to say it out loud. "A doctor and his wife. They have a little one," the housemother said. "She's seventeen months." When I didn't respond, the woman went on. "You'd be their second unwed mother. The last one lived with them for the last four and a half months of her pregnancy, and it worked out so well they've decided to do it again." When I still didn't respond, the housemother tightened her lips and stared at me.

"Can't I just stay here?" I asked.

She gave me the fakest of fake smiles. "Now, dear, why would you want to do that when you can live with a nice family? Besides, Raven House is not meant to be permanent housing; it's just a place for girls to stay while we look for a family who's willing to take them. We wouldn't have room to keep all the wayward girls here the whole time."

Since my mom dropped me off, I'd met a couple girls who'd been at Raven House for months. That seemed pretty permanent to me. When I mentioned this fact, the housemother explained it was because they were too far along when they first arrived at Raven House. "No one wants to bring an unwed mother into their home only to have her turn around and leave a month or so later. And that happened with a handful of the unwed mothers who are here now. They got here too late, but that's not the case with you. You have your mother to thank for that, and I hope you express your gratitude the next time you write to her."

"Yes, ma'am."

"Let me explain the facts of life to you, young lady. All the girls who come to Raven House spend a couple weeks with us before going to a family, and then they return to us their last month or so. That way, unless something goes haywire, the family you're living with doesn't have to be inconvenienced by you once your labor begins.

"This, of course, assumes we have volunteers in our community who are willing to open their homes to a fallen woman in the first place." Before I could respond, the housemother picked up a pen from her desk and pointed it toward me, emphasizing her every word. "That's. Just. How. It. Works."

I WAS ALREADY THREE AND a half months along. "Please be reasonable," my mother said as we crossed from Michigan into Ohio, headed toward Raven House. "It's just for five months, or thereabouts. And once this is over, you can come back home and no one will be the wiser." She turned toward me, taking her eyes off the road, which always makes me nervous because she isn't a very good driver and is always stopping fast and extending her right arm out to keep me from falling forward. "You haven't told anyone, have you? Not even Karen?" my mother asked for what felt like the millionth time. She then went on with a litany that I could recite almost word for word. How, in her day, if a girl found herself in the family way, she and the boy got married. Immediately. "You know why they call it a shotgun wedding?" my mother asked. "Because the girl's dad stood there with a shotgun and the boy had no choice; it was do or die. You're lucky you have options."

"Like you'd even let me get married," I said.

"I don't appreciate your tone, young lady." Her voice was stern, the way it got when I was younger right before she grabbed the back of my neck and washed out my mouth with soap. "You're fifteen years old, for God's sake. Do you really want to get married?" She didn't even give me time to answer. "You'd be throwing your life down the drain, and for what? You don't even enjoy babysitting. You have no idea how much work a baby is. Don't toss away your whole future over one silly mistake."

One silly mistake. God, I hated it when she was right. I barely even liked the boy, and I sure didn't love him, and I absolutely, positively didn't want to marry him.

HE WAS FROM OUT OF town, visiting some of his cousins for the summer. We met on the basketball court on the playground at the local elementary school when I was on the foul line, practicing my free throws, not that it would matter—none of the boys ever let me play basketball with them. Still, the rhythm of lifting my arms and tossing the ball into the air, watching it hit the backboard and fall in, or twirl around the rim, or sometimes just swish through the net—well, it made me happy, even though it really ticked off my parents, who never missed a chance to tell me I was too old to still be a tomboy. The boys and girls at school (minus my friend Karen) more or less agreed with my parents, but mostly, they just ignored me. So, when this out-ot-town boy challenged me to a game of HORSE, I said yes right away, and then I beat the pants off of him, H-O to H-O-R-S-E. "What's that even mean?" Karen asked when I told her about my victory. "It means I'm Wilt Chamberlain." It was clear from her cockeyed expression, and the fact that Karen knew absolutely nothing about sports, that she didn't know what I was talking about, but just didn't care enough to ask.

"HORSE is simple," I said. "You alternate taking shots. When you sink one, your opponent has to make the same shot, standing in the exact same spot. If they miss, they get a letter. First one to spell out H-O-R-S-E loses."

Karen said, "Far-out," but it was crystal clear that she didn't find it at all interesting.

Karen had a part-time babysitting job as a mother's helper four days a week, so even though it was summer, she wasn't around a lot. And when she was around, she only wanted to ride bikes to the town pool, which was actually weird because Karen didn't even like to swim; she just liked to walk around showing off her new bikini, or maybe what she liked showing off was her new body. This summer, Karen had suddenly sprouted boobs, and her bathing suit barely covered them.

On rainy days, we were stuck indoors, so we alternated houses and passed the time playing board games like Trouble, Monopoly, or Mouse Trap. But because she was babysitting most days of the week, I had lots of time to shoot hoops and rack up more victories playing HORSE against the out-of-town boy.

One day, he told me he liked me. I figured this was how it all worked. A boy told you he liked you (which he did after I beat him in HORSE on the third day), and so you said you liked him, too. Sometime later, the boy started to kiss you and you kissed him back. More time went on and he got handsy and asked you to touch him "there," so you did. And on it went until his last week in Kalamazoo, when the boy told me it was time to go all the way. I knew what that meant, but only sort of. I certainly didn't know I could say "no," but I'm not sure it would've mattered; I was curious, so I didn't say anything. Sex and babies and the link between the two were not topics my mother ever mentioned. And it certainly wasn't something they taught at school, although that didn't mean it wasn't talked about. "Do you think it's true that girls can get pregnant when boys put their pee-pees where the girl goes to the bathroom?" Karen once asked me. We rolled around the floor, laughing about such an absurdity, completely upending the small houses and hotels on the Monopoly board.

But I wasn't a total moron. I was a couple months past my thirteenth birthday when I finally got my period. Although my mom hadn't yet talked to me about menstruation, she had warned me that one day, when I went to the bathroom and wiped, there would be blood on the toilet paper. "It probably won't be a lot, at least not at first, but when it happens, come tell me." When she said that, she turned red all around her neck, where she sometimes got a rash when she and my dad "had words," as she put it. "And if I'm not home or you're at school or at Karen's house, just ball up some toilet paper and put it in your underpants until you get home. That should do it."

So, when I started to bleed, it wasn't a complete shock. Still, it wasn't easy to tell my mother, and I remember mumbling something like "You said I should come tell you about it when it happened. You know. When there's blood."

She was on her way out the door, going somewhere or another, and said, "Betsy Ann, I have no idea what you're talking about. You have something to say, just spit it out."

And so, in those rushed minutes before leaving, my mother gave me the briefest summary of menstruation, which amounted to little more than some talk about bleeding, using a sanitary belt, and how often the pads should be changed. "And for God's sake, Betsy, make sure to wrap it up good before you throw it in the wastebasket. I keep some brown paper lunch bags in the cupboard under the sink. That's why they're there. Your father doesn't need to see your dirty business." That was it. Nothing about how to keep a calendar so I'd know when to expect my monthly cycle, although that came a couple months later, when I was caught off guard at school and my mother stressed the importance of having a sanitary napkin in my purse around my time of the month, or at least some exact change so I could buy a pad from the Modess machine in the girls' bathroom. But she said zilch about how you get pregnant.

"We're lucky you didn't find out about this business until after he left," my mother said. "Because if you told him, then his cousins would also know, making taking care of this far more complicated."

I wanted to ask how she (and my father?) planned to "take care" of my problem, but I didn't have a chance. My mother was already rattling off her speech, the one about shotgun weddings and how lucky I was. How very, very lucky. Pregnant girls, she informed me, are not allowed in school, even if they've had a shotgun wedding. But lucky me, she had figured out a way for me to complete my education and get on with my life, but first, I needed to put this "disreputable business" (her words) behind me. And since no one knew I was in trouble (again, a quick check, using an arched eyebrow to make sure this was indeed the case), I had options.

Although I didn't have a spinster aunt somewhere out of town, they could invent one. This woman, my mother explained, was her father's sister. She was all alone, poor thing, and in failing health. Still, she managed to care for herself until she took a nasty fall and broke her hip. I was just what the doctor ordered—someone young and strong to help care for the woman until she was back on her feet, quite literally. The spinster aunt was a way to give me a future—a babyless future—with options. It was also a way to avoid bringing shame to myself and to my family. I would go to Raven House, have the baby, give it up for adoption, and return home. "Just like it never even happened," Mom said.

So now here I am. In the utility room of the Bergs' basement, where I'll live until a month before the baby is supposed to arrive, which is when I'll go back to Raven House. And the out-of-town boy who spent the summer visiting his cousins is back at his home, doing whatever he wants, completely unaware that he left behind a parting gift.

Mrs. David Berg

(Lily)

Becca was the one to tell me about the Raven House Maternity Home for Unwed Mothers. "Before our boys started elementary school, having that extra set of hands was a lifesaver," she said after I tried to put into words just how overwhelmed I was feeling. I only had Jo-Jo and felt almost silly complaining, but Becca seemed to understand. "Housework is a lot. Add to that just the laundry a baby creates and, well, I know what you're going through." What Becca left unsaid was the fact that, unlike most women in the neighborhood, I didn't have a mother or even a mother-in-law to step in to help. My mom passed away when I was fourteen, and David is from Milwaukee, where his parents still live. Becca wrote down the phone number of Raven House and made me promise to call.

When I initially contacted them about getting an unwed mother, they said they keep each girl at Raven House for two weeks before placing her with a family, assuming a family is available to take her. Then the woman on the phone told me about Kathy—only she didn't use her name, but called her "the girl I have in mind for you." She said the girl needed to stay with them for another ten days before they'd release her. "During their two weeks with us, we make sure the girls are fed, examined by an obstetrician, and mentally sound. We don't want to send anyone into your home who might have a disease"—she cleared her throat—"down there, or, God forbid, a girl who is unstable and could harm you or your child. Isn't that right?" These were things I hadn't considered when Becca told me about Raven House. When I heard them verbalized, I admit to having some second thoughts.

"What if it doesn't work out?" I asked. "Or what if we just don't get along?"

"You're in the driver's seat," the woman replied. "If, for any reason, you and your husband decide you don't want her, just send her back to us. Remember, you're doing her a favor, and, frankly, us as well. But you're also helping some lucky couple who will adopt the girl's unwanted baby, and that's no small thing. I only wish there were more people like you and your husband, willing to open your home to a wayward girl."

I was worried how David would feel about an unwed mother living in our house. He gave me permission to make the preliminary call, just so I could find out what was what. I understood his reluctance. After all, having a pregnant teenager under your roof—well, it could be riddled with problems. But after buying the house, we had to do some belt-tightening, and I really needed some extra help, especially since I didn't have a mother around to step in. I begged David to give it a try, and promised him that if he felt uncomfortable, we could always send the girl back to the maternity home. I also promised he'd never have to be alone with her in the house, because that would be awkward, for obvious reasons of impropriety.

Fortunately, Kathy liked to have an early dinner with Jo-Jo, and then she retreated to her room in the basement, so by the time David got home for dinner, it was just the two of us. David rarely saw Kathy on the weekends, since David was often at the hospital delivering a baby or occupied with reading medical journals or paying our monthly bills. He also had a regular handball game at the YMCA, and after playing, he and his friend typically had lunch together. Since David and Kathy rarely saw one another, it didn't take a lot of convincing to get my husband to agree to let me take in another unwed mother, especially when I told him I was pregnant with our second child.

When Kathy first arrived, she was miserable and cried almost nonstop. As a result, her eyes were always red and swollen, and it was weeks before I realized that she looked closer to fourteen than her actual sixteen years. She had long blond hair, and I could tell that when she wasn't pregnant, she had a slender, petite frame, and nice long legs. Her parents sounded like real doozies, and when they learned of her condition, they tossed her out of their house. I couldn't imagine such a thing, and if I hadn't heard it straight from Kathy, I wouldn't have believed it. I thought about my little Jo-Jo and wondered what I would do if she found herself unmarried and in the family way. It was too much to contemplate, considering she wasn't even a year old at the time, but one thing I knew for sure: I certainly would not kick her to the curb.

When Kathy got here, Jo-Jo was on the verge of walking. My little girl also did her own share of crying. I was giving serious thought to calling Raven House and telling them this wasn't working out. Finally, after four days of nonstop tears, I sat Kathy down. "Look," I said. "I understand if you're homesick, but you've got to get yourself together. I can't have both of you crying all the time. Is there something I can do to make it better? Would you be happier if you went back to Raven House?"

That's when she told me she wasn't just homesick; she also missed her boyfriend. "We were going steady and I haven't talked to him in almost a month," she said, while playing with the class ring she wore on a chain around her neck. The ring was clearly her boyfriend's as it had a good amount of pink mohair yarn wrapped around it, sizing it so it could also be worn on her finger.

"So, you and your boyfriend were serious?" I asked.

She nodded. "I wanted to marry him, and I still do, but my

parents won't let me. Since I'm only sixteen, I need their consent." Kathy told me that in the weeks between telling her parents she was "knocked up" (her words, not mine) and her mother dropping her off at Raven House, she was forbidden to have any contact with her boyfriend, or anyone else. "The only reason my mother even drove me to Raven House was to make sure I didn't run off with him." Kathy pulled a clean tissue from the box she held in her lap. "How could I run away with him if I can't even talk to him and tell him where to come get me?" She unballed the tissue in her hand and blew her nose. "They only have one phone at Raven House, and they stand guard over it all the time, and they listen to all your phone calls, so I couldn't even talk to him!" I reached out to hold her hand, but she pulled me in for a huge hug, the kind my sister, Rose, used to give me when we were little girls. "You're only allowed to call your parents, and then you have to call collect, which is so expensive," she said into my shoulder. Not knowing what else to do, I stroked her long blond hair, something I also used to do for Rose when she was upset, and something I now do for Jo-Jo when she's crying.

I remember placing a collect call on my honeymoon, letting my dad know that David and I had arrived safely at Niagara Falls. I gave the operator his number, and when he picked up, the operator said, "I have a collect call from Lily. Will you accept the charges?"

"Yes," he said. Immediately followed by "You're arrived?"

"Yes," I said.

"Thanks for letting me know. Have fun." And that was it. I knew calling collect was more expensive than regular long distance, which was plenty expensive by itself. I just didn't realize how much more costly it was until my father all but hung up on me.

I wondered what Kathy's parents said when she called them. Did they even accept the charges? I told Kathy that the housemother at Raven House had given me firm instructions: "Kathy is not to call her boyfriend."

"But Kathy," I said, "there are going to be times when I'm not here and I won't know what you're doing." I explained that it was all but impossible for me to police her actions. I did not say this in a "wink-wink" way of giving her permission without expressly giving her permission. I said it was a matter of trust between us, as she was a guest in our home, and we all had to show trust and respect for one another. What I did not tell her was that I had a soon-to-be year-old daughter; I didn't need, nor want, to be a parent to a teenager, too. I already did that with my sister, Rose. I did, however, tell Kathy there was nothing wrong with writing letters, and I would not be reading any correspondence she sent out nor anything she received. I asked if she had stationery and stamps, and when she said she didn't, I supplied both. By the end of the day, she asked if I had any outgoing mail. When I told her I didn't, she took the envelope I'd given her earlier that day, walked down the driveway, inserted her letter into the mailbox, and put up the flag. I wish I could say I never saw another tear in her eye, but over the next few months, until the time her water broke, her daily crying jags ended.

I am a bit ashamed to admit that there was more than one occasion when I was out of the house with Jo-Jo, coming back from a pediatrician appointment, for instance, or a walk around the block, when I returned home wondering if that would be the time when I opened the front door and found a note from Kathy, telling me she and her boyfriend had eloped. But it never happened. In fact, just the opposite. About three months after Kathy had her baby, I got a letter from her. Post-birth communication between an unwed mother and the family she lived with is strongly discouraged by Raven House, who impress on both parties that the best way for the unwed mother to get on with her life is to put this unfortunate chapter behind her.

Kathy ignored Raven House's (strong) recommendation. In her letter, she thanked me for everything we did for her and told me that after having a baby boy and giving him up for adoption, she moved in with her boyfriend and his parents, with every intention of getting married once she turned eighteen and no longer required her parents' permission. Two months after she reunited with her boyfriend, they broke up. Kathy said her parents allowed her to move back home, and she was going to make the most of this second chance. That "second chance" business sounded more like her parents talking than Kathy, but I was glad to know she was in a safe place. Everything, it seemed, turned out exactly as it was meant to be.

Mrs. Marty Seigel

(Rose)

Marty and I didn't start dating until after I graduated from Kent State. He was already in law school, and I was interviewing for my first teaching job. Even though we didn't date until I was twenty-two, I had literally "known" Marty my entire life.

Marty's mom, Doris, and my mom, Joan, went to high school together. Doris was a year older, so they ran in somewhat different circles and weren't close friends. That changed when years after graduation, they bumped into one another and decided it would be fun to catch up and compare notes about their classmates. Doris was already a mom to three little boys (Scott, Daniel, and Marty), and Mom had Lily and was pregnant with me. Before long, the two women—along with their young kids—started getting together every week for coffee and mommy chit-chat. Once I was born, their coffee klatsch grew by one. So, in some ways, I've known Marty and his brothers my entire life, even if I didn't really *know* them.

For our first date, Marty took me to the movies and we saw *Mary Poppins*. By the end of the movie, when Mary leaves the Banks family, I could hear Marty sniffle (he was sensitive) even though he denied it (he was manly). I know it sounds corny, but he really did sweep me off my feet (he was handsome and charming). I, like most girls, was familiar with Disney's *Snow White* and was looking forward to the day when my prince would come; I felt certain Marty was who I'd been waiting for. That notion was further reinforced two weeks later when we saw *My Fair Lady*. Afterward, we went to the Howard Johnson ice cream parlor, and Marty did an imitation of Audrey Hepburn, telling our waitress that he'd like twoooo scoooooops of the butter pecan ice cream. (He was funny.) Whenever we were at his parents' house, I not only felt at home, but genuinely welcome as well. His mother shared stories about my mom that I didn't know, and being with her was almost like having a real mother, not a future mother-in-law. Long before we were married, I already felt like part of the family.

At our wedding reception, during his toast, Marty's dad said that for as long as he could remember, "Doris used to say she hoped at least one of her boys would grow up to marry one of the Mitchell girls." He paused, at which time Marty's brothers, Scott and Daniel, and his mom all nodded their heads, leading me to believe this gesture was scripted. But maybe not. After all, it was true. "And then David took Lily off the market," he said. "So, Doris told the boys they'd better hurry before someone snatches up Rose." Everyone at the reception laughed at that remark—including me. Of course, as I often did during family gatherings and celebrations, I thought about Mom, about how much I missed her, and how she should have been with me, under the chuppah, standing next to Dad as Marty slipped the ring onto my finger and repeated after the rabbi, "With this ring, you are consecrated to me according to the law of Moses and Israel."

Marty's dad concluded his toast with "Good thing we raised our Martin to listen to his mother."

Although I've known Marty since I was in my mom's womb, he was obviously older than me, so we were never in school at the same time. When I asked him about his dating life prior to going steady with me, he said there was no one serious before me. "You, Rose, are perfect." I laughed and told him I wasn't perfect, but I would try my best to be a perfect wife, and someday a mother, but he should be forewarned: Roses have thorns, and sometimes he might find me prickly, at least according to my sister. He laughed it off and said he thought he was man enough to handle me.

I never fell hard for anyone before Marty, but that doesn't mean I was a wallflower who sat home. I dated a lot. Marty, who always claimed there was no one special before me, had the same girlfriend, Linda, all throughout college. That seemed pretty serious to me. When I questioned him about it, he agreed. "Everyone figured we'd get married, but she wasn't the right girl for me. I guess I knew there was a Rose-Bud in my future." (He was romantic, too.)

After Marty proposed, I asked him what went wrong with his college sweetheart. He told me that Linda put out and he didn't want spoiled merchandise; he wanted to marry a virgin. He didn't tell me why that was important, and I didn't ask. I simply filed it away as a lesson: Marty didn't need to know everything about me. It was the '60s, after all. What difference did it make whether I was a virgin? *All the world's a stage . . . and one (wo)man in her time plays many parts.* If my future husband required a virgin, well, *as you like it,* Marty.

Marty is a good, good man. He works hard to provide a nice life and lifestyle for us and tells me all the time how much he looks forward to the day when I won't have to work. It doesn't matter how often I tell him that I love teaching; he tells me he wants to be the sole provider.

Marty's an attorney. Four months into our marriage, I referred to him as a lawyer. "A lawyer is someone who went to law school but hasn't passed the bar," Marty said, correcting me. "An attorney has passed the bar."

"Oh, look at you, puffing out your chest like a proud peacock," I replied. That's when he slapped me across the face. I was stunned, but not more so than he.

"My God, I'm so sorry," he said. "I don't even know where that came from. I guess I'm under more stress at work than I thought." His hands were shaking, and his voice caught in his throat. "Please, Rose, please forgive me." And that's when I noticed his eyes were filled with tears. He took me into his arms and cried.

"Of course," I assured him. "Of course I forgive you." And I meant it. So, the next day, when he returned from work with a bouquet of flowers and a box of chocolates, again professing his sorrow, I again told him it wasn't necessary. And again, I meant it. After that, we had month after month of marital bliss, with some normal newlywed quarrels mixed in. But mostly, we were happy and we began talking about starting a family.

Miss Betsy Ann Eubanks

When I arrived at Raven House, the housemother gave me a cheap wedding ring that she bought at Woolworths, the local five-and-dime. "Wear this for the next two weeks while you're here," she said as she handed it to me. "That way, when you're out and about, no one will know you're not married." A good plan, but it didn't matter. People in the neighborhood knew who we were and why we were there, and if we left for a walk or to go to the corner market, they'd yell names at us, calling us whores and sluts and sometimes throwing things at us, like rotten fruit and even eggs. But when it was just us girls, and we were indoors, there were times when I forgot why I was there; it felt almost like a giant slumber party. Unfortunately, that usually didn't last, and before long, I remembered my situation and started to feel guilty about the shame and embarrassment I was causing my parents.

At first, my mom was just mad at me and kept asking how I could have been so stupid. "But I didn't know," I said. "How was I supposed to know?" She didn't have an answer for me, and alternated between hugging me and sending me to my room so she could think. A few days later, she told me about Raven House.

My dad wouldn't even look at me and only talked to me if I asked him something directly. Even then, he kept his nose buried in the newspaper when he answered me. Then, one day, he surprised me and asked me if I had anything to say for myself. I told him I didn't understand his question. "What," he said, "do you have to say for yourself?" I still didn't understand, but I told him I was sorry. He shook his head.

"I just want to know one thing," my dad said. "Is this the first time you've compromised yourself with a boy or just the first time you've been caught and had to pay a price?"

EXCEPT FOR SLEEPOVERS AT KAREN'S, I had never been away from home before Mom left me at Raven House. I was surprised there were almost a dozen girls at the maternity home when I arrived; it made me realize I wasn't alone in my troubles. A couple of them were close to the two-week mark when they could be placed with a family, but more than half were at the end of their pregnancies, and had moved back into Raven House while they waited to have their babies. In spite of there being so many girls, no one was outwardly mean, like so many of the girls at school.

A few nights after I got there, a girl named Sheila came up with the idea that we all share how and why we wound up at Raven House. It was dark in the dormitory, except for a little bit of moonlight that crept in through the curtains. The room was not nearly well lit enough to be able to see faces, and since I was new, I didn't even recognize anyone's voice. But I think it was the darkness that allowed everyone to just say whatever she wanted.

We started at the far end of the room, with the girl in the bed closest to the door. More than one girl said she was raped; two said it was by people in their families. I wasn't sure what rape was, but one girl talked about being held down and how she kicked and tried to fight, but he put a hand over her mouth so no one could hear her scream. That gave me enough of an idea about what "rape" meant. For the first time since I found out I was expecting, I felt lucky, if you can believe it. As we got closer to me, I worried over what I would say, as I didn't really understand exactly what had happened. The out-of-town boy rolled on top of me, and, well, whatever happened was so quick, I wasn't even sure what *had* happened. But I thought if I said that, everyone would laugh at me. I decided to just string together bits and pieces from what others said and wound up with something like "My story is boring. A boy from out of town came to visit his cousins for the summer. We met, and you know how it goes, one thing led to another"—that was what I cribbed from one of the girls who spoke before me—"and here I am, knocked up"—which is another expression I stole from another one of the other unwed mothers.

After everyone shared her story, one thing was clear: No matter how we wound up "preggers" (another word I stole that night), one thing we all had in common was that our parents didn't want us anywhere near them where we would bring shame to them or to ourselves.

Mrs. David Berg

(Lily)

I knock on the front door of Becca's house, and without waiting for a response, I let myself in. I don't know when we gave up on formalities and started just popping by without waiting for doors to be answered, but it's been so long that I don't even remember *not* just walking in. Mostly, it's a good thing, and honestly, I only minded once, and it was only because I wasn't feeling well that morning and took my sweet time starting my day. When Becca showed up right before lunch and I was still in my nightgown, it was embarrassing. "Oh, please," Becca said. "Look how I walk around?" She pointed to her head, where she had wrapped her hair in toilet paper and clipped it into place, hoping to preserve her set. Topping it all off was a black hairnet that looked like she'd walked through a spidery web. "It's our anniversary tonight, and I wanted to look put-together instead of my usual disheveled self. Do you think I succeeded?" Before I could even answer, Becca began laughing, and not for the first time, I thought about how freeing it must be to be Becca. Not only can she laugh at herself, but she never seems to care or worry about what other people think of her.

When I enter her house, I'm struck, as always, by the smell of smoke. Even if she's not smoking, the place always reeks. I back out and breathe in the fresh fall air. With Jo-Jo, and apparently with this baby, too, walking into Becca's is going to be touch-and-go, as far as my morning sickness is concerned. I force myself not to give in to my queasiness. I breathe in through my nose, out through my mouth. I know some women who like the smell of cigarettes, but that's never been me, even when I'm not in the family way. Whenever I host canasta, as soon as everyone leaves, the first thing I do is reach for the ashtray. It is always filled to the brim with cigarette butts that are smeared with Becca's and Sarah's lipstick. I empty it into a brown paper lunch bag and walk the bag into the garage, where it sits in a trash can, mercifully out of my house, until garbage day.

Once I feel confident that I'm not going to get sick all over myself, I enter Becca's house and catch the screen door so it won't slam behind me. When I turn, I see my friend sitting at her kitchen table. Her eyes are red, and there's a coffee cup and a box of tissues in front of her. "Becca? Did I come at a bad time?"

She shakes her head. "There isn't a good time."

I slip out of my jacket and hang it on the back of the chair closest to her and sit down. I'm not so big that I can't bend toward her, and when I do, my face is inches from hers. "What's wrong, honey? Is there something I can do?"

Again, she shakes her head. "You know what's wrong." She places her hand over her stomach; the bangles around her wrist jingle like tiny bells. "How could this happen?" The skin between her brows tightens, and I can see her trying hard to keep from crying.

"I know, Bec. It's not what you expected, but . . ."

And then, because Becca is Becca, she falls back on her sense of humor. "I mean, I know how this happened, but *how*?" She runs her hands through her hair, which was back-combed at one point but is now sticking out in at least four different directions. "I take my Enovid pill every day, even though it makes me nauseated and even dizzy. But I take it anyway because I didn't want this to happen." She places her hand on her stomach.

I tell her it will be okay. "And we'll have babies so close in age. That will make it easier, don't you think?"

When she still doesn't answer, I promise her I'll help. "One day a week, I can babysit both kids, and you can do the same. Or we can watch the babies together so neither one of us is alone."

Becca still doesn't respond. Instead, she clenches her fist and begins punching her stomach.

"Becca, stop." I pull back on her arm and cover her fist with my hand. "Stop. You don't want to hurt the baby."

She looks me directly in the eye. "Who says I don't?" She then says that she needs some privacy and asks me to leave.

I called Becca later that afternoon, just to check in. She assured me she was fine and apologized for what she called "the drama" of the morning. "Please," she said, "don't worry about me. You're right. It will all work out. Apparently, I still need some more time to adjust to the idea of another baby." I reminded her I was just down the street if she wanted to talk about it, but I'm pretty sure that Becca is right, she simply needs time.

TONIGHT, AS WE DO EVERY Friday night since even before Mom died, we are going to Grandma Mollie's house for Shabbat dinner. The first Friday after Betsy came, I didn't mention anything about it being Shabbat and just told her we were going to my grandma's for dinner. I suggested she warm up the meat loaf in the fridge. But in the last week, I realized just how sheltered Betsy grew up, and it occurred to me that she's likely never even met a Jewish family before, so I decided to give her a little background about us (no, we don't have horns), and a crash course in some of our customs (no, we don't eat pork or shellfish, at least not in our home, since David and I keep kosher) and our beliefs (no, Jesus Christ is not our Lord and savior, but we do believe in God).

Betsy seemed interested, so I continued. "You know how for Christians, Sunday is the Sabbath?" She nodded. "Well, for Jewish people, our Sabbath is from sunset Friday night until sunset Saturday night. And we start the Sabbath by lighting candles and saying a prayer."

Now, holding Jo-Jo, with David by my side, I do just that, covering my hair with a lace doily, lighting the candles, waving in the light, and saying the prayer in Hebrew. "We also say a blessing over wine and bread, but we're running late, so we'll skip it here and just do that when we get to Grandma's." I grab Jo-Jo's toe and wiggle it. "Isn't that right, Jo-Jo?"

"Remember the diaper bag," Betsy says, pressing it into my arms.

"Oh my goodness, thank you! These days I feel like I wouldn't remember my own head if it wasn't attached by my neck. That forgetful fogginess happened when I was pregnant with Jo-Jo, too. Do you ever feel that way?"

Betsy shakes her head. I get a sick feeling and realize that I've been so busy the last two weeks trying to make Betsy feel comfortable, showing her how I like things done, and how to help with Jo-Jo—most notably, how to change her diaper without impaling her—that I haven't given much thought to her pregnancy and how it might be affecting her. Even though Betsy's further along than I am, this is her first time. I remember when I was expecting Jo-Jo. I had so many questions and most of them went unanswered because I didn't have a mom to turn to and I was too embarrassed to ask Becca. But still. How could I have not focused on the fact that while I'm excited and thinking a million different things about having a new baby: Will it be a boy or a girl? How will this baby change our family? How will Jo-Jo do in her new role as a big sister? How will she adjust to her big-girl bed and her new bedroom? Well! I just didn't consider that Betsy is having a very different experience, and her outcome doesn't end with a baby in her arms.

I surprise both Betsy and myself by reaching out and giving her a quick hug before we leave the house.

Mrs. Marty Seigel

(Rose)

Grandma Mollie is my dad's mom. Dad's younger brother, Uncle Calvin, and his wife and their three kids live out of town, so our weekly Shabbat dinners at Grandma's house typically include my dad, Lily, David, Jo-Jo, and, of course, Marty and me. Grandpa died when I was two, so neither Lily nor I have any memory of him. Grandma doesn't talk a lot about him; I think it just makes her sad. When she does mention him, it's mostly to say, "Oy, my Max. He was so good and he always loved me."

Grandma is a great cook, but more importantly, she knows all our favorite foods, and we can count on them being on the table each week. When Mom died, Grandma made it her business to be around for us and did more than her fair share of cooking and cleaning. But even before that, Grandma Mollie was always the real center of this family.

Grandma doesn't talk a lot about her past, but I know she came to America when she was fifteen and married my grandpa when she was sixteen. Her future mother-in-law saw her sweeping out the alley behind her parents' house and immediately decided that Grandma would make a good wife for her son. That's it. They got married. I get different answers, depending on when I ask her, but Grandma met her husband, Max, either on their wedding day or a few weeks before. Another thing Grandma isn't clear about is when she came to the United States from "the old country." She thinks she lived for a while in Poland and Russia and maybe Romania, but is unsure because "Jewish people moved around," getting thrown out of one country or another, or just leaving when it wasn't safe for Jews. What she doesn't say, but I know, is that the boundaries for many of the countries in Eastern Europe were also constantly changing, making it hard to know where you were, where you came from, and where you were going. Grandma also has no idea when her birthday is since she came to America without a birth certificate. Frankly, I don't even know if they had birth certificates back then.

Dinner conversation rarely varies and typically begins with Dad asking, "How are my petite fleurs this week?" He never called us his "petite fleurs" until Mom passed away, but I like that he adopted her way of referring to us, and I'm glad he's kept the expression alive. Lily, being the older daughter, goes first, and once she's weighed in about her week, it's my turn. Then someone asks about Grandma's week, and she always says the same thing: "Busy, busy. Cooking, cleaning, shopping. You know . . ." And then we all say in unison, "A voman's vork is never done!" Yes, we say it using *V*s, because Grandma has an accent and can't say her *W*s.

You'd think that since Lily is the firstborn grandchild, Grandma would favor her, but even though she tries to hide it, it's abundantly clear to everyone she likes me best. I sometimes feel bad for Lily because Grandma pretty much says whatever pops into her head, and it's often a thinly veiled suggestion that Lily somehow be more like me. Last Friday night, for instance, Grandma went on about how much she likes the curl in my hair and that I wear it natural, like she does, "vithout any teasing it up and so much hairspray." Of course there was Lily, fresh from the beauty shop, where she goes every Friday morning to have her hair shampooed and set. Lily has her hair back-combed and smoothed to form a dome on top of her head. She typically adds a colored velvet headband to match whatever she's wearing. Her look is very mod, but Grandma is old-fashioned and doesn't like what she calls "newfangled styles." I always try to counter Grandma's flattery of me with kind words about my sister. "I would never be able to pull off Lily's hairdo, which is so pretty and suits her personality." Lily just giggles when I do that. She swears she doesn't mind when Grandma *jujjes* her, which is our made-up word for when Grandma ribs, criticizes, or backhand compliments me in order to *jujje* Lily.

"I love Grandma, and I know Grandma loves me," Lily always says, trying to assuage my guilt over being the obvious favorite. "I think it's admirable that, after all she's been through, she's come out an independent woman who is not afraid to speak her mind. In some ways, I wish I could be more like her."

I agree. When Hamlet said, "Frailty, thy name is woman," it is clear to me that he never met Grandma Mollie. I can't pretend to understand the details of it, but years ago, when Lily and I asked Dad how Grandma can afford to live alone when she doesn't even have a job, he explained that Grandpa Max owned a car dealership, and even though he passed away, everything was set up to take care of Grandma. Dad, being an accountant, assured us that "it's all under control," and I've never asked him about it again.

Grandma's story *is* inspiring, at least to me. That's partially why I told her I want to write it down. I'm afraid if it's not documented, it will be lost, and I want to be able to pass it along from generation to generation, *l'dor v'dor.* Unfortunately, so much of what made Grandma the woman she is today happened to her when she was young, so it comes out in dribs and drabs. When we're washing and drying dishes, for instance, she'll tell me about how her mother taught her to make matzoh balls, and if I ask her questions about it, I've suddenly got an incredible new story to document. Unfortunately, Grandma can't read or write in English; Yiddish is her primary language, but she only learned to speak it so she can't jot down her memories. Since I'm the one it matters to, I've taken on the role of scribe.

While I do want future generations to know about Grandma Mollie, that's only part of why I feel this yearning to write down her story. The other part is more selfish. When my mom died, I was so young, and even though there are pictures of her, my memories feel a little fake. Sometimes I'm not even sure if something is a real memory or if it's just an anecdote that Lily told me and I've sort of stolen it, taking it on as my own. What I would give if someone had written down my mom's story. Even better: What if Mom kept a diary? When I have a baby, I am going to start a journal so, God forbid, if something happens to me, my child will know all about me and who I was. Lily knows how I feel, and whenever I encourage her to start a diary for Jo-Jo, she tells me she's busy enough at home and "you'll see when you start your own family." Of course she always ends with some variation of the question "When will that be again?"

Miss Betsy Ann Eubanks

I t's me," Mrs. Hudson says in a half whisper as she comes down the basement stairs and into the family room, where I'm building block towers with Jo-Jo. The truth is, I'm doing most all of the building and Jo-Jo is knocking down the blocks.

"Oh, she's awake. I was whispering because I thought Jo-Jo might be napping." Mrs. Hudson's bracelets jingle-jangle as she tries to smooth her hair, which is flying every which way.

I look at my watch. "Wow, I lost track of time." I scoop the little girl into my arms. "Jo-Jo, how did you not remind me it was your nap time?"

Jo-Jo, who is a great mimic and just started putting two words together, says, "Nap time."

"That's right, kiddo."

"I actually came over to see you," Mrs. Hudson says. "But you go ahead and put her down. I'll wait right here."

When I return, Mrs. Hudson tells me she's dropped by to offer me an apology.

"What for?"

"I said some very unkind things to you after canasta."

"That was a couple weeks ago. And besides, you already said you were sorry."

Once again, Mrs. Hudson tries to smooth her blond hair, which is sticking out over her ear. "Yes, but I wanted you to know I feel truly awful. I was . . . disappointed, shall we say? . . . to find out I was pregnant again, and I took out my frustrations on you. That comment about how you should know what it's like to have an unplanned pregnancy was completely out of line, and it's been bothering me."

"Well, I accept your apology a second time."

Then Mrs. Hudson does something I didn't see coming in a million years. She invites me to her house for Thanksgiving. "I know Lily and the family always go to her grandmother's house for the holiday," Mrs. Hudson says. "And I should warn you that I'm not a great cook, but we'd love to have you join us, if you'd like."

Just when I'm about to say yes, Mrs. Hudson says I don't have to let her know right this minute; I can think about it. But I tell her I've already made up my mind and ask what time I should come over.

BEFORE I LEFT HOME, MY mom gave me a boxed set of stationery and some stamps. She said she expected to hear from me at least once a week. She also told me to write to Karen. "You don't need to do it every week, but just enough so she doesn't get suspicious."

I didn't understand.

"Betsy Ann, pretend you really were taking care of a sick aunt. Wouldn't you write to your best friend back home?" She didn't give me a chance to answer. "Of course you would. You'd write to her and say things like what your chores are, and how your poor aunt doesn't seem to be getting better very fast, and how it looks like you're going to have to stay longer than you thought. You might even tell your friend that you don't miss school and doing the homework, but you sure do miss her and look forward to seeing her. And here's the important thing: You'd tell Karen that you're sending her letter inside the envelope along with the letter you sent to me because you're trying not to use a lot of stamps, since the post office is far from your aunt's house. And you would tell her that if she'd like to write back, she should just give her letter to me and I'll mail both letters together, and that way Karen won't have to spend her babysitting money on stamps."

"But why can't I just send my letters to Karen at her house? I know her address."

"Because I don't want her to see a postmark or your return address. The less she knows, the better. Besides, I want to read the letters you send her to make sure you don't slip up and say something that might lead Karen to know why you're in Akron and what's really going on."

I tell my mom I wouldn't do that. She doesn't say anything but makes that "hmmm" sound, which she does when she doesn't believe me.

Dear Mom,

In your last letter you asked me a lot of questions about Raven House, so here goes:

You were right. Most of the girls were from Ohio, but there were also some, like me, from Michigan, and even a couple from Pennsylvania. All the girls were teenagers, at least that's how they looked to me. We all pretty much had the same cover story: We left town to take care of a sick relative.

You'll be happy to know that when we introduced ourselves, we only used our first names—that was the housemother's idea. Actually, her idea was that we use fake first names, or even our middle names, to help keep us top secret. (It's like each girl was a real-life James Bond!!)

Anyway, that's why, whenever anyone asked my name, I told them I was Ann. The housemother said we shouldn't use our last names AT ALL, because that way no one could ever spill the beans about who was at Raven House. She said it would protect us because "you don't want to risk spoiling your reputations now, or in the future." She didn't have to add "any more than they are already," if you catch my drift. We all sure did . . . loud and clear.

Happy Thanksgiving (a little bit early) to you and Dad. One of Mrs. Berg's neighbors invited me to Thanksgiving dinner with her family. Isn't that cool? Not to brag or anything, but it must mean that she likes me. Still, I'm sure gonna miss your cranberries and stuffing.

Write back soon!!

Love,

Betsy

(Since I moved into the Bergs' house, I'm back to being just regular Betsy. Not Ann.)

Dear Dad,

I know you're still mad at me and I'm sorry about that. I'm really, really sorry about all of it.

Happy Thanksgiving (a little bit early) to you and Mom. I'm sure gonna miss Mom's cranberries and stuffing.

Please write to me and tell me how things are going at the hardware store.

Love,

Your daughter, Heavens to Betsy

(Remember when you used to say that to me all the time???)

XOXXXOOOXXXOOO

Dear Karen,

Happy Thanksgiving!!!! Are you having any company this year? It's going to be weird to be here with just my aunt for the holiday, but them's the breaks, right? I promise to write a long, newsy letter as soon as I can, but she's calling for me so I better go. I just wanted to wish you a happy turkey day.

Love,

Betsy

XOXX

December
1965

Mrs. David Berg

(Lily)

I sometimes wonder why David chose me—not that I'm complaining—I'm glad he did. But as Rose, who I sometimes refer to as my Rose-Petal, loves to remind me, I am rather prudish. You would think that a doctor, one who delivers babies and looks at women's private parts all day, would have preferred a wife who, well, doesn't blush when referring to private parts or even call them "private parts."

"Are you ever attracted to your patients?" I asked David after we'd been dating a couple months. I'd met him at a restaurant that was just around the corner from the hospital where he was doing his rotation in obstetrics and gynecology.

I was surprised when he said yes. "But let me clarify. If there's a beautiful woman sitting at a table next to me"—he gestured at me—"I notice her, even admire her," he said. "The same is true if I see her at the hospital. But when that woman has undressed and I'm examining her, she is my patient, and she becomes nothing more than parts."

I admitted that I didn't completely understand the distinction. "Pretend you're making chicken tonight for dinner," David said. "You buy it from the kosher butcher. You wash it, and use a knife to pluck any feathers that are still visible, right?"

I nodded, wondering how he knew the first thing about preparing chicken.

"You season it and put it in a rotisserie pan. Maybe you cover it with some tinfoil. You preheat the oven. Am I right?"

This is when I realized David really did not know the first thing about cooking. "Basically," I said, not wanting to insult him. "You skipped all the gross parts, though. Like dismembering the various pieces and pulling out the insides and removing some of the skin."

David laughed. "The point I'm trying to make is that when you've got to cook a chicken, you just do what you need to do. You don't think about what precisely anything is or what you're doing, per se. You just do what needs to be done. Am I right?"

I understood the point he was making.

"That's how it is when I'm examining a woman or when she's giving birth. I just do what I've been trained to do."

I fiddled with the stem of my water glass. "I guess that makes sense," I said, hoping he was being truthful.

He reached across the table and placed his hand on top of mine. "Let me try again." He cleared his throat. "People typically see the doctor because something has gone wrong," he said. "Nobody really wants to go. They do it because they're sick and not getting better. They're often in pain and sometimes they need an operation."

He had a point. I never liked going to the doctor and getting shots, or having a stick shoved down my mouth to see if I had strep throat.

"Women see an OB-GYN mostly just for checkups. If they're married, they might want to be fitted for birth control or get a prescription. And of course they see me when they're pregnant. The point is, I'm not constantly treating sick people, the way an internist or urologist does." David withdrew his hand from mine and began gesturing, somewhat frantically—a habit I'd noticed he reverted to whenever he was either extremely excited or very interested in something. "I'm seeing women who are medically sound, and usually, they are happy to see me. They are doing the most healthy and natural thing in the world: having babies."

In addition to his somewhat wild gesticulations, David also had a tendency to talk fast when he was into something and his voice got higher, which was what happened when he explained his enthusiasm about obstetrics and gynecology. I've often told him he sounds like a record that was meant to be played at 33 rpm but is spinning on the turntable at 45 rpm. "Plus, when a woman can't deliver vaginally and needs a cesarean section, I get to do surgery. So, for me, being an OB-GYN is the best of all worlds."

I felt my face heat up when David said "deliver vaginally" and was relieved the restaurant had dim lighting.

Not for the first time, I wondered why David was interested in me. He had all those nurses at the hospital to choose from—women who probably weren't the least bit prudish—and they were likely much closer to him in age, not that I minded David being five years my senior. To me, that only made him more mature and worldly and, yes, more desirable. He wasn't like the boys I dated throughout high school. He was a man.

When I asked him about all those nurses around him every day, David said it was his desire to marry a woman who wanted to be a housewife and mother, not someone who was striving for a career. That's exactly what I wanted, and why I was more than happy to accept David's proposal, which happened right after my high school graduation. But after a year or so of marriage, maybe because I hadn't yet had Jo-Jo, I started to wonder if I'd made the right choice. Don't misunderstand; not about David—I never questioned marrying David. It was the fact I didn't go to college that I wondered about. Sometimes I still do. It nagged at me so much I made Rose promise me that she would not just go to college, but wait until she graduated to get married. So many women were going to school to find Mr.

Right and to get their MRS degree, never bothering to finish their studies. I wanted to make sure Rose didn't fall into that category.

Like most of my girlfriends, I kept a dating diary in a steno pad. It included the boy's name, where we went, and the date of our outing. At my bridal shower, I followed the custom of counting up all my dates (111) and was applauded by my friends for making triple digits. The point is, I did more than a little dating and I knew my own mind and I knew exactly what I wanted. David ticked all the boxes. Only lately have I started to think about what might have happened if, like Rose, I, too, went to college. Then the reality hits me: I'm the mother of one with another bun in the oven. What would I possibly do with a job?

Miss Betsy Ann Eubanks

I'd never met anyone who wasn't Catholic, or at least a Christian, and when I told that to Mrs. Berg, she asked if I'd like to learn a little about the Jewish religion while I live with them. Before I could answer, she laughed and said, "Well, living with us, you're going to pick up some things here and there whether you want to or not." That was why she started talking to me about being Jewish.

But lately, if I ask her something about her religion, she gets all serious and tells me I can ask her anything and it doesn't just have to be about being Jewish. "When my mother died, it was up to me to be sort of a mom to my sister, Rose," she says. "So there's nothing you could ask me that I probably haven't already heard."

I don't need to be asked twice since there is something I've been dying to know: "How did the baby get inside me?"

Mrs. Berg shakes her head. "You didn't talk about it in your health class at school?"

"Naw. We separated into girls and boys, and the gym teacher got the girls. She mostly talked about how our bodies were changing and that we should wear deodorant, on account of BO, and take a bath or shower every day for the same reason. And to let her know if we had cramps and needed to skip gym. That sort of thing."

Mrs. Berg shakes her head again and pinches her lips together. Then she launches into a story about birds and bees and something called pollination. I tell her that even though it was a unit in our science class, I wasn't very good at horticulture. "Besides, what does any of this have to do with how this happened?" I rub my belly, which has gotten even bigger in the month since I moved into the Bergs' house.

"You know what?" she said. "You're absolutely right." And so, thanks to Mrs. Berg, I now know how the baby got in there. Even though she said I could ask her anything and I wouldn't surprise her, that was only a little bit true. She knew the answer about how it all happened, I could tell, but man oh man, did she have a hard time spitting it out. Her neck and her face kept getting red and blotchy and then pale and then blotchy again when she told me about the "male member." It took me a little while to figure out she was talking about a dick. Mrs. Berg also showed me how I can use my menstruation calendar to figure out when my egg is coming down the pike, and to make sure never to do the sex thing for those days. "It's called the rhythm method," Mrs. Berg explained. "But since you're not married and since you want to avoid becoming with child again, the best way is to practice abstinence." (Then she explained what that word meant.) "Agreed?"

She was right. And since I didn't even like it when it happened that one time, I promised her I wasn't going to do it again until I got married and had to.

Mrs. Berg took in a big, deep breath and let it out. "Good. Well, I'm glad we've got that behind us." She started stroking her neck, almost like she knew it wasn't its normal color and she was trying to hide it.

"You know, Betsy, since we've talked so openly about . . . things . . . I feel like it's time you stopped referring to me as Mrs. Berg. Why don't you call me Lily?"

"Groovy." I felt a gas bubble in my stomach, but it wasn't like the kind that makes me feel like I've got to use the bathroom. And I still had a question, so I just tried to ignore it. "Mrs. Berg, um, I mean

Lily. I've got this dark line running from my belly button down into my crotch. Is that normal?"

Mrs. Berg smiled and said she had the same line. "I got it when I was expecting Jo-Jo, and it faded after she was born but was still there. And now with this baby"—she rubs her stomach—"it's back. So yes, Betsy, it's completely normal."

I know it's silly, but I liked hearing M— . . . Lily tell me how similar we are. I got that gas bubble feeling again.

"Can I ask another question?"

Mrs. Berg smiled, reached out, and squeezed my hand. "Of course. And just so you know, there isn't an expiration date. You can ask me questions tomorrow or next week or whenever they occur to you." She patted my hand. "I can't promise I'll always know the answer, but if it's about the baby, and it's something I don't know, I can always ask Dr. Berg."

I explained about the gassy, bubbly feeling I'd been having the last couple days. That's how I found out the baby was moving in there.

Mrs. Marty Seigel

(Rose)

Lily and I went shopping last weekend, and I let her talk me into buying a fall—a hairpiece of sorts—to add some fullness and length to my hair. I said it wasn't exactly my thing, but she kept pushing me to just try it on, which, finally, I did. "Wow," Lily said. "You look so glamourous. Like Raquel Welch."

"More like Sally Field in *Gidget*," I said. But the truth is, I liked the look. I just didn't like the idea of fake hair; it wasn't me.

"Don't be a spoilsport. Go ahead and buy it," Lily said. "Try it on for Marty and see what he thinks. If he doesn't like it, you can always return it."

As usual, my sister was right, so I bought the hairpiece.

That night, I told Marty I had a surprise for him. I thought he might enjoy being with "another woman." I forget exactly who said what, but I remember making a joke about Marty being jealous that I could wear a fall, while he, poor man, couldn't do anything about his receding hairline. That's when he shoved me against the dresser. At least that's how it seemed to me. It all happened so quickly. Marty pulled me back toward him, hugged me against his chest, and asked if I was all right. I was stunned, and just nodded.

"Hon, you need to be careful. How did you even manage that?"

Again, I didn't respond.

"I don't understand how you tripped backward, over your own two feet, smack-dab into the dresser. That takes talent, Rose. Real talent."

But I didn't trip. At least I didn't think so. Still, why would my husband shove me and lie about it afterward? He loves me and I love him.

"By the way," he said as he left me to unclip the fall. "You should return the hairpiece. Not to be mean, but I know you'd want me to tell you the truth. It looks like you're wearing a dead animal on your head."

Miss Betsy Ann Eubanks

During my first couple weeks at the Bergs' house, I don't think I said more than fifteen words to anyone. And if you think I'm exaggerating, you'd be wrong because one day I actually counted the words. Now it's been a little over a month since I got here, but in some ways, it feels longer, mostly because of Mrs., um, Lily. Sometimes she's more like the older sister I always used to wish for. But I'm not gonna lie; that first week or so was rough for a lot of reasons. First, it was bad because I was still having some morning sickness, even though I told Lily it was gone. I don't know why I lied; I think I was scared she'd send me back to Raven House, and I was pretty sure the housemother would be really mad about that. I also don't know why they call it morning sickness because it happened to me at all different times of the day, not just in the morning. Sometimes it hit me after lunch, and a few times, it even snuck up on me before dinner. Also, when I first got to the Bergs', I was so nervous and afraid of making mistakes. I knew Lily was keeping a real eagle eye on me after I stuck Jo-Jo with the diaper pin. I felt awful when I did it, but I didn't know the right way to put a diaper on a baby until Lily showed me how I had to keep my hand between the diaper and Jo-Jo's leg, which is how I found out about how really sharp those pins are.

I was also nervous because for the two weeks I was at Raven House, before I got dropped off at the Bergs', the size of a few of the girls freaked me out. Some of them looked like they had beach balls under their sweaters, and I wondered what would happen to them or their babies if someone bumped into them. Would they burst wide open? It sure looked like it! Knowing that would be me in a few more months scared the bejeezus out of me. Some of the girls at Raven House asked whether I was homesick, and I guess that was it, even though I'd never heard the word for it before. But it was true. I missed my mom and dad. I even missed going to school, and of course I missed Karen.

Mrs. David Berg

(Lily)

I wonder if Rose would reassess her opinion of me if she'd heard me explaining the facts of life to Betsy. I imagine her response would be something along the lines of *When you can refer to it as "sex" and not "the facts of life," come see me and we can talk about your progression into the 1960s.* Yep. That's exactly what Rose would say. Regardless, I'm rather proud of myself, even if it was hard—so hard—and I stumbled over my own tongue just trying to spit it out. At least I didn't shy away from the discussion, and that *is* progress, even if it's not where Rose is. I could have asked Becca to talk to Betsy, but I pretended Betsy was Jo-Jo as a teenager and asked myself what I'd want my own daughter to know. That made it just a tad easier, I think.

I poke my nose into the utility room, where Betsy is resting on her cot listening to the radio, which is playing the Beach Boys' latest hit, "Help Me, Rhonda."

"I hope I'm not interrupting, but I was just about to sit down with my soap." I debated about whether to ask Betsy to join me. Since this is when Jo-Jo naps, it's an opportunity for Betsy to have time to herself. But I get the feeling she's lonely, or homesick, or both, and maybe she'd like the company. But I also don't want her to feel obligated. Having her in the house is tricky. I'm trying to strike a delicate balance—being hospitable but not smothering, while also making sure I'm approachable, yet not too familiar.

"If you'd like to join me, you're welcome to. But I don't want you to feel obligated, like it's something you have to do if you'd rather not. I just don't want you to feel pressure to do something you don't really want to do." It's not lost on me that I sound like a teenage boy, stumbling through asking a girl out on a date. Not for the first time I thank goodness I was born a girl and never had to muster the courage to ask out a girl, and to risk having her say no.

"Have you ever watched *General Hospital*?"

Betsy shakes her head.

"Well, come then and give it a try." I motion for her to join me in the family room, which is where the TV is, and also where most of Jo-Jo's toys are. I'm pleased to see that without my having to ask her, Betsy has picked up Jo-Jo's alphabet blocks and stacked them against the wall.

I turn on the television, wait for it to warm up, then twist the dial to ABC. If the reception today isn't great, which it might not be because it's rainy and windy outside, there's a separate box on top of the TV, an antenna rotor that allows me to move the antenna, which is on the roof. Again, I feel lucky to live in a time when I can enjoy such luxuries. I think about Grandma Mollie and how she grew up; these inventions must blow her mind. David and I have a small black-and-white TV in our room, but this television is much larger and it's in color, so this is where I watch my soap every day at three p.m., except for Tuesdays, when I'm playing canasta.

"What's *General Hospital*?" Betsy asks.

"It's a soap opera. It's been on for about two years." I take a seat on the couch and tap the cushion, indicating that Betsy should sit next to me. "The show is a half hour and is set in a hospital, which might be why I like it so much. It gives me an inside look at what

David does. It focuses mostly on three couples and their marriages and their problems, and it's also got a lot of hanky-panky." I laugh realizing what I've just said. "Oh man. I hope that's not what David does when he's at the hospital!" Betsy laughs, too.

"Anyway, there's Steve and Audrey Hardy, who just got married. He's a doctor. Jessie and Phil Brewer and . . . you know what? I'm just going to tell you who's who while we watch. It'll be easier. It might take a week or so, but you'll get it. You're smart."

"Groovy. Thanks for letting me watch with you."

The credits are rolling when I hear the front door shut, and I go upstairs to find Becca in the entryway. As usual, she's holding a pack of cigarettes.

I'm glad she's here. Even though we've talked on the phone and have seen each other the last couple weeks at canasta, we've avoided the elephant in the room: her feelings about another baby. I told myself to just give her some time, and when she was ready to talk about it, she would. But the truth is probably closer to the fact that I was relieved not to talk about it. I didn't know what to say.

"Coffee?" I walk into the kitchen and Becca follows. She takes her usual seat as I open a cupboard and remove the tin can of Maxwell House. I add water and coffee to the percolator and settle into my seat across from her.

"That elephant is taking up so much darn room," she says.

"Honestly, I swear there are times when I think you can read my mind."

Becca's laugh is deep and throaty, but a little wet, like so many smokers I know. "Do you mind putting on the radio?" she asks. "Just in case there are ears listening." She points over her shoulder and toward the basement.

I turn on the radio, which is tuned to WKYC and what sounds like the Jay Lawrence show. I spin the dial until I locate a station that's just music.

"I've practiced what I'm going to say for the last hour." Becca smooths her hair, not that it helps; it's just a nervous habit.

"I was pregnant with Gregory when Bradley and I got married. There. I've said it." She looks at me, waiting for a reaction, but I'm caught so completely off guard I don't know what to say. We've been friends for years, and she never mentioned getting in trouble and having to get married before.

"I could have been Betsy, or any one of the other girls at Raven House," she says. "There but for the grace of God go I. That's not just a set of words. It's the God's honest truth. And don't think it wasn't my mantra the entire time we had unwed mothers living with us before the boys were old enough for school. But Bradley did the right thing and married me."

Still, I'm speechless and feeling a bit nauseated. Whether it's morning sickness striking in the afternoon or whether it's Becca's news, who knows? I take the banana sitting in the bowl of fruit in the center of the table and begin to peel it. Maybe putting something in my stomach before another cup of coffee is a good idea. I break off the top half of the banana and tilt the other half toward Becca, raising my brows. She shakes her head. That's the kind of friendship we have—where we can communicate without talking. At least that's the kind of friendship I thought we had.

"When Bradley and I started doing it in high school, we weren't stupid, and we sure weren't careless. Bradley either used a rubber or I douched right afterward. So this"—Becca gestures toward her belly— "isn't the first time that contraception has failed me."

I feel myself heating up. Becca may be plainspoken, and I may have recently been patting myself on the back after my birds-and-the-bees talk with Betsy, but all this talk about doing it, rubbers, and douching makes me uncomfortable, even with Becca.

Becca places a cigarette between her lips, slides out the matchbook nestled between the pack and the cellophane wrapper, and lights up.

She inhales deeply. "But the condom obviously broke or had a hole in it or whatever happened." Becca exhales just as deeply and brings her hand up to her hair again. "I just don't want you to think I'm an idiot who was simply rolling the dice." Becca asks if I have a tissue, and when I hand her the box, she removes one and dabs at her eyes. "When I told Bradley I was in trouble, he was wonderful about it. Said we were planning on getting married anyway, so we'd just have to hurry up the timetable. The only good luck about the whole thing was that my high school graduation was three weeks later, so getting married right away didn't raise too many eyebrows. My mom was suspicious, I'm sure. But she didn't say anything outright and I didn't volunteer anything. Do you know, to this day, she's never asked me?"

"Not even when Gregory came early?"

"Nope. He was a healthy size and I acted like *I know nothing.*" She maintains her deniability by imitating Sergeant Schultz from that new show *Hogan's Heroes.*

"When we moved from Cleveland to Akron, Bradley and I agreed never to tell anyone. And just in case, we moved up the date of our anniversary. We tell people I got pregnant right after we got married on . . ."

"April first," we say in unison, because of course I know her anniversary. Getting married on April Fools' Day is (A) not something I'd forget and (B) so typically Becca and her sense of humor.

"It's our private little joke—that we're the ones fooling everyone," Becca says. "But now we're not fooling you. Not anymore." Becca removes another tissue from the box, brings it to her nose, and gives a couple noisy blows.

I try to lighten the mood. "Listen to you, you sound just like me when I was teaching Jo-Jo to blow her nose."

My attempt at humor clearly has no effect because Becca doesn't even offer me a polite smile.

Becca stubs out her cigarette and begins to remove her bracelets, one by one. She carefully puts them down on the table as she pushes back the sleeve of her sweater. Then she turns over her left arm.

The skin is thick and almost white, and the scar, which is clearly not recent, reaches from one side of her wrist to the other and is almost half an inch thick.

I'm stunned and feel my mouth turn dry. My heart is beating faster, and it takes a moment before I finally manage to speak. "Becca, is that what I think it is? Did you once try to, um, to hurt yourself?"

"It looks that way, doesn't it?"

As I reach for her hand, she pulls back her arm and pushes down the sleeve of her sweater. "That's why I always keep my wrist covered with my bracelets. If the weather is cool, I also wear long sleeves. When the boys were young and couldn't swim, if I had to get in the pool with them, I'd just keep the bracelets on."

"Because you don't want anyone to know?"

Becca laughs. "Relax. I'm fine." She smooths her hair, a hopeless task. "I hide the scar because, based on where it is, whenever anyone sees it, they jump to the wrong conclusion and have the very same response you just did. At least that's what always used to happen— before I started wearing the bracelets. I don't want people assuming I tried to kill myself, especially since they'd likely be too well-mannered to ask me directly if it's true."

"So you didn't try to . . . you didn't attempt suicide?"

"Absolutely not! Although the truth is far less dramatic." She picks up the bracelets and slips them over her hand and back onto her wrist. "When I was in fifth grade, the city was replacing a portion of the sidewalk in front of my school. There were chunks of jackhammered cement everywhere. Anyway, I was riding my bike with Suzy Card, my best friend at the time, and one of us, I don't remember which idiot, thought it would be fun to ride over the rocky path. To call what happened a wipeout is an understatement. Fortunately, some office worker was at the school, saw what happened, and called an ambulance. Suzy wound up with a broken arm and a lot of missing teeth. I got the booby prize, tearing the flesh off my wrist. The doctor thinks that I instinctively put out my hands to try to brace my fall and it was simply a case of bad geometry. I hit the edge of a razor-sharp chunk of cement that left me with this." She holds up her left hand and jiggles it, causing her newly replaced bracelets to jangle.

"So, are you wondering why I never told you before, or are you wondering why I'm telling you now?"

I'm wondering about both, but she's sort of addressed why it's easier for her to keep the gossips at bay. "Why now?"

"Because I really, really can't have another baby," she says. "And not just because I'm overwhelmed with the ones I have and keeping them . . ."

"Out of juvie," we say at the same time.

Becca smiles. "Yes. Not only that." She fiddles with the spoon on the saucer. "Do you have any cookies or crackers? I'm already having heartburn, if you can believe it."

I can. I started having it almost the second I realized I'd missed my monthly. In fact, heartburn was my first clue that I was expecting again.

I notice that the soda crackers are almost gone and pull open the drawer next to the refrigerator where I keep the grocery list and add the word "saltines."

"Bradley's been having problems with the store," she says. "I wasn't going to say anything because it's not the sort of thing I want people to know." Becca takes the plate of crackers I hand her.

She clears her throat. "I repeat. It's not the sort of thing I want people to know."

I promise that her secret is safe with me.

"We've been belt-tightening for a while now. We stopped putting money into the boys' saving accounts for college, and we're not even letting them order books from the Scholastic flyers they give out at school; they each get their *Weekly Reader* and that's it." Becca chews a cracker and washes it down with a sip of her coffee.

"Oh, Becca. I'm so sorry."

"Of course you are, Lily, and I appreciate it. But it's gotten so bad that last month Bradley had to let go of one of his employees, and I'm going to start working at the store to replace him." She holds up her hand. "Don't worry, I told Bradley my canasta day is sacred." She laughs. "For now, I'm going in on Mondays, Wednesdays, and Fridays. The plan is for me to help out with inventory and shoe returns and whatever else Bradley teaches me to do. I was going to tell the neighbors that with the boys in school and Bradley being busier than ever, we decided to see how I liked being part of the workforce and I'm trying it out, part-time. Think they'll buy it?"

I assure her that if she hadn't just told me otherwise, I would believe it. "And you might love it. I sometimes wonder what I'll do when Jo-Jo and this new baby are in school full time. Do you ever feel like you should or *could* be doing more?"

"Honestly, I haven't given it much thought. But I guess we're about to find out, aren't we?"

I feel so horrible that my best friend has been going through this and I had absolutely no idea. "I wish you'd told me sooner. I could have helped."

"I don't know how. Unless you're sitting on a gold mine you're not telling me about."

I admire Becca's ability to joke about something so serious. If this were happening to me, I don't know if I could ever stop crying.

"Obviously I won't get paid, but hey, I don't get paid now. Right? But seriously, if I go into the store, I can partially make up for the man Bradley had to let go. What I'm trying to say is . . . well, what I mean is . . ."

"Becca, it's me. Whatever it is, just spit it out."

"Even if I wanted it, and I definitely don't, we absolutely cannot afford another baby."

Before she walked into my kitchen, I would have told you there's no explanation Becca could offer up that could in any way convince me that her reluctance to have another baby was anything but selfish. She was just being dramatic and overwhelmed with her three boys. Now I can see I was wrong. This is the opposite of selfish. She can't afford the children, the house, and the lifestyle she has now. Adding another baby to the mix, well, this is unexpected. "So, what are you going to do?"

The coffee is percolating, so I have an excuse to get up and turn my back on my friend. "Are you going to put it up for adoption?"

"No, Lily. I'm not going to have it."

I don't understand, until I do.

"But it's illegal." The words are out of my mouth before I'm even aware I said them.

Becca smiles. "You won't even say the word, will you?" But Becca doesn't expect an answer and keeps right on talking. "There are guidelines for abortions," she says. Her speech is interrupted by her near constant sniffles, trying to keep her mucus from leaving her nose. My motherly instinct takes over, and I pull a tissue from the box and push it toward her.

That's it! That's what I can't understand. Where is Becca's motherly instinct?

Becca again smooths her hair. "I'm going to get a therapeutic abortion. I'll save you the question. They're legal and they're done by doctors. They're allowed if, and I quote, 'pregnancy would gravely impair the physical and mental health of the mother.' I need letters from two psychiatrists saying that if this pregnancy continues, I'll be suicidal, or something like that. I need to find out exactly what I have to do to prove it, but I have a feeling the scar from my bicycle accident will come in handy." Becca plays with the bangles around her wrist. "I've promised Bradley I won't go off half-cocked, which he says is something I'm prone to doing."

"Bradley knows you're planning to get an . . . that you're planning to get rid of it?"

Becca nods. "I'm pretty sure my gynecologist will do it if I have letters from the psychiatrists. If he buys it, I'm home free."

"What do you mean, 'if he buys it'? Becca, this isn't a game. There's a baby's life at stake." I look at my friend and wonder if I even know her at all.

"It was a poor choice of words." She sounds beaten down and utterly exhausted. "And believe me, Lily, I am well aware this isn't a game."

I'm surprised by how quickly her mood has changed, taking on a more scolding, almost condescending tone toward me. There is a long silence, mostly because I don't know what to say. I feel reprimanded, but I haven't done anything wrong. And Becca? Well, she just seems spent. I fill the silence by placing a fresh plate of crackers in front of her. I refill the creamer with milk and put it next to her saucer. I try to keep my hands steady as I fill both of our cups with fresh coffee. The radio, apparently, has been eavesdropping on our conversation, because Vic Dana begins singing that he wants some red roses for a blue lady.

Mrs. Marty Seigel

(Rose)

During Shabbat dinner, Marty sits next to me with his arm draped around the top of my chair. Lily talks about her week and shares a cute story about Jo-Jo: She was playing with her pop beads and shoved one up her nose, and thank goodness they've already taught her how to blow her nose because it was rough getting it out. When it's my turn, I decide to tell everyone about one of my second graders.

"Since the start of the school year, every week I teach the class a new letter sound or combination of sounds. This week it's the letters *s-h*."

I suddenly realize that for my broken-English-speaking grandma, who can't read, my story may be difficult to follow, but it's too late now.

"As usual, I announce, 'It's reading time,' which is the cue for everyone to drag their chairs over to the corner and put them in a circle.

"I tell my students that when they see the letters *s-h*, they should think about being quiet, and I put my finger up to my lips and say, 'Shhhh.'" I demonstrate for everyone at the dinner table.

"Anyway, I ask them all to practice. So all the children put their fingers over their mouths and everyone says, 'Shhhh.' Next I take out my flash cards. I tell the kids that we're going to go around the circle, and when it's their turn, they should try to read the flash card. I remind them that all the words start with *s-h*. And again, everyone practices by saying, 'Shhhh.'"

"There's a point to this story, right?" Marty asks, and everyone laughs.

"Marty," Lily says, "don't be so impatient. Although it would be good to wrap this up before dessert." Everyone laughs again, including me.

I give Marty a playful pretend punch in the arm. "We go around the reading circle. I start with a flash card that says 'she' and the little boy says 'shhhh-ee.' So far so good. And then we get to 'share' and 'shape' and 'shy,' and then it's Nathan's turn and he gets the word 'shot.' It's clear he's having trouble and I remind him to sound it out. That's when he says 'shhhhhit!'"

Everyone at the table laughs, even Grandma Mollie, who doesn't like foul language but clearly understood the story, or enough of it, to be genuinely amused.

"Can my wife tell a story or what?" Marty says to no one in particular. He moves his hand from the top of the chair and strokes my back a few times. He leans down near my ear and quietly whispers, "The next time there's a party at my office, tell that story. Everyone will love it."

Marty leans back, and to the rest of the table he says, "That was great, hon, but I thought you were going to tell them about how you tripped and fell into the dresser."

"Oh, no," says Lily. "What happened?"

Marty doesn't give me a chance to answer. "Well, my gorgeous wife is not so light on her feet these days," he says. "She tripped over herself and fell backward into her dresser. Poor thing." He continues to lightly stroke my back and asks my sister if I was always so clumsy.

This, to me, is further proof that Marty was 100 percent right about what happened. He didn't push me; I tripped.

Once table clearing has commenced, Lily takes me aside and asks whether I might be pregnant. "You know," she says, "when I was expecting Jo-Jo, I was always dropping things or banging into furniture. Do you think that's what's happening with you? It would be so fun to have babies together!"

I assure my sister that no, I'm not pregnant, and that yes, it would be fun to have babies together. And that yes, I promise to be more careful when I'm near dangerous objects, like bedroom dressers.

Miss Betsy Ann Eubanks

I can't believe it, but I actually like living with Mrs. Berg, I mean Lily—I'm still not used to calling her that. I think after the day she invited me to watch *General Hospital* with her, it all just started to get better. Now, even if you don't count the stuff I say to Jo-Jo—which is usually just me singing nursery rhymes or talking baby talk or wishing her sweet dreams when I put her down for a nap—I'm saying a lot more than fifteen words a day, mostly because I've been talking more to Lily. During the day, she's really busy with household chores, cooking, and taking care of Jo-Jo, and Dr. Berg, of course. But she always finds time to ask me how I'm doing, and sometimes even asks me to sit down and have some pop with her when she has a cup of coffee. And since that first time, we always watch *General Hospital* together unless it's canasta day. Then Lily counts on me to fill her in with what happened. I still don't know all the characters' names very well, but I know enough to be able to give Lily what she calls "an excellent recap."

Still, just because I say more than fifteen words a day doesn't mean I don't miss my parents and my house and my bedroom. I also miss Karen and being with people my own age. But one thing I've figured out: I'm a good letter writer, and sometimes I even write two letters in a row before I get one back.

Dear Mom,

I got the bras and the underpants. THANK YOU so much for sending them. They are so much more comfortable than my Days of the Week underwear, which sure weren't made to stretch over my big stomach, which is getting gigantic. And it's fine with me if we do what you said and just consider the bras and underwear an early Christmas present.

That reminds me, did I tell you that the Bergs are Jewish? If I did, you can just skip this next part. But the Bergs are Jewish! They don't even celebrate Christmas. And they don't believe in Santa, either. I mean, I know Santa isn't real, but they don't even tell their little kids about Santa. I told Lily (and yes! I'm sure it's OK with her that I call her that!!!) that I never met anybody who was Jewish before. She didn't seem surprised and told me it wasn't that big a deal. That people are just people. STILL! No Christmas???? She did tell me they celebrate Hanaka (sp?) instead and how it lasts 8 days, and Jewish kids get a small gift every night, so it doesn't sound so, so terrible. Lily said that Jewish people don't celebrate the Sabbath on Sunday, either. They do it on Friday night and Saturday, for who knows why, but every Friday night they go have a special Sabbath dinner with Lily's grandma and I'm on my own. It's sort of groovy to have the quiet house all to myself, and I sometimes pretend that I'm Lily and this is my house. I know that sounds silly, and it is, but it's better than boo-hooing over being so far away from home and being left all alone. Oops. That's the train whistle . . . I'll be right back.

OK. I'm back. Did I tell you about the train? It's behind the house, but not right behind. But close enough that we can see the color of the caboose. Whenever the train comes, we guess what color the caboose will be. It's either red or green. If you guess right, you get to make a wish and it's supposed to come true. I don't know if it's like the wishes you make before you blow out the candles on your birthday cake, and you're not supposed to tell anyone your wish, or it definitely won't come true. But I think you can probably guess what I wish for.

Do you think Dad will speak to me when I come home? Maybe we can do what you always say about this and just pretend it never even happened. Do you think you can tell him that?

Only 4-ish more months until I can come home. I can't wait.

I'm going to write a letter to Karen after this. Please give it to her.

I'm gonna jet. Please write back.

Love,

Your very own Betsy Wetsy doll

(Remember when you used to call me that??)

Dear Karen,

I think it's so groovy that you like Mark. But it's not like you can just walk up to him and say, "Hey, man. I like you. You wanna go on a date?" I mean, that's what boys do to girls, not the other way around. But I've been thinking about it. You said that since I'm away this year you've been hanging out with some other girls. Who are they? You can tell me. I won't be mad that you're making other friends. I promise, I get it. It's not like you even have a choice. ANYWAY . . . .

Maybe you could ask one of your new girlfriends to ask

one of Mark's guy friends if he knows if Mark likes anyone. At least that way you'll know if he has his eye on you or whether he's got a crush on some other girl right now. Isn't that a good idea?

I can't take total credit for it, though. I've been watching this soap opera with my aunt that she likes. It's called General Hospital. One of the characters, who's a nurse, liked this doctor who just happens to be married. But the nurse wondered if she had a chance with him anyway, and what did she do? She made friends with one of the doctor's friends and started asking nosy questions about the doctor and his wife. Not the same difference, but sort of the same. Anyway . . . .

It's worth a try, don't you think?

Write back soon.

Miss you!!!!!!!!!!!!!!!

Bets

Mrs. David Berg

(Lily)

W e're at Sarah's house because it's her turn to host canasta. She's wearing a bright orange pantsuit ensemble, which, of course, she made. That woman is truly a wiz with a needle and thread. But every time I compliment one of her outfits, I can't help but think: *Honey, you have too much spare time on your hands. You should be taking care of your babies and sewing clothes for them!* I've given Sarah more than a couple openings to tell me whether she's having trouble starting her family or if she's just one of those girls who doesn't want children, but she's never taken the bait. And Rose is right: I can't just come out and ask; that would be so rude. Still, I was there when Robin once suggested that Sarah open a clothing store with all her fancy outfits, but Sarah just laughed and said her job was taking care of Joel. She didn't even mention the word "babies."

Sarah interrupts my gossipy thoughts, which I immediately feel guilty about. "Is it just me, or has the game today seemed glacial?" she asks.

"Slower than slow," Becca says.

"Come on, ladies." Robin jumps up from her chair at the game table. She lifts her arms over her head, clasps her hands together, and rocks her hips back and forth in a mock dance. "It's time to get our grooves on." We all exchange looks with each other. It's clear that not one of us has any idea what Robin's talking about.

Becca glances at the Timex on her wrist, which causes her bracelets to jingle. "It's too late to start another game, but we still have time before the boys get back from school. What did you have in mind to help us get our grooves on, Robin dear?"

"Something fun and out of the ordinary. Something that we've never done before, at least not together."

I must admit, I'm more than a little curious. "Okay, Robin. Whatever it is, count me in."

"And for that, you get to go first," Robin says. "Truth or dare?"

Sarah laughs and then offers soft applause. "I haven't played that since I was a little girl."

"Me, neither," I say.

Robin points at me. "So, Lily. What's it going to be? Truth or dare?"

"Watch it," Sarah says. "Knowing Robin, if you choose dare, she'll probably ask you to go to a protest march with her."

Everyone laughs about that. "Can I trust you to be nice?" I ask Robin.

She just looks at me, clearly trying hard not to give away anything.

"This isn't the Staring Game," I say.

"I remember that one, too. I used to play it with my sister all the time," Sarah says. "I always blinked first."

"Sounds like me and the Quiet Game," Becca says. "I always lost."

"Not like that's any surprise," I say, and we all have a good laugh, thinking about Becca trying to remain silent.

"You think I don't know that you're stalling?" Robin says. "Soon we'll have to head home for our kids, so let's get on with it. What's your pleasure, Lily, truth or dare?"

"I'll pick dare," I say. As soon as the words are out of my mouth, I wonder why in the world I didn't select truth. These are my closest friends, and they know everything about me. Well, okay, not everything, and certainly not anything about the intimate parts of my life with David, which is what I suspect Robin would question me about.

Robin cocks her head to the side. "Hmmm. You completely surprised me, I thought for sure you'd say 'truth' and I was all set with a couple of great questions."

"What were your truth questions?" Becca asks before I have a chance.

Robin wags her index finger back and forth. "No way. I'm saving them for next time." She uses her fingers to lock her lips before she thrusts her arm over her shoulder, tossing away the invisible key.

"So, what's the dare?" I ask.

Robin slaps the top of both of her thighs hard enough to leave red marks just below her miniskirt. She gets up from her seat and makes a sweeping gesture with her arm. "Come with me." Robin walks into Sarah's kitchen, and like lemmings, Becca, Sarah, and I all follow.

Robin rests her hand on the handle of Sarah's refrigerator door. "I'm going to open this," Robin says. "And remember, this isn't my house, so I don't know exactly what's inside, though I could guess and be 95 percent right. But it doesn't matter. I'm going to pull out everything that's liquid and pour some of each of those things into a glass and mix it all together for you to drink."

Even before Robin opens the door, I do a mental list of what I know is in my refrigerator: milk, leftover Campbell's chicken noodle soup, orange juice, Kool-Aid. I wonder if the juice that's in the jar of maraschino cherries or olives counts as liquid. What about salad dressing or condiments like mustard and ketchup? I'm already feeling sick to my stomach when Robin tugs on the handle and opens the refrigerator door.

Mrs. Marty Seigel

(Rose)

As we leave the movie theater, the crisp night air cools my nostrils. I'd heard from Sarah and Becca that *Doctor Zhivago* was good, but I'm surprised by how touched I was by the love story. I'm still feeling weepy as we walk through the parking lot, but I know if I make a big deal about the movie making me cry, Marty will tease me. Mercilessly. So when I sniffle, I pretend I'm simply inhaling, albeit deeply. "I love this time of year, don't you? It even smells like winter is coming, doesn't it?"

"If you say so." Marty removes the car keys from his pocket. Once he's behind the wheel, he reaches across the seat and pulls up the knob, unlocking the passenger door.

"Oh, the good old days." I yank the door shut. "Remember when we were dating and we went to the movies and you always walked around to open my door?"

"I'm sorry," Marty says. "I guess my mind is just elsewhere."

"Don't be silly. I'm joking. I'm fully capable of doing it by myself. Needing help opening doors is part of the feminine mystique."

"The what?"

"Feminine mystique. It's the title of a book I'm reading. It's the term the author made up to describe what we're all taught to believe about what it means to be truly feminine. It's written by this woman Betty Friedan."

"What's the point of it?"

"Well, I'm still reading it, but it's based on a survey she did with other women who graduated from Smith College, where she went to school. She identifies something she calls 'the problem that has no name.'"

"What's the problem?"

"How we're all sort of programmed to think that real women are only truly feminine if they're happy being housewives and mothers. And if they're not happy with that, then there's something wrong with them."

"And that's not true?"

"Not according to this book. The author says a lot of women feel unfulfilled and suffer because they think there's something wrong with them if being a wife and mom isn't enough. And everyone thinks they're the only one who feels that way. I think part of what she's wanting women to know is they're not alone. I'm still reading, like I said."

Marty taps the space next to him, indicating I should slide across the bench seat. When I do, he wraps his right arm around my shoulder. "But I'm asking you, what do you think?"

"I think it's part true. I mean, I went to college and I love my job and I certainly enjoy being married to you. I can't honestly say I like cooking, keeping the house clean, or doing the laundry or going to the grocery store and some of the other things that are my responsibilities as a wife. Of course I don't know yet about whether having kids and managing the house will make me feel happy and fulfilled, but once I get pregnant, I'll have to go on mandatory maternity leave, so I'll have plenty of time to prepare. I think it will all work out. I mean, look at Lily. She's happy. But she could do so much more, don't you think?"

Marty taps me on top of my head. "I'm not sure I agree, silly goose." He returns both of his hands to the steering wheel. "David has a very demanding job and is running off to deliver babies at all hours of the day and night. He needs someone to prepare his meals, run his house and keep it clean. And don't forget about Jo-Jo, and soon the new baby. If Lily doesn't take care of all the things on the home front, then David can't be as successful as he needs to be in order to provide for everyone. Women keep the home flames burning, and it's up to men to make a living and support everyone. Don't you agree?"

What Marty says makes sense. And I experienced, firsthand, how hard life was without a mom in the house for us, and without a wife in the house for Dad. But we managed. We had Grandma Mollie, of course, and Dad hired Esther-Lee to come in and clean a couple times a week. She, along with Grandma, cooked all our dinners and put them in the freezer for Lily to heat up. I think we did okay.

"It's complicated. I honestly don't know how I feel," I say. "The Negros have been protesting and marching in Washington asking for rights. That speech a couple months ago by that man who talked about not judging people by their skin color, but by who they are inside, still sticks with me. I'm starting to feel like women are next."

"What does that mean?"

"That women shouldn't be judged based on the fact that we're women, but by who we are and what we can contribute—and that might be more, or at least something different than wife and mother. At least for some women."

Marty doesn't respond, unless you count his "hmm," but he does reach down and pat my thigh. "You're a good teacher," he says. "Your students are really lucky to have you."

I'm glad it's dark in the car and he can't see me blushing. This is so silly; he's my husband, and I feel like a schoolgirl on a date with my crush. "Aw, honey, that's so sweet of you. Thank you for saying that."

"I only said it because it's true. And it's not just those kids who are lucky to have you." He pats my thigh again. "I am, too. I want you to know that. I might not always remember to say it or show it, but you're the best thing that's ever happened to me."

"I want you to know, I feel the same way, Marty. I love you and I think we should have more talks like this."

"Oh, you do, do you?" Marty pulls me closer, and I have to move my shoulder to avoid hitting the steering wheel.

"Yes, I do. I absolutely do."

Miss Betsy Ann Eubanks

One thing Lily and I have figured out is that we're both hungry all the time, so we've added a snack to the schedule. Every day after *General Hospital*, we go upstairs to the kitchen and see if we can find what Lily calls "a little something to hold us over till dinner." That's when we talk, mostly about Jo-Jo, but sometimes about how our big bellies get in the way, especially when we have to bend over to do something that used to be easy, like tie our shoes. Today I tell Lily how groovy I think it is that she and her sister are both named after flowers. "Technically," she says, "we're named after my mom's grandparents. Her grandpa's name was Levi, so my mom used the *L* from Levi and named me Lily, and her grandma was Ruth, so she took the *R* from her and named her Rose. The fact we both have flower names was something my mom just added. Her special twist. My mom referred to Rose and me as her petite fleurs." Lily stops long enough to take a bite of the Hostess cupcake she cut in half for us to share. "I once asked her what she would have done if one of us had been a boy, and she just laughed and laughed and finally said, 'What? You've never heard of a boy named Tulip?'"

That was funny, a boy named Tulip. I'd never heard about using someone's initial to choose a name, not that it matters because (A) I don't want the baby inside me and wish it wasn't there about a million times every day, and (B) I'm giving it away as fast as I can and

I don't really care what the people who adopt it name it. I have not thought even one time about this baby's name. The only thing I know for sure is I wouldn't name him John, since that's another name for toilet or bathroom and I really don't get why people do that to their little boys. I think I'd go with Michael if it was a boy and maybe Lisa or Karen if it was a girl. But that's off the top of my head because, honestly, I'm sure whoever adopts my baby couldn't give two hoots about what I think.

"It's part of being Jewish," Lily says, interrupting my thoughts about the unnamed baby in my stomach. "Jewish people think it's bad luck to name our babies after someone who is still living, so we name after someone who died. It's a way to honor their memory."

"Groovy. I'm named after my dad's mom, Elizabeth, who lives in upper Michigan. We mostly just see her during the big holidays, like Christmas and Easter. But when I was born, my parents decided that Elizabeth is a lot of name for such a little baby, so I've been Betsy right from the get-go."

All this talk leads me to ask who Jo-Jo is named after. I immediately know I put my foot in my mouth when Lily's beautiful blue eyes start to shine because there's a thin layer of tears piling up.

"My mom," she says.

Alarm bells go off in my pea-sized brain. She just told me that you only name after someone who's died, and yet I opened my big mouth—which my mom used to say gets me into trouble, right before she'd wash out my mouth with soap or smack me across the face, telling me to "watch your mouth, young lady." I make matters worse when I ask, "How'd she die?" My parents would be mortified, and I can practically hear my mom using her whisper-scream voice asking, *What, exactly, is wrong with you, Betsy Ann Eubanks?*

But Lily doesn't seem to take offense. She taps the area between her breasts. "The C-word."

Mrs. Marty Seigel

(Rose)

We are having a small gift exchange at Grandma's, and by "small," I mean we are each bringing a gift for Jo-Jo. Dad said that once we got married, it was up to us to decide what, if anything, we wanted to do as far as gift-giving with our spouses, but Grandma has always insisted that Chanukah is for children, the *kinderlach*, which was why, once I hit eighteen years old, the edict came down: We were no longer to buy presents for each other, and certainly nothing for her. But last year, when we gave Grandma a gift, we made it clear that we didn't buy it, "buy" being the operative word.

We created our gift for Grandma using some Magic Markers from my classroom and some airmail stationery that Lily picked up at the post office. We made Grandma an official, unofficial birth certificate. On it, we wrote down her birthday as July 4. We selected that date because, for one thing, it would be easy to remember. We had to pick a year for her birth, so we just guessed. She seems certain that she was sixteen when she had our dad and, using his age, that put her at sixty-seven, give or take. But what woman doesn't want to be younger?

We wrapped the birth certificate in colorful tissue paper and told her it was a gift from all of us. "Be careful unwrapping it, you don't want to tear it," Dad said. Since she can't read, when she opened it, she didn't know what it was. "It's a birth certificate," I said. "And this year, on July 4, you'll be turning sixty-five." She seemed a bit confused, albeit pleased. But when July 4 rolled around and we took her to see the fireworks, she was downright giddy. And when Lily told her "the whole country is celebrating your birthday and that's the real reason for the fireworks," I wondered whether Grandma would ever *jujje* Lily again.

Mrs. David Berg

(Lily)

This year, Chanukah falls on Saturday, December 18, so it will overlap with Christmas, assuming we celebrate all eight days, which we do. I think it's always more fun when the holidays fall roughly at the same time, rather than when Chanukah is really early or very late. At least when they're close to each other, all Americans can just celebrate and be festive the entire holiday season. Betsy didn't understand why Chanukah jumps around while Christmas is always December 25, so I explained how the Jewish calendar is based on the lunar cycle, whereas what she called "the regular calendar" revolves around the sun. She gave her standard response of "groovy," but I could tell by her puzzled look this wasn't something she understood. Another reminder to me that she's only fifteen.

Sarah, Becca, Robin, and I all agreed not to meet for canasta during the two weeks that Becca and Robin have their kids home for the school vacation. "Not a problem," I said. "I can be patient and wait a few weeks to exact my revenge for Truth or Dare, Robin." We all laughed, remembering that crazy day.

After Robin mixed together the concoction of liquids from Sarah's refrigerator (olive juice counted, as did the spaghetti sauce, salad dressing, and all the other condiments), she handed me the glass. My hand was literally shaking as I brought it up to my lips and tilted it up, preparing to take a sip—just a small one.

"Stop, you ninny," Robin said, grabbing the glass from me. "I didn't tell you that you had to drink it. I told you I was going to mix the liquids together *for you to drink*. Those were my exact words."

"She's right," Becca said.

"Of course I'm right." Robin tucked her hair behind her ear. "I'm married to a lawyer. You think I haven't learned that words matter and what you don't say is often more important than what you do?" Robin rolled her eyes. "You don't really think I'd ask you to drink that crap? Holy moly. What kind of friend do you take me for?"

We all wound up laughing and hugging each other. Not for the first time, I was struck by how much these girls mean to me.

Since we won't be meeting for cards during the school vacation, we decided to get together for our First Annual Canasta Group Secret Santa Gift Exchange. When Robin initially mentioned the idea, she asked if, since Sarah and I are both Jewish, she'd be ruffling feathers. I'm not sure who laughed first, but Sarah and I were in agreement: It wasn't the least bit offensive. So today before we play canasta, we're going to figure out the details of the gift exchange.

Since I know how tight finances are in Becca's house, something the others aren't privy to, I'm not crazy about asking her to spend money, so I offer an alternative. "How about instead of buying each other something new, we find something we already have around the house and give that as a gift to whoever's name we draw from the hat?"

Robin nods. "Ooh. That will make it even more fun. We get to see what everyone decides to get rid of."

"Or to pawn off on her poor unsuspecting friend," Becca says. "But you know what they say about one man's trash being another's treasure." She extends her wrist and dangles her bracelets. "Whoever gets me has it easy. A girl can never have too many bracelets. Hint,

hint." Becca offers an exaggerated wink. Looking at Sarah, she says, "And I'm a size eight, just in case you have some extra fabric lying around."

I'm pleased that Becca's in such a good mood. In fact, this is the most chipper she's been since telling us she was pregnant. I wonder if she's seen those psychiatrists yet, and if she has, maybe they've given her the good news she's looking for. I assume that's the case, but I haven't asked her about it directly because, as much as I want to be a good friend, I don't want to be a hypocrite. I don't think ending her pregnancy is the answer—especially since it's illegal. But then I remind myself that she's seeing the psychiatrists because that would make it legal. Except she's lying to those doctors because it is illegal. And if it's illegal, then it must be against the law for a reason. And it goes to follow that it's against the law because it's wrong. Then I remind myself of their precarious financial situation. But it's still illegal. 'Round and 'round I go in my mind, always winding back up in the same place, which is in a state of confusion.

Still, I can't shake the feeling that Becca seeing the psychiatrists is akin to what my dad calls cheating the system. As an accountant, he says that many people, especially people who have lots of money, try to do that. And how it's his job to make sure they don't cross any red lines. All of this is, of course, Greek to me, because Dad's never really explained his work. When I was a little girl and asked him about his job, he usually answered by saying, "Nothing to worry your pretty little head over." When I got older, he told me that he prepares taxes for people and companies, which helped a bit but not a lot since David takes care of all our finances and I just make sure that the pay packet he gives me on the first of every month covers our expenses.

But the bottom line, I tell myself, is that Becca is my best friend and I should support her, whatever she chooses. It's just hard for me to push aside my beliefs and get behind what I feel in my heart is wrong, so I find myself simply dodging it entirely, mostly because it's easier not to be involved.

We all agree that starting a Secret Santa tradition will be fun.

"As long as we're all going through our treasures," I say, emphasizing Becca's word choice, "can I ask everyone a favor?"

I explain that Betsy recently got an early Christmas present from her mother. "It was maternity bras and underwear, which she definitely needed. But still." I pick up the cards in front of me, figuring I may as well give them a few shuffles since at some point we will actually play canasta today. "Betsy's only fifteen, and she's away from her family and friends, and I just don't want her to have a miserable holiday on top of everything else she's dealing with."

Robin immediately senses what I'm asking yet not stating directly. "We should each bring something from home for Betsy, too. Just so she knows we're thinking of her."

Becca and Sarah agree, and Robin jumps up to get a small notepad. She hands us each a piece of paper and tells us to write down our names. She folds each paper in half and looks around for something to put them in. She comes back with a saucepan. "It'll do. Now, if you get your own name, throw it back in, and hopefully this will all work out. And since there are only four of us, don't tell anyone whose name you picked, because if you do, it'll be too easy to figure out who might have your name."

"Ooh. So much intrigue," I say. "This is even more suspenseful than *Perry Mason*."

That's how, two weeks later, I wind up with a copy of *The Feminine Mystique*, my gift from Robin. I fan through the pages and see a great deal of underlining, as well as a lot of dog-eared corners. "Promise me you'll read it," she says. "At least the first chapter. Remember, I didn't make you drink that concoction, so please? Promise?"

I tell her I'll read it, and she gives me a huge hug. "I think you'll get a lot out of it. I really do."

I drew Sarah's name and immediately knew I wanted to give her a tube of lipstick. I chose one I thought would suit her complexion but didn't flatter me the way I'd hoped when I bought it. When I present it to her, she seems genuinely excited and blots off the lipstick she's wearing to model the new one for us. It's a perfect shade for her! I also give her a package of needles and some buttons. "Not that you need sewing notions," I say. I hope Sarah will get the inside joke and understand how much I appreciate that she has never shared my secret: Since she moved into the neighborhood, she's helped me with at least a half dozen repairs, including one just last week, when I popped a button on my winter coat, thanks to my ever-growing belly.

Becca had Robin's name and gives her a brownie pan. "If you think that's a hint to make me some, you're right!"

Finally, Sarah gives Becca a pair of patterned stockings still in their original packaging. "Giving you a bracelet was too boring," Sarah says. "You did say you're working a few days a week, right? Well, you'll have to supply your own girdle or garter belt, but I thought you could use them."

"But they're new," Becca says.

"Yes. But the rule was the gift had to be something already in your house. These meet the criteria. I hope they make you feel more like a professional woman and less like a mom." Then Sarah takes a piece of silky fabric from her bag. "And I made you this scarf to tie around your neck. It'll look great with your blond hair."

Becca, for once, doesn't have a smart-aleck response. In fact, she seems truly touched.

Miss Betsy Ann Eubanks

I am not a happy camper, as my dad would say, except I don't know for sure what he'd say because I still haven't gotten a single letter from him.

That's just one thing that's ticking me off. Also:

- None of my clothes fit, and I have to wear these horrible dresses, left over from the Bergs' last unwed mother, that look like they came from Goodwill.
- My mom sent me new bras and underpants for pregnant ladies, but they're completely scuzzy.
- Whenever I'm trying to sleep or take a nap, that's when the baby gets its groove on in there and won't stop moving, just to keep me awake.
- Every night, it kicks me so hard that I have to pee right away; otherwise, I'll wet my pj's.

When I mention all this to Lily, she just laughs and says, "Welcome to the club."

A couple days ago during our snack after *General Hospital* (a Little Debbie Swiss Roll!), Lily asked me how I found out I was pregnant. What was really surprising is she didn't say "expecting" or "with child"; she actually used the word "pregnant."

I told her that when I didn't get my monthly visitor at the end of August, it was the first time I'd ever skipped. I figured Aunt Flo was just late, but then it still hadn't come through all of September. "My stomach was upset and I was puking a lot, but I figured I was only sick because my monthly was so late."

"Oh, you poor thing." Lily rests her hands on her belly and starts petting it, like it's a cat or something.

"Then one morning when I was still puking, my mother stormed into the bathroom and asked if I was in trouble. I had no idea what she was talking about. When I asked her 'What trouble?,' she grabbed my arm and practically dragged me into the car and right to our family doctor. He had me pee into a paper cup, but when I handed it to him, there wasn't any blood in the cup, so I knew my monthly still hadn't come.

"Two weeks later, the doctor called my mom. She just listened, then thanked him for calling. Then she used her whisper-yelling voice and said, 'Come with me, young lady.' We went into my bedroom and she closed the door. That's when she told me I was pregnant and she didn't want my dad to know anything until she figured out what we were going to do."

Lily purses her lips, and her eyes are watery-looking. I'm pretty sure she's going to start crying, but she doesn't. She just asks me to tell her what happened next.

"Well, a year earlier, there was this cheerleader, Donna, who was at my school, and everyone knew all about her. She, um, well, she got her pregnancy unstuck by falling down the stairs, so I decided that's what I'd do, too."

"I thought your house was one floor."

"It is. But we have stairs that go down to the basement, there are seven or eight of them, but I was too scared to do it. So I got an idea and just started spinning and spinning in circles. Then, when I was good and dizzy, it was a cinch to just make myself fall forward."

Lily gasps and puts her fingertips over her lips. "Did your parents know what you did?"

"Naw. I had some bruises the next day, but when my mom asked me about them, I told her it probably happened when I was playing dodge ball. She just shook her head and said something about how I was too old to still be a tomboy.

"The thing is, I just assumed that falling down the stairs would work. So whenever I went to the bathroom, I looked to see if the baby had dropped out yet, but nothing ever happened." I glance down at my hands, which are folded in my lap, because it's better than locking eyes with Lily, who looks the most down in the dumps as I've ever seen her during the entire time I've been here.

She sighs. "I'm sorry, Betsy." Lily reaches across the table, grabs my arm, feels for my hand, and then rubs the top of it. "Did you ever tell your mom what you'd done to get the baby, um, unstuck?"

I shake my head and ask Lily if we can share another snack. I'm not really hungry, but I don't want to talk about this anymore.

Lily takes the metal tray out of the freezer and pulls back the handle to release the ice cubes. When she returns to the table, she hands me a glass of orange pop and a Little Debbie Oatmeal Creme Pie, my favorite cookie.

"Betsy, I don't mean to pry, but throwing yourself down the stairs is pretty desperate. I just want to make sure you're okay and don't feel that way now."

I don't know what to say. It's true that I wish I never met the out-of-town boy and I hate being pregnant and how uncomfortable I am all the time. But if I wasn't pregnant, I never would have met Lily and Dr. Berg, and they're just the grooviest. And Jo-Jo is such a cutie-pie. But if I tell Lily that, I'll sound completely pathetic. So instead, I tell her how being around Jo-Jo has shown me how much work it is to have a baby. "Since I'm not ready to keep it, I'll give my baby to a couple who wants it, because I sure don't."

Lily puts her hands over her stomach like she doesn't want the baby inside her to hear what I've just said. *Like the baby can hear!* I shouldn't make fun of her. Lily is actually outta sight. She's not my mother, and it's not her job to be my friend—at least that's what Mom keeps writing in her letters. But I know Lily likes me. She got her whole canasta group to look around their houses to see if they had anything they didn't need anymore that they thought I could use. Mrs. Thompson gave me two of her old maternity dresses. She also gave me a pamphlet about a civil rights protest march to help Negros get the right to vote. "It's coming up," she said when she passed out the brochures like playing cards. She invited the whole canasta group to join her, and even though everyone said they'd think about it, I could tell they really meant no. "What do you say, Betsy? Don't you think Negros should be able to vote just like you and me?" Mrs. Thompson asked. I reminded her that I was only fifteen and not allowed to vote at all. Everyone had a good laugh about that.

Mrs. Hudson said she gave away all her dresses years ago because she never expected to be pregnant again, but then she handed me a pair of moccasins. "My feet hurt and grew after each pregnancy, so I practically lived in these," she said as she pressed them into my hands. I almost asked her why she wasn't keeping them, since she'll probably want them this time, too. But instead, I just tried them on, and she was right. They made me feel like I was walking on really fluffy cotton.

Since Mrs. Bloom doesn't have any babies, she didn't have any pregnancy stuff to give me, which is fine since I won't be like this forever. Just three more months until I go back to Raven House and then another month until I have this baby, give or take. Mrs. Bloom gave me a bunch of headbands in all kinds of bright colors that she made especially for me. She also gave me all twelve months of *LIFE* magazine from this year. "I don't know why I save them after I've read them," she said. "But I do, so now you can enjoy them."

Lily said it was a terrific gift. "And when Betsy's done, she can share them with me."

Everyone laughed when she said that. But then Mrs. Thompson reminded Lily that she gave her a book for the Secret Santa exchange. "I expect you to read *The Feminine Mystique* first."

January
1966

Miss Betsy Ann Eubanks

Lily and Dr. Berg were invited to a party for New Year's Eve at Mrs. Thompson's house. I thought it would be pretty funny if she wrote "Happy New Year" on some of her protest signs and hung streamers off of them. I planned to tune in to Guy Lombardo on the boob tube and watch the ball drop, but I fell asleep before it happened, and when I woke up, it may have been a new year, but everything else was exactly the same. On New Year's Day, all the Bergs went to their grandma's house, so I had hardly any diapers to change, which was fine with me. Today we're back to our normal routine, which makes it especially weird when Mrs. Hudson pokes her nose in the front door and asks if Lily's around.

It's weird because everyone knows that Lily has a standing appointment at the beauty shop on Friday mornings.

"Of course," Mrs. Hudson says when I remind her about where Lily is. Mrs. Hudson puts her hand against the side of her head and adjusts her hair. I don't know why she does that; if she was so concerned about her mess of hair, she could use hairspray, like my mom does. I smile, thinking about my mom and how she calls it shellac.

"Silly me. Betsy, there are days when I think I've lost my mind completely."

"Lily says that when she's pregnant, she would lose her head if it wasn't attached to her neck."

"How about you? Are you forgetful, too?"

When I tell her that it's nothing I've noticed, she says something about how nice it must be to be young. "I swear, sometimes I think raising those three juvenile delinquents has muddled my brain!" She laughs, although I don't really get the joke, and I really don't know why she always talks about her boys like they're criminals. When I was at her house for Thanksgiving, they seemed nice to me, except she must have said about a million times that they should sit still in their seats. But of course they didn't listen to one word she said, and by the time the meal was over, there was gravy spilled all over everything. Even still, when we went around the table and it was time for them to say what they were thankful for, every one of them said, "My mom."

"Well, dear, as long as I'm here and I have some time on my hands, why don't you tell me about yourself?" Mrs. Hudson taps her pack of cigarettes, pulls out one, and places it between her lips. Not to be mean, but I notice that her lipstick is smeared across her front teeth.

You don't have to know Mrs. Hudson well—and I don't—to know she is acting cuckoo. Back home, whenever someone was going mental, we circled our index fingers around the side of our foreheads, but I know better than to do that now. But still, she acts like I've just arrived. "I think you know just about everything. What else is there?"

Mrs. Hudson walks from the entry hall and into the living room, where she sits on the love seat. "I'm afraid I'm not very good at this," she says.

I truly have no idea what *this* is. "Are you feeling all right, Mrs. Hudson?" Without waiting for her to answer, I head into the kitchen to get her some water and an ashtray. She takes the water first, downs a gulp, and then rests her cigarette in the ashtray.

"Oh, Betsy. I'm just a bit overwhelmed, is all. I have this friend, and I'm trying to help her." Mrs. Hudson begins to smooth the crushed-velvet fabric on the love seat with her hand, moving the nap one direction and then the other. Then she uses both hands to tap herself on her upper thighs. That's something my mom always does once she's made up her mind about something.

"My friend—" She goes back to petting the couch. "There's no delicate way to say this, so I'll just spit it out. She's pregnant." She makes a half-circle gesture in front of her stomach.

"Well, she can go to Raven House, like I did."

Mrs. Hudson goes back to smoothing her hair. "No, dear. Raven House is for unwed mothers, and my friend, well, she's married and she wants to get rid of it."

I try not to freak out. First off, I have no idea why Mrs. Hudson is telling me this, and second, I know Mrs. Hudson is unhappy about her baby on the way, and now she has a friend who is, too? I may not be a genius, but I'm also not an idiot. I suddenly feel like my mom who whenever she caught me in a lie would say, "Do I look like I was born yesterday?"

Before I even have a chance to ask her why her "friend" doesn't want her baby, Mrs. Hudson starts talking again. "I was wondering if abor— . . . if getting rid of their babies was something that maybe you've discussed with your friends at Raven House."

"Well, they're not really my friends. I was only there for two weeks before I came here."

"But you go back there once a month to see the doctor, isn't that right? That's what my girls from Raven House did." Again, she doesn't even give me a chance to answer. "So, I was just wondering if it's something maybe you heard some of the girls talking about and, if so, maybe you could get a telephone number, so I could give it to my friend." Mrs. Hudson takes a puff of her cigarette and exhales like she's so glad to be done talking. She looks at me and smiles.

This is heavy, man. "Well, ma'am, a couple girls talked about taking some pills or herbs or something to make them puke, but afterward, they were still pregnant. Obviously. I mean, if they're at Raven

House, they're preggers, right? And one girl said she was going to try using a knitting needle, but then she freaked out. I don't even know what she was talking about, but is that the sort of thing you mean?"

"Not really, dear." Mrs. Hudson takes a sip of her water, and I notice her hand is shaking. "I was thinking more along the lines of a doctor or nurse who's been trained to, you know, get rid of it. Have you heard about anything like that?"

"Getting rid of a pregnancy?"

"Yes, dear. Exactly."

I shake my head. "The next time I go there, I can ask them, though. But you know what? Lily might know. She's told me all kinds of things about babies and how they get made." That's when I have an extra great idea. "But I'll bet someone who could really help is Dr. Berg! I think he's an expert about everything there is to know about babies."

Mrs. Hudson makes a face like she's just sucked on a lemon. "You're right, dear. Dr. Berg would be the perfect person to ask . . . for my friend." She stands and smooths her skirt, just like she was smoothing the couch. "I'm going to head home now." She rubs my cheek with her thumb. "You really are such a pretty girl. Has anyone ever told you that?"

"No, ma'am."

"Well, you are. And I will talk to Lily or Dr. Berg about my friend, but I'd really appreciate it if you didn't mention anything about it to them first. So this talk can stay just between us. How's that sound?"

I nod, still struck by the fact she thinks I'm pretty.

Mrs. David Berg

(Lily)

Canasta was supposed to be at Robin's house today, but she used the Bissell to shampoo her carpeting this morning, and since it's still not dry, she and I traded. I start to shuffle the deck we just used. I've been dying to ask Becca whether she got her letters from the psychiatrists yet, but I figure if she had an update—an update she wanted me to know about—she would tell me. But deep down, I know it's equally likely she wouldn't say a word, one way or the other. Not after the way I behaved when she told me her plan.

Becca is telling a story about how things have been going at the store. "So, I said, 'Bradley, you can either be the boss of me at home or be the boss of me at the store. But it can't be both, or I quit!'" Everyone at the table laughs. It's good to see she hasn't lost her sense of humor. Maybe things with the psychs went well.

Becca begins to deal and calls for last hand. I'm always impressed by her ability to talk and deal out thirteen cards at the same time, and she doesn't disappoint. "My boys will be home from school any minute—*ten*—and if I'm not there soon, they'll—*eleven*—find the cherry pie I made for dessert and—*twelve*—there won't be anything left by dinner—*thirteen*. Everyone count your cards to make sure I'm right."

Of course she's right.

"I know exactly what you're talking about," Robin says. "I wasn't going to mention it, but you all are my very best friends, and this is just too great not to share." Everyone leans in close until our chins are almost colliding over the card caddie in the center of the table. "This happened a couple weeks back. I had just finished baking a pan full of brownies," she says. "They were cooling on the counter. Honestly, I turned my back for just one second—one second—and those little hands each managed to steal a brownie. Before I could say a word, the twins were shoving them into their mouths."

I laughed, as did everyone else, picturing those tiny faces smeared with chocolate. "Don't laugh," Robin says. "They were not your ordinary Betty Crocker brownies!"

Rose says that sometimes I can be slow on the uptake, but I'm not this time. "Your twins ate brownies filled with dope?"

Robin has a smile that shows not just her beautifully white teeth but also her gums. Whenever she smiles, she typically holds back; she worries "my big gums make me look horsey." But today she doesn't seem to care. Her smile is genuine and wide. "Thank goodness they're just five, so they didn't manage to get too much into their mouths." She winks and starts laughing so hard she can barely speak. "But I swear to you, those kids . . ." More laughter. "Those kids . . ." More laughter, screeching really. "Those kids slept very well that night." Robin is rocking back and forth in her chair, laughing harder than I knew possible. She calms down but then she starts up again, and we all follow suit. Our laughter is so uproarious that I'm not at all surprised when Betsy appears from the basement.

"Lily, I thought I heard Jo-Jo. Was she crying?"

"No, dear." I try to get a handle on myself, but I can't help it. Still laughing, I manage to communicate that Jo-Jo is still napping, unless we just woke her. We start laughing all over again. We are like teenagers playing that game "try not to laugh," only once someone starts, you can't stop. "No, Betsy," I say, trying again. "You just heard a bunch of housewives laughing and enjoying each other's company. Isn't that right, girls?"

Robin wipes away tears from her eyes, she's laughing so hard.

"Jo-Jo should be up from her nap any minute, though, so why don't you just take a seat on the love seat and wait for her."

"Groovy."

I have to admit, while Betsy's seemingly constant refrain of "groovy" is more than a tad annoying, she has opened up so much since she first arrived. No one can deny that she grew up quite sheltered, but there's something refreshing about being around a teenager who is still somewhat wholesome-looking—not that there's anything wholesome about a pregnant unwed teenager. But at least she isn't like the drugged-out, long-haired Vietnam protesters I see whenever I watch the news on TV.

I try to make it a point to spend time with Betsy every day, even if it's just ten minutes here or there. I think it's important she has a role model who can teach her that this pregnancy doesn't need to define her for the rest of her life. I've encouraged her to go to college, something I didn't do because I got married. But Rose went, and look at her. She so enjoys teaching, and she's learned to think for herself.

"You've got a good head on your shoulders," I'm constantly reminding Betsy. "Don't be afraid to put it to work."

While she used to just nod her head, lately Betsy has been asking my opinion about all sorts of things, and I can practically see her growing up and maturing a bit more with every passing day. The truth is, I find her quite lovely; in fact, I even enjoy her company. Let there be no mistake: I love being a mom to Jo-Jo, but it gets lonely, since sometimes I don't see another adult until David comes home. Before Kathy, and now Betsy, there were times I took Jo-Jo out for a stroll, hoping to bump into another mom just so I could hear an adult voice and use mine. Pre–unwed mothers living in our utility room, there were days when David came down for breakfast and I'd ask him how he slept, what he wanted for breakfast, what he might want for dinner (so I could take it out of the freezer and defrost it during the day), and other bits and pieces of our daily chatter. And that was it unless someone telephoned or I left the house. This isn't something I talk about with the girls; I wouldn't want them to think less of me for complaining that being a housewife and mother is, well, not very stimulating. But today I just found out that Robin and her husband get high on marijuana! Or at least Robin does. I know Robin is a bit of a rebel, always running off to protest something or another. In fact, it wouldn't shock me to see her one night on the news with all the hippies and their signs about Vietnam. But this? I had no idea she ate dope-filled brownies, and the next time I'm with Becca or Sarah, I'm going to find out if this is something they knew about. That's when it occurs to me that maybe they not only know, but they do it, too. Then I remember our Secret Santa gift exchange. Becca gave Robin a brownie pan and asked her to bake her some. What if I'm left out because they think I'm just a prissy prude, as Rose has accused me of being more than once? But if I have to be honest, I guess I am. Eating brownies with dope? Robin's not a hippie. She's a housewife and mother, just like me. Except, clearly, she's not just like me.

"Oh, no. Mrs. Bloom, did you sit in ketchup?" Betsy asks, having maneuvered around the card table to her place on the love seat. "It's all over the back of your pretty yellow skirt."

Sarah springs up from her chair and twists her torso around. "Oh, no, no, no, no." She plops back down in her seat and tucks her lips inward, around her teeth. Before she places her hands over her face, I notice that she's gone pale.

Becca takes charge. "Sarah, are you okay? Are you having cramps?" She drapes an arm around Sarah's shoulder.

Sarah shakes her head and bites her lower lip. "But I'm pregnant. Or I was."

"No, no, honey," Becca says. "There's no reason to think the worst. I had some bleeding with one of my boys, and everything turned out just fine."

Sarah brushes away Becca's arm and removes her hands from in front of her face. "It's not just fine," she says. Even if you'd never met her, you could hear there is deep anger in Sarah's voice. "This is the fifth time this has happened."

I quickly exchange looks with the girls. A glimpse into their eyes tells me that this is news to them, just as it is to me.

"My body just doesn't know how to stay pregnant. I was hoping this time it would stick, but wanted to wait and see. That's why I didn't say anything to any of you."

Becca helps Sarah to her feet. "Let me walk you home, sweetie."

Sarah stands up and looks down at the chair, which has a bright crimson bull's-eye in the middle of the cushion, fading out to a pinkish tint. "Oh, Lily. Look what I've done to your chair. You'll have to let me replace it."

"Don't be silly," I say, because what else can I say? "A little soap and water and a touch of vinegar and it'll be good as new."

Robin stands up, too. As she heads for my front door, she speaks over her shoulder to Becca. "I'm going right over to your house to protect your cherry pie from your boys. I've got the sitter until five p.m., so take your time. Key still under the mat?"

Becca confirms what we all know—we seldom lock our doors during the day, and if we do, the key is under the mat, or under the flowerpot, if one exists. As Becca and Sarah head out the front door, I grab hold of my stomach and give that baby in there a couple of good, comforting pats.

As soon as the door closes, Betsy says, "Funny how things work, huh?"

"What do you mean?"

"Mrs. Bloom wants a baby so bad and can't get it to stick. And look at me? I couldn't get mine unstuck."

This is when Jo-Jo lets out a shriek that tells me she's not only awake from her nap, but she's likely gotten her leg twisted and wedged between two of the slats in her crib.

Mrs. Marty Seigel

(Rose)

After dinner, I'm typically the one who helps Grandma clean up since Lily likes to get Jo-Jo home for bed. But there's a special football game on TV that started before dinner, and the men decide they will stay and watch it together until halftime. Then everyone will go home to see the end of the game at their own houses.

While the men adjourn to the living room, my sister and I help Grandma clear the dining room table. "Hey, Rose-Petal, since it's your birthday tomorrow, I'll give you an early present and I'll wash," Lily says as she squirts some Palmolive onto the dishes. As the sink fills with water, she puts on the yellow rubber gloves. I grab a couple of towels from the drawer, and Grandma stands ready to put away the dry dishes and serving pieces. We move along like an assembly line. Wash, dry, put away. Wash, dry, put away.

"If you don't watch it, you'll be fired," I say when I detect a smear of lipstick on the rim of a wineglass that I hand back to Lily.

"I'll ignore that, but only because it's almost your birthday. Any special plans?"

I shrug. "Marty won't tell me anything more than to be dressed and ready to leave the house at noon. Oh, and that I should expect to be gone all day."

Grandma nods her head in approval. "Surprises are good, no?"

"Yes," I say. "It's the upside of having my birthday fall on Saturday this year. Neither one of us has to go to work."

THERE'S SUDDENLY A ROAR FROM the living room. To say the men are rambunctious is an understatement. I feel certain they'll wake Jo-Jo, who is sleeping on a blanket Lily put down in the corner, mere feet from the television. My niece proves to be a good sleeper, though, and the men continue their banter.

Before long, David appears. "Grandma, my beeper went off. Okay if I use your phone?" He's already dialing before she grants him permission. His call is brief.

"Marty, I've got to get to the hospital. Can you and Rose drive Lily and Jo-Jo home for me?" Once there are reassurances and all plans are in place, David gives Lily a peck on the cheek. It's clear this is a normal part of his routine: His beeper sounds, he calls into the service or the hospital, and then he dashes out. "Don't wait up" are his last words to Lily before he grabs his coat from the bed in the spare bedroom and heads out the front door.

Marty announces that it's halftime and we should help Grandma remove the leaves from the dining room table. Dad chimes in that he's decided to stay until the game is over and he'll be happy to take care of the table. "Go, go," he says.

"There are so many football games," I say. "What's so special about this one?"

Marty laughs, and it's definitely at me, not with me. "Dad," Marty says to my dad, "how did you manage to raise a child who doesn't know the difference between a normal football game and the Pro Bowl?" The men resume their laughter as Lily grabs the diaper bag, picks up Jo-Jo from the floor, and tries to position her against her shoulder without waking her.

"Now hurry up," Marty says playfully to Lily. "Thanks to your important husband, I don't want to miss any more of the game than I have to."

"Does that mean you don't want to stop for ice cream on the way home?" Lily says, giving it right back to my husband.

We all laugh so hard. Golly, I love my family. And oh, how I wish Mom were here to enjoy moments like this.

Miss Betsy Ann Eubanks

Lily lets me get the mail every day since she knows how much I look forward to letters from my mom. The truth is, it's not just my mom's letters that keep me excited to get to the mailbox; it's Karen's. Unfortunately, today there isn't a letter from home, but during Jo-Jo's nap, before *General Hospital*, I write, hoping that will remind them that it's really their turn. Also unfortunately, since I send my letters to Karen through my mom, I can't write only to Karen (well, I could, but that would be mean), so I always have to write two letters. And triple unfortunately, my mom reads every word that Karen writes to me and every word I send to Karen, so we need to be a little sneaky in what we say and how we say it. Still, I'm careful to keep the big secret: where I am and why I'm here. Even Karen can't ever know that.

Dear Mom,

Thank you for your last letter. Things with the Bergs are still copacetic. Lily looks like the same size as me, on account it's her second baby and she said that's how it works. She's teaching me about how a lot of things work and I now understand how this trouble happened. I'm so sorry, if I would have known, I wouldn't have let him go all the way with me, which I now understand is only something to do when I'm married.

I know you think it's not a good idea that I'm watching General Hospital (which you only know because I wrote it in my private letter to Karen . . . ahem, about reading my mail, just joking). But I get what you mean when you said those people are immoral, and I agree. You know who else thinks so? Lily! But she says it's fun to watch the boob tube, and we always talk about how there are consequences for people when they do bad things, like Dr. Baldwin is doing now on the show. And you know what's really far-out? If I'd watched General Hospital before last summer, I would've known about babies and how they get made. Hahahahaha!!! Who'd think you could learn anything from a soap opera?

Well, that's all for today. I'm including a picture that Lily took of me and Jo-Jo so you can see how cute she is and what I look like, in case you forgot. Just joking. Lily says absence makes the heart grow fonder and I know she's right because I miss you AND DAD. Please tell him I said hello and to try not to be so mad at me. Maybe you could send me a picture of you guys.

Love and kisses (or smooches, as Lily says),

Betsy

Dear Karen,

Thank you so much for your groovy letter. It sounds like things at school are outta sight! Fortunately, Aunt Tilly is healing, but it's very slow, on account of her age. The doctor told her that she will probably be able to manage on her own by the late spring, so I should be back in Kalamazoo this summer!!! I never thought I'd be excited about going to summer school, but I've got some catching up to do. Maybe you could help me with my schoolwork, since it will be all the stuff you're learning now. So PAY ATTENTION.

I can't believe Mark asked you to go steady already! I thought for sure he'd wait and ask you after homecoming. Have your mom take pictures so I can see you in your dress cuz it sounds groovy. Are you going to wear gloves that go up past your elbows or haven't you decided yet? I agree, that would be very Audrey Hepburn, but it all depends on whether you're wanting to look sophisticated or if you're going for more of a psychedelic vibe? Either way, just remember about that cheerleader, Donna Murphy, and those stairs. What a bummer! We don't want anything like that to happen to YOU!

Miss you tons and tons. Keep on truckin' and WRITE BACK SOON!

Love,

Bets

XOXX

Mrs. David Berg

(Lily)

During the drive back from Grandma's, I hold Jo-Jo in my lap and give her gentle smooches while I rub the top of her head with my chin. Miraculously, she stays asleep. I thank Marty and Rose for the ride home and try to close the car door without slamming it shut and undoing this miracle.

Since I changed Jo-Jo into her footie pajamas when we were at Grandma's, I debate about whether she needs a dry diaper before I put her into her crib for the night, but I decide against it. She went down on the floor at Grandma's around the same time she goes into her crib when we're home, so she shouldn't be that wet. But I don't want her to get diaper rash, so maybe I should change her. I give my head a strong shake, keenly aware I'm obsessing about . . . what? Nothing. What is wrong with me that I'm making every choice into such a big deal?

I lower the side of Jo-Jo's crib and set her inside before giving the mobile a tap with my finger, causing the clowns to spin. I pull up the side of the crib, hoping against hope that the clicking noise it makes when it falls into place doesn't wake her. "Sweet dreams," I whisper before closing the nursery door halfway, so I'll be sure to hear Jo-Jo if she needs me.

David said not to wait up, but that's what he always says. I decide I'll get ready for bed, start the book that Robin gave me during our

Secret Santa exchange, and, depending on how I'm feeling, catch at least the monologue on *The Tonight Show with Johnny Carson*.

As I wash my face and wrap my hair with toilet paper—I was just at the beauty shop this morning, after all, and I want to protect my hair so the set will last—my mind drifts back to dinner. My dad and David have always gotten on just swell, but since Rose married Marty last year, I can tell how much David likes having a contemporary to chat with at dinner. Even though Marty's a lawyer and David is a doctor, they always have plenty to talk about, and it's clear they've become friends. David always makes sure that at some point the conversation includes sports, which is my dad's favorite topic. That way Dad has an opportunity to chime in and feel like one of the boys. I love how David thinks about everyone and goes out of his way to make them feel comfortable. I've heard from people everywhere—at the beauty shop, at the pediatrician's office, even people I've met at parties—that David's patients love him, and I'm not surprised. I married a wonderful man, and I think I love him even more now than on our wedding day. That doesn't mean, however, that I don't mind his constantly having to rush to the hospital to deliver a baby. But his practice just hired another doctor, and he's promised me there will be fewer nights when he's on call.

Once I'm situated in bed, I crack open *The Feminine Mystique*, already feeling relief over knowing that when Robin asks me if I've read it yet, as she is sure to do, I can honestly tell her I've started. Robin has underlined every word in the first paragraph, except for the last sentence, which she has underscored multiple times; she's also put a series of exclamation points in the margin.

The problem lay buried, unspoken, for many years in the minds of American women. It was a strange stirring, a sense of dissatisfaction, a yearning that women suffered in the middle of the twentieth century in the United States. Each suburban wife struggled with it alone. As she made the beds, shopped for groceries, matched slipcover material, ate peanut butter sandwiches with her children, chauffeured Cub Scouts and Brownies, lay beside her husband at night—she was afraid to ask even of herself the silent question— "Is this all?"

I slam shut the book and try to steady my breathing. I have a vivid memory of my mother reading *Peter Pan* to Rose and me when we were young. After that first time, whenever she got to the part with Captain Hook and the crocodile and the "tick, tick, tick," I forcibly closed the book. Of course my mom repeatedly asked me what was wrong. "Don't you like that part?" she asked. "I can skip it, if you want." I was too embarrassed to admit that, though I knew the captain couldn't jump off the page and claw me with his hook and the crocodile also couldn't emerge from the pages, it *felt* like it could happen and I needed to shut them in the book, where they'd stay buried and I would be safe. I have that same sensation now. *"Is this all?"* is not a question I want to even think about.

Mrs. Marty Seigel

(Rose)

Marty enters the bedroom, a little more than an hour after we've dropped off Lily and Jo-Jo. "Who won the game?"

He smiles. "You don't care. You don't even know who was playing."

He's got me there. I giggle and admit he's right.

"It was the Pro Bowl. East beat the West 36–7. It was a real shellacking. But the best part is that the star of the game was Jim Brown."

He says his name like it should mean something to me, but he knows my knowledge about sports is pitiful. "He plays for the Browns. The *Cleveland* Browns," he says. "So we've got reason to crow."

"Oh, *we* do, do *we*? Well, cock-a-doodle-do."

Marty shakes his head and quickly undresses. He jumps into bed next to me and takes the book I'm reading from my hands and places it on the nightstand next to me. "Time to celebrate." He kisses the back of my neck, his sign that he wants to make love.

"It's not a good time of the month, just so you know," I say.

He continues to kiss my neck. "Come on, honey. I thought you wanted to start a family." He pulls up my nightgown and nudges me onto my side, facing him.

I turn my face so our lips meet. I can smell the beer on his breath, and when I give him a long, passionate kiss, I can taste it, too. We kiss like we did when we were dating. Back then, whenever things got too steamy, all I had to do was think of his girlfriend Linda, whom he called spoiled merchandise. That was what it took to remind myself to put a halt to things before we got carried away. But now we're married and there's no reason to stop.

After another deep kiss, I sit up and fluff the pillow behind my back. "I've been thinking about it." I grab my knees and pull them toward my chest. "I'd rather finish out the school year before I get pregnant. I feel like I've finally connected with my kids, and if I got pregnant, I'd have to have to resign and turn them over to someone else."

"They're not *your* kids."

"I know. But still." I reach across Marty, open his nightstand drawer, and pull out a condom. "I know it's only January, but I want to be able to see the year through. Let's wait until this summer to start our family." I jiggle the wrapped condom between my fingers. "In the meantime, think of all the fun we can have practicing." I raise my eyebrows, Groucho Marx style. "Please?"

He takes the condom from me and flings it across the room, as if it's a Frisbee. "Who's in charge here?"

I can tell he's playing with me. I give him a coy smile, showing no teeth. "You are, my love. Most of the time."

And just like that, his mood changes and any trace of a smile is gone. "You are my wife, damn it. You belong to me. You do not tell me what to do." His voice is stern as he overenunciates each word. And it happened so quickly. He doesn't blink; he just glares at me. "You are my wife and you will do what I say. Is. That. Clear?"

I nod my head. Although there are times Marty has lost his temper with me, I've never seen him this enraged. And it's never before happened in bed. Our lovemaking has always been just that—a tender expression of love and kindness.

"Marty, what's going on? Why are you talking to me like this? If you don't want to wear a condom, that's okay. I can get my diaphragm and jelly from the bathroom, or you can just pull out."

"What is wrong with *me*?" Saliva is pooling in the corners of Marty's mouth. "What's wrong with *you*? Since when do you get to tell me what I can and can't do to my own wife, in my own bed, in my own home?"

I'm truly speechless. But a voice inside me tells me this is not the time for discussion. *Just placate him.* I apologize, but he seems not to hear.

"I'm the man of the house and you'll do what I say when I say it. Are we clear?"

I again nod my head. With lightning speed, he pushes me back down against the bed, grabs my nightgown, and pulls it over my head, where it becomes entangled with my arms. My instinct is to fight back, but he's holding my wrists over my head, pinning them against the mattress. I arch my back and start bucking like a bronco, trying to jostle him off me, but it's useless; he's too strong. I kick my legs, but I fail to make contact. I bend my knees, like I'm going to sit Indian style, and try kicking from that position. I'm able to hit him with my feet, but I lack any momentum to do any damage.

Still, I know he feels my resistance because that's when he screams, "Hold still."

Instinct takes over and I scream right back at him, "What is wrong with you? Get off! You're hurting me!"

"Rose, I swear, if you don't hold still, you're going to get hurt."

I'm already hurt—did he not just hear me say that? I don't understand what's going on. That's when I feel his grip on my wrists relax and the weight of what feels like a cinder block hits my mouth. I feel moisture on my chin, and the metallic taste of blood fills my mouth.

Where is Marty? Did this man who is doing this to me break into our home while we were at dinner, and did he kill Marty? This man on top of me is a monster; it cannot be Marty. My thoughts are irrational, I know, yet I cannot make sense of anything. Once again, the monster grabs my wrists, and with both arms pinned over my head, he penetrates me with such force it feels like my flesh is tearing. As he thrusts in and out of me, I am convinced that he's not only mutilating my insides, but he's also set my pubic hair on fire. And then it occurs to me, maybe I am on fire. But there is no flame. There is just hot, searing pain. And then there is nothing.

Mrs. David Berg

(Lily)

By the time David arrives home from the hospital, I'm in bed watching *The Tonight Show with Johnny Carson*.

"Oh, good," he says. "I didn't want to wake you."

"I was asleep, but then Jo-Jo started crying, and, you know . . . by the time I managed to calm her down, I got a second wind and decided to wait up for you." I study my husband's face. He looks tired, but that's not unusual. I try to recall if I've ever seen him without dark circles under his eyes, but I can't remember. Regardless, lately they seem worse.

"Hey, favorite doctor. I'm worried about you. Are you okay?"

David looks down at the carpet. His scrubs are splattered with blood. The fact he didn't change before coming home is a tip-off that something is definitely wrong.

In the past, I would have prodded David with questions, but after years of marriage, I've learned if I just give him time and let him go at his own pace, he will, eventually, talk. I just need to be patient.

He peels off the bloodstained top over his head and holds it out, unsure of where to put it.

I get out of bed and take the shirt from him. "Best not to toss it down the chute with all that blood. Why don't you take off your pants and I'll run them both downstairs."

David does as I suggest and I reach for his bottoms, which are not as soiled, and wrap them around his top so I don't have to touch the blood. I take the scrubs downstairs, and then I remember that Betsy, who is likely sleeping, is in her cot right next to the washing machine. I leave the bloodied clothes on the linoleum floor, at the foot of the basement stairs, figuring they'll keep till morning.

As I enter our bedroom, I run into David coming out of the bathroom. He's holding a towel and patting dry his hair. He wears only his pajama bottoms, his typical garb for bedtime. "I just needed a quick shower."

David closes the door behind me, walks across the room, and shuts off the television. I pull up my nightgown around my thighs as I get back into bed, where I put both of our pillows against the headboard, making myself a comfy spot to sit. "So," I say. "Tell me."

David looks at the carpet. "Oh, Lil. It was just awful." He shakes his head, and when he looks up again, he uses the pads of his fingers to press against his eyes, which is how I know he's trying to keep his tears in check. Still, I wait for David, forcing myself not to fill the silence.

"A young girl was admitted. She was only fifteen. Fifteen, Lil, and she tried to give herself an abortion." I immediately think of Betsy, who is also fifteen. David again hangs his head and looks down at the carpet. I want to scream, *What is so interesting down there? Look at me!* But I know David needs to do this his way, on his timetable.

"She did it with a hanger."

I feel certain I've misunderstood. I've heard of women drinking concoctions of drugs and poisons, hoping to get rid of a baby. I've even heard about women putting knitting needles into their bodies where a tampon should go, hoping to—well, I'm not sure what they're trying to do. Hurt the baby so it will die? Damage it in some way so it will fall out? But a hanger? This is definitely news to me.

"I don't understand," I say. "What did she do with the hanger?"

He walks over to our closet, grabs a wire hanger, and begins to twist the curved part that hangs over the bar and then he uncoils the whole thing. He comes over to my side of the bed and holds it inches away from my face. "She spread her legs and stuck it up . . .

"I'm sorry," he says, allowing the hanger to drop onto the floor. Then he sits on the side of the bed next to me and envelops me in a strong hug. "It's just been a long, horrible night," he says into my neck, with his head against my shoulder. I stroke his hair and whisper into his ear that it's all right and that I understand.

He pushes away from me. "No, honey. You don't understand."

"Mean" is not the right word to describe how he sounds, but it's close enough. So, just as I do when Jo-Jo is pitching a fit, I counter David's stridency with as much calm in my voice as possible. "Then explain it to me."

David's expression is hard to read. It looks like he, himself, hasn't decided how to answer me. If you'd asked me whether he'd simply shut down and say "Never mind" versus actually tell me what happened, I'd say the odds were fifty-fifty. Finally, he decides on option two. "She punctured her uterus and got an infection and . . ."

He is silent long enough for me to realize he's not going to complete his sentence. I am almost too afraid, but I ask anyway. "Did she die?"

He shakes his head. "No. But she's in bad shape. We admitted her into the septic abortion ward."

"There's an entire floor for people who use hangers?"

David shakes his head again. "It's for anyone who needs to be admitted after complications from an abortion. The ward is new at our hospital, and this is the first time I've had to admit someone." David gets up and begins to pace alongside the bed. "We've had so many girls and women come in needing special care that it made sense to start putting them all together so the nurses can keep a closer eye on them." David returns to my side of the bed and sits on the mattress, grabs my hand and rubs small circles, around and around. "Sometimes they're women who drank chemicals or poison, and they end up with burns or fatally sick. Some of them use long objects, like knitting needles, crochet hooks, or . . ." David glances at the unwound hanger on the floor by his feet. "They often get infections or don't stop hemorrhaging." He runs his hands over his face, and I notice his five-o'clock shadow. "But some of the women wind up in the ward after seeing someone else," he says.

"Like who?"

"There are doctors, midwives, and just regular people who give women abortions all the time. Some are better at it than others; some are real butchers. But there is always the risk of complications, and when things go south, they wind up in our hospital."

There is no doubt in my mind; the way he says "butchers" tells me he is filled with loathing for these people. "Why didn't you ever mention this special floor before?"

"Septic abortion ward," he says. "And I wasn't keeping it a secret; we just opened it. But you're right. I didn't think it was something you wanted to hear about. I was trying to protect you. Honey, you know women get abortions, and you know they sometimes die from them. Did you really want me to share the nitty-gritties?"

I don't answer because of course he's right.

"There's a reason women aren't called for jury duty," he says.

Just when I'm about to ask what jury duty has to do with anything, he completes the thought. "It's because women are more delicate, and listening to the details about crime can be upsetting. It's not something that we, as a society, want women to have to hear about."

I ignore this jury duty detour that, knowing David, is a clear sign there's more he's trying to avoid talking about. I refuse to take the bait.

"That girl from tonight, do you think she'll be okay?"

"I can only hope. I told you she punctured her uterus with the hanger. So, if she manages to survive, she won't ever be able to have children." David looks me in the eye. "Is that the sort of thing you want me coming home from the hospital and telling you about when you ask about my day?"

Again, I hear—what is it?—that tone to his voice. I'm unsure whether he's actually looking for a fight or if he's just spent. I decide it's most likely the latter, or maybe I'm just not willing to make his awful day even worse. "I don't know," I say. "Maybe it is. How else can I be a good wife to you if I don't know what's going on?" What I don't say, though, is that he's right; this isn't the sort of thing I want to hear about. Who would?

"Lily." David interrupts my silent musings about what I do and don't want to know. "I've got something else I need to tell you, and I've danced around it long enough. But I need you to promise me something. I need you to be strong. Can you do that? Can you be the strongest you've ever had to be in your entire adult life?"

Now he's got me scared, so scared that I can't speak, so I just nod my head.

"It's about Becca."

Mrs. Marty Seigel

(Rose)

I'm certain my eyes are open, yet I see only black. I attempt to turn over, and I land on what must be a pocketknife that's stabbing me between my legs. What happened? My mind is fuzzy, and I try to focus on remembering, but it's just out of reach. My mind goes blank and then I feel nothing.

I MUST HAVE FAINTED BECAUSE the next thing I'm aware of is Marty, sitting on the bed next to me, holding a cold washcloth against my forehead. He lowers the cloth into a bowl filled with ice water that's propped against my left hip. Suddenly, it all rushes back. I jerk away, hitting the headboard and grabbing for the covers, which I pull up to my chin. The bowl of water sloshes onto the mattress and leaves me sitting in a shallow puddle. The cold feels good between my legs.

My head is throbbing, but not more so than when I scream, "Get away from me."

Marty has clearly been crying. There's something wrong with my vision, but from what I can make out, his eyes are puffy and red, and his face is soaked in sweat and tears. He gets up from the bed, stands over me, and utters the same phrases over and over: "I'm so sorry . . .

What have I done? . . . Please forgive me." I don't know if he repeats himself ten times or ten thousand times, but at some point, I start matching each of his apologies with my own commands: "Leave. . . . Go away. . . . Now. . . . Leave. . . . Go away. . . . Right now." I will not stop; there will no stalemate. He finally turns and leaves. I win.

Mrs. David Berg

(Lily)

As soon as David says Becca's name, I know what he's going to tell me, and yet I still have a moment of shock where I can see his mouth moving, but I cannot hear his words. It only lasts a few seconds, but by the time I'm able to focus on what he's saying, I have heard enough to know that Becca was admitted to the septic abortion ward.

"She asked for me by name," David says. "And she repeatedly begged me, and I quote, 'Tell Lily not to be mad at me.' She also told me to ask you not to call her or visit her at the hospital. She said she'll telephone you when she's ready."

I nod, just so David knows I've heard him. The baby gives me a good hard kick, and I jump up from the bed, hoping the change of position makes it stop. I want to ask if Becca's going to be okay, but I'm too afraid of the answer. Fortunately, David anticipates my question.

"Here's what I know. Becca got an abortion somewhere in downtown Cleveland. She went home and thought she was fine, but then she started bleeding, and when it didn't stop, she got scared. She called Robin, who came over to stay with the boys, and Bradley drove her to the hospital, where, as I said, she asked for me."

I know this isn't the time to get ruffled feathers over the fact that when Becca needed help she reached out to Robin instead of me. Because I know exactly why she didn't call me. And it makes me feel both guilty and ashamed. I told myself that Becca knew where to find me, and when she was ready to talk, she would. I convinced myself that was the case. I used Rose as my excuse—after all, didn't Rose tell me that Sarah would talk to me about her infertility if and when she was ready? I told myself the same was true with Becca, too. But I knew better. It was just a lie I told myself to make it easier for me to bail on my best friend when she most needed me.

Again, I remind myself this isn't about me. "Is Becca going to be okay?"

"I think so, I really do." David gets up from the bed and walks alongside me. He slings his arm around my shoulder as I pace back and forth, rubbing my belly, hoping the baby stops pushing around in there. "She lost a lot of blood, but we were able to control the hemorrhaging, and they were transfusing her when I left. We're also running a line of antibiotics, to help with infection. With a little bit of luck, she'll be discharged in a day or two." He kisses the top of my head and then turns me toward him so he can give me a full-body hug. He rubs my back in large circles, creating an even, predictable rhythm. "Listen, you," he whispers into my ear. "I promised her you wouldn't call her, so don't make me look bad, okay?"

I nod.

"She just needs time, Lil. Whatever's going on between you two, you'll work it out. Just give her time. And don't be hard on yourself."

I nod again.

"No, honey. Say it."

"I won't be hard on myself." I wonder if David would think I shouldn't be hard on myself if he knew I had more than an inkling that Becca might go down this path. Isn't that why I never circled back with her about the psychiatrists and also why I never mentioned Becca's desire to end this pregnancy to David? I know my sister is the one with the Shakespeare obsession, and yet I cannot help but feel that, just like Lady Macbeth, I have blood on my hands.

And with that thought, I burst into the tears that I've somehow managed to hold at bay for the last ten minutes.

IN THE MORNING, BY THE time Jo-Jo wakes me with calls of "Mama-Mama-Mama," David is gone. Even though it's Saturday, I'm not surprised he's not here; I'm sure he's at the hospital, checking on the fifteen-year-old girl. And Becca . . . *Oh, Becca. I've never wanted to talk to you more than I do right now, but at the same time, I feel such relief that I don't have to talk to you right now.*

As I pad down the hall, I feel like I did right after Jo-Jo was born, back in the days when I didn't get more than two hours of sleep at a time. I'm so exhausted it's like I'm living outside of my body.

I grab Jo-Jo from her crib. She's gnawing on her fingers, and her nose is runny, a clear sign she's cutting another tooth. I remove her diaper, and because life isn't fair, she has what I call a "sleep poop," and it's smeared all over her. "How about a special treat this morning? How would you like a bath?"

Jo-Jo loves her baths and couldn't be more delighted. "Bath, Mama. Bath."

When we are both dressed, I take Jo-Jo down to the kitchen and find Betsy leafing through one of the *LIFE* magazines Sarah gave her for Christmas. Sensing that something is off, maybe because we're running late with breakfast, Betsy closes the magazine and steps right in. "Jo-Jo, we are out of orange juice. Would you like to help me make some more?"

"Yes. Make juice," Jo-Jo says, clapping her hands. Only it comes out "Make dooce."

Betsy gets a can of OJ from the freezer, and I hold up Jo-Jo so she can watch the electric can opener, which, for some reason, she finds fascinating. Once Betsy has opened the can and tossed the lid, she scoops out the frozen concentrate and spoons it into the glass pitcher. As she fills the empty can with water, she counts aloud. "One." She refills the empty can. "Two." She fills it a final time. "Three." Jo-Jo does her best to count along.

Then comes the stirring, which is Jo-Jo's favorite part. Exactly as I've taught her to do, Betsy stands behind Jo-Jo, each arm extended forward, forming a secure barricade along each side of my little girl so she won't fall off the chair she's standing on. Betsy holds the pitcher—one hand on each side—so it won't go flying off the table, thanks to my almost-two-year-old "helping." Using the wooden spoon, Jo-Jo does a "good job" and "excellent mixing!"

Of course my mind isn't on making breakfast—Pop-Tarts for everyone! I'm still silently berating myself for being a bad friend who wasn't willing to support Becca when she was obviously desperate. But even if Becca had come to me, what would I have said? *Becca, you've turned to the right person. Just let me take a spin through my Rolodex. Yes. Right here under the As, for . . . you know . . . that procedure I'm too prudish to call by its name but rhymes with "contortion" . . . Yes, that word! Well, it must be your lucky day because I, of course, know just the person you're looking for! I've heard good things about him, so why don't you give him a call?*

Mrs. Marty Seigel

(Rose)

I have to pee. The mere thought makes me think of Lily. I can practically hear her reprimand: *Rose, that's so crass. Can't you just say you have to go to the bathroom, or that you need to use the restroom?*

Oh, sister, you're always so worried about looking and sounding proper. What would you say if you saw me now?

I try to lift my head from the mattress, but it's so heavy, and every time I move, even the slightest bit, I get either a shooting pain running from my shoulder up through my neck, or just a weightiness that makes it impossible. Instinct takes over, I guess, and I use my arms and hands to prop myself up so I can get out of bed. From what I can tell, Marty isn't here, which allows me to work my way, slowly, into an upright position. Finally, I manage to sit up, and then I swing my legs to the floor so I'm perched on the side of the bed. Though everything is blurry, I was right. No Marty. *Why is it so hard to see?*

In an effort to evaluate my vision, I place one hand over my right eye, remove it, and then I cover my left eye. When I cover my left eye, I can't see anything.

Mrs. David Berg

(Lily)

After breakfast, I tell Betsy that I need to do some baking and ask if she'll take Jo-Jo to the basement, lest she want to help. "It's Saturday morning, so you should be able to find some cartoons she likes, or she can just play with toys. I'll let you know when I've got a spoon for her to lick."

"We're going to have special adventures this morning, aren't we, Jo-Jo?" Betsy says, distracting Jo-Jo with the promise of something exciting so she won't attach herself to my leg.

My plan is to do some serious baking. Two cakes. One for Becca's family—she might have asked me not to call her, which I will honor, but I can drop off a dessert that I know her boys will enjoy while their mother is away. The least I can do. The other cake is for Rose's birthday, which is today. While I'm waiting for the cakes to cool before I frost them, I decide to bake some cookies for Sarah.

I don't want Sarah to think I'm being a buttinsky, but I also don't want to pretend she didn't lose a baby—in my living room. If anything, this whole business with Becca has taught me that silence isn't the answer. I figure that, once the cookies are done, I can drop by Sarah's house, and if she wants to invite me in to talk about what happened, I'll be there to listen. And if she doesn't, that's okay, too. At least she'll know I'm not avoiding her, the way I avoided Becca.

She invites me in. She's wearing a shift dress, which of course she made. It's loose around the waist, which makes sense, considering what she's been through. Unlike her usual psychedelic prints or bright solid colors, this dress is a muted shade of apricot. She seems genuinely happy to see me, and we exchange some small talk. I, of course, ask how she's feeling. She assures me she's just fine, and after some more chitchat, I work up the courage to inquire about what's really on my mind. "Sarah, you said this was the fifth time this happened. Why didn't you ever tell me anything about your difficulties before?"

"I don't know." Sarah bites at her lower lip. "I guess I figured we'd moved to a new state and it was a fresh start. I told myself if I didn't talk about the past, well, I'd have a different outcome this time. Funny what we can make ourselves believe, isn't it? Do you think I'm crazy? Because saying it out loud, it sounds pretty wacky."

I assure her there's nothing crazy about any of this.

"But then I had a couple losses last year and it looked like my Ohio luck was going to be just as bad as my Indiana luck. Still, I didn't give up. And what's really strange is it almost worked. This time I made it farther than I ever have before. I really thought this would be the time we'd have a baby."

We're sitting at Sarah's kitchen table, because where else would we be? As she fiddles with the salt and pepper shakers, I think about how many of my friendships revolve around kitchens and coffee and sharing confidences. I think of Becca.

Sarah gets up to grab the coffeepot that's percolated and nods toward the cup and saucer she placed in front of me when I arrived— my cue to move it toward her so she can pour. Once Sarah sits down, she makes a show of looking at her wristwatch. "Ten o'clock. Is it too early to sample your chocolate chip cookies?"

We both laugh, and between bites of the still warm, gooey cookies, I decide to step off the sidelines. "What does your doctor say?"

"My doctor in Indianapolis kept telling me that miscarriages happen for a reason. That when a baby doesn't thrive, it means it's defective in some way, and it's nature's way of taking care of it. Then he told me I should be happy that getting pregnant was not a problem for me." She blushes when she tells me this. I probably do, too.

"But it's time to get back on the horse," she says. "My doctor here says the next time I get pregnant, he's going to put me on a drug. I can't remember the proper name for it, but he kept calling it DES. He said it's been around for a while, and it helps prevent miscarriages, going into labor too soon, and all kinds of other complications, so I'm really hopeful. I just wish someone thought to give it to me sooner."

I lean across the table, grab her hand and give it a squeeze. "I'm sure it will work," I say. "And if you ever want another opinion, David could help. I mean, it might be awkward for you to see him, but maybe you could see one of his partners. Or you could see him." Oh God. I'm rambling. "Whatever you're most comfortable with."

"Thanks, Lily. But I feel good about my doctor and don't want to make him angry by going to see someone else. I really do think I've turned the corner. Besides, you know what they say about staying relaxed and positive if you want to get pregnant." Sarah lights a cigarette and swivels toward the counter to grab an ashtray.

I think about David, who, on more than one occasion, has reminded me that unwed teens are anything but relaxed and positive, and yet they manage to procreate at an alarming rate. Hence, Betsy and other girls like her filling up Raven House.

"Your time will come," I say. "And when it does, you're going to be the most wonderful mother because of everything you've had to go through to have a baby."

I look at Sarah, who I know, without question, would trade places with me if she could, and I feel more than a little bit guilty that lately I've been thinking, *Is this all?*

Mrs. Marty Seigel

(Rose)

I force myself to stand and immediately collapse back onto the bed. On my third attempt, I'm able to remain upright. Our bedroom isn't large. Even though it's called a master bedroom, it's smaller than the room I shared with Lily when we were little girls. Now, however, it seems enormous. Every step is an effort. Walking pulls at my crotch, which is on fire, but is also throbbing to an almost drumlike beat. It's what I imagine it must feel like when a woman's been raped. And there we have it. That's exactly what happened. Last night my husband raped me.

Somehow I manage to get to the hall bathroom. I deliberately avoid looking into the mirror until after I pee, and that's when I see a face that isn't mine staring back at me. My right eye is swollen shut, which I sort of expected based on my vision. What I wasn't expecting was the rest of it. There's dried blood under my nose and all around my lips. My lower lip is split, and there are lots of scratches across my cheekbones. I open my mouth and am relieved to find all my teeth intact. A miracle. I should try to clean myself up, I know, but I'm so, so dizzy and tired that I decide to get myself into bed before I fall down and have to crawl back to my room.

I open the bathroom door, taking a moment to brace myself before the long journey back to my bedroom. He's there. I try to close the door, but in my physical condition, any one of my seven-year-old students would win the battle.

"I heard the toilet flush, so I knew you were awake. You should have called me to help you."

For some crazy, illogical reason, I think about the Bugs Bunny/ Looney Tunes shorts they sometimes show at the movies, and I swear I can feel steam coming out of my ears. This is when Marty falls to his knees in front of me and grabs me around my thighs and begs for forgiveness, saying absolutely nothing I haven't heard from him before.

I stare at the man on his knees in front of me. I reach out and place my hands on his shoulders, and I use every bit of the strength I have to push him. He falls over backward. "I deserved that," he says when he gets up off the floor.

"Marty, I want you to leave. Right now." My voice is a monotone, devoid of emotion.

He mumbles something about going into the office, even though it's Saturday, and how we'll talk about it tonight when he comes home. But as he turns to go back down the stairs, his final words to me are "You're my wife. I'm allowed to have sex with my wife."

Mrs. David Berg

(Lily)

After my visit with Sarah, I return home to frost both cakes. If Jo-Jo was happy to lick the spoon after I prepared the batter (she was), then she was beside herself when she got the spatula after I completed the frosting.

To make sure I pull this off undetected, I will take the cake to Rose's house sometime after noon, when I know they'll both be out doing whatever surprise romantic thing Marty told her to be ready for that she alluded to last night. I know Rose said she planned to be out all day, but I don't want to take any chances and get there too early or too late. I just want her to be surprised for her twenty-fifth birthday, regardless of when they get home. But first, I've got to drop off some dry cleaning and stop at the hardware store to get more Pledge for dusting. Plus, I want to get a balloon for Rose. I can then find something to eat, maybe at McDonald's. I figure I'll be at Rose's around one-o'clock-ish and on my way out ten minutes later. Then, when I get home, I can drop off the other cake at Becca's. I silently congratulate myself on my organizational skills. Then I scold myself for feeling pride over such nonsense. *Is this all?* I push the question from my mind.

Rose's cake is sitting on the floor of the front seat of my car. A single balloon, which I got from the dime store, is floating around in the back. We'll celebrate Rose's birthday as a family next Friday night at Grandma's house, but I wanted to do something today, on the actual date. David asked why we didn't celebrate last night, and I had to remind him that, just as Mom taught us, if we're not celebrating on the actual date, we only celebrate after the actual birthday, never before; otherwise, it's bad luck. Only since becoming a mom do I understand that by celebrating after the real birth date, Mom was essentially making sure to prolong the birthday.

To make this an efficient get-in-the-house-and-get-out-of-the-house errand, I could have brought Betsy, but with Jo-Jo teething again—no doubt that's part of why she enjoyed chomping on the rubber spatula so much—I wasn't confident she wouldn't melt down and become a Miss Cranky Pants, turning this outing into a nightmare. So with Betsy at home, it's up to me to pull this off on my own.

I get out of the car empty-handed and walk up the sidewalk to my sister's front door. The grass is already brown since it's January, but there are weeds poking up from between the cement slabs on the walkway. Marty might be a rising attorney, but his landscaping skills need work. There is a flower box near the front door that contains a few artificial flowers. Clearly Rose's domain, "just to add some color." I feel around for the key under the pot closest to the front door and grab it. I unlock the house, leave the door ajar, return the key to the flowerpot, and go back to my car. "That's how you do the breaking part of breaking and entering," I say, narrating in my best *Dragnet* voice.

Back at my car, I pick up the cake from the floor and use my hip to close the car door, but only after making sure the balloon has cleared the door and won't fly back inside my Chevy. Once I'm back at the house, a simple kick of my foot is all it takes for the door to swing open. "The suspect entered the house at roughly 1:15 p.m." Ah, the silly games I play to keep myself entertained. This is my first recitation from Sergeant Joe Friday, however. More typically my mind wanders to Gomer Pyle, U.S.M.C., who uses my favorite expression, *Sur-prise, sur-prise, sur-prise!* When I say that after unpinning one of Jo-Jo's dirty diapers, she can be counted on for a giggle. That little *bubbeleh* is my best audience. Not for the first time, I wonder whether all women narrate their lives. Is it a side effect of spending so much time at home alone or with children who cannot yet talk? But I've got Betsy. Since she moved in with us, do I narrate less? *Is. This. All?*

THE CAKE IS STILL SECURE under the Tupperware carrier, and the balloon hasn't popped. So far, so good. I use my hip to close the front door behind me, and I make my way into the kitchen. I bought two birthday cards. I plan to leave one on the kitchen counter next to the cake and the balloon. I'll put the other on Rose's pillow, so she'll find it as an extra surprise when she gets into bed tonight. I take a pen from my purse and sign the card for the cake.

> *We can't believe you're a quarter century old already. Happy, happy birthday, twenty-five times over.*
>
> *With love,*
>
> *Lily, David, and Jo-Jo*

I debate about whether to include Betsy's name, but decide that, although she's become almost like family in our house, at least to me, Rose doesn't have that kind of relationship with her, so I leave off her name. Next I fill in the card I'll take upstairs. This one is just from me, so I add a more personal note:

My dear Rose-Petal,

Even if you weren't my only sister, you would be my favorite sister, thorns and all. Have a wonderful birthday!
　　I love you.

The other petite fleur . . . Lil

I lick both envelopes shut. I place the first card under the Tupperware and grab the other card and run upstairs. When I reach the landing, I'm surprised to see the door to Rose and Marty's room is shut. I always leave our bedroom door open just so the air can circulate. While I'd normally knock on a closed door, I know Rose and Marty are out on their romantic date, so I walk right into their bedroom.

Apparently, my sister doesn't believe in making the bed before she leaves the house because the covers are all balled up. I guess I can give her an extra birthday present and make it for her. I put down the card on her dresser, and as I reach for the mound of blankets, I see that Rose is under the covers, but she's turned away from me, apparently still sleeping. "Rose," I say, gently touching her shoulder. "Why aren't you and Marty out for your birthday? Are you okay?" As the words leave my mouth, I realize how stupid I sound. Of course she's not okay. It's after one p.m., and she's sleeping when she should be out celebrating with her husband. She sighs and without turning toward me she calls my name. At least I think that's what she says. It's hard to tell, as her voice is barely above a whisper, and "Lily" sounded more like "Ill-ee."

Then, ever so slowly, she turns toward me. In just an instant, I take in the horror that's in front of me. Her entire face is swollen and bruised. Her once green eyes have all but vanished—at least one of them has. Her right eye is completely shut. There are scratches along

her face, and dried blood is crusted in her hair and all around what I
know is her mouth yet looks like a menagerie of cuts against a back-
drop of purple and yellow skin tones. In truth, if she weren't in my
sister's house, in my sister's bed, I'm not entirely sure I would know
she was, in fact, my sister.

"Rose, honey. What happened? Did someone break in? Should I
call the police?"

In spite of her clearly weakened state—she is trying to use her
elbows to lift herself up without success—she shakes her head, then
moans and grasps her head. Clearly the act of moving has increased
her pain. As she holds what must be a throbbing head, I notice her
wrists are also swollen and heavily bruised.

"Rose! What the hell happened? Tell me."

Before she can answer, I taste the sourness bubbling up into my
mouth, and I make it to the hall bathroom just in time to vomit into
the toilet.

Mrs. Marty Seigel

(Rose)

There isn't anywhere that my body doesn't hurt, yet strangely, I feel a sense of relief. Now at least Lily knows—or she will once I tell her. I quickly wonder how much to reveal, but my brain feels heavy, and as soon as that thought enters my mind, it's gone before I can formulate an answer.

"Rose. Please, please tell me what happened." Lily reaches for the phone, or that's what I assume she's done. My vision is even worse than it was earlier, which means my eye is even more swollen, if that's possible. I move my head slightly to the right, testing whether my vision is better when I try to use just one eye. "I really think I should call the police," Lily says. "Or at least I should call Marty. Do you know where he is?"

"No." It feels like I am yelling, but when I hear it, my voice sounds thin and weak. "Marty. Marty did this."

Lily doesn't respond. For a moment, I wonder if I've said it out loud. If so, did she hear me?

I feel a depression in the mattress, and before I can register what is happening, Lily is sitting next to me. She jumps up immediately. I remember the basin filled with water that wet the mattress earlier. No doubt Lily has discovered it, too. She grabs the blanket and bunches it next to me before she sits down on it. She wraps her arms around my shoulders and smooths my hair away from my cheek, ever so gently. "Oh, Rosie." And then it is her voice that is thin and weak. She is trying so very hard not to fall apart—not to let me know she's crying. "Why didn't you tell me?"

Why indeed? Do I explain it's not all the time; in fact, it's not even that often? How do I make my sister understand that Marty is not just violent but a master manipulator? So good, in fact, he's had me convinced, on more than one occasion, that he didn't hit me or push me; it was my own carelessness or clumsiness that caused my injury. How, I wonder, could I be so incredibly stupid? But I don't say any of those things.

"Rose. Do you have a camera?" Lily asks.

I tell her where I keep my Instamatic. "But it's almost out of film," she says when she finds it.

"There's another cartridge and a flash bar downstairs. It's either in the credenza in the family room or the junk drawer in the kitchen."

After I assure Lily that I'll be okay, she leaves me to retrieve both items. It doesn't occur to me to wonder why she wants my camera; it doesn't even enter my mind to *ask her* why she wants my camera. I am focused only on trying to remain upright in my bed; I'm fearful I might faint again.

When Lily returns, she says she wants to take pictures of me and what Marty has done.

I turn my head and ask her not to—this is all so embarrassing, and I would never want anyone to see pictures of me looking like this—but I'm not in much of a position to object.

"I think it was on *General Hospital*, or maybe it was on another show, but a woman was assaulted and her best friend took pictures so it could be her proof when she went to court.

"I want you to have that option," Lily says. "Photographs can give you grounds for a divorce."

Although Lily said the word—Lily said "*divorce*"!—she suddenly seems flustered. "I mean, if a div— . . . , if that's what you want. You don't have to decide now."

My sister drops the film cartridge into the back of the camera and uses her thumb to wind it forward. She attaches the flash bar to the top and begins to shoot.

Mrs. David Berg

(Lily)

I call Betsy to let her know I'm running late and to please feed
Jo-Jo mac and cheese for dinner and to take the tuna-and-
noodle casserole out of the freezer so it will defrost before dinner.
"I fully expect to be home before David arrives. But if I'm not back
by six p.m., please just put some foil on the casserole and put it in
the oven at three hundred fifty degrees for forty-five minutes." I
also ask Betsy if she'll take the cake I frosted earlier, which is still
sitting on the counter, to Becca's house. Then, without thinking,
because my mind is completely consumed with Rose, I say, "Just
leave the cake with Bradley and tell him I'm thinking of him and
the boys." Of course that prompts Betsy to ask, "Why, what's
wrong?"

"She . . . Becca. She had a miscarriage." I figure that will
end any conversation, and it's probably what Becca told Robin and
anyone else who might discover she was admitted to the hospital.

"Whoa, wow. Then I guess she won't need me to ask anyone at Raven House if they know someone who can get rid of a
pregnancy."

"What?" I feel certain I misheard.

"Mrs. Hudson came over a couple weeks back, when you were

at the beauty shop. She asked me to find out about whether any-one at Raven House knew a doctor or nurse who could get rid of a pregnancy. She said it was for a married friend of hers, but I was pretty sure she was the married friend, if you know what I mean."

I've heard the expression "my head is spinning," but never fully comprehended its meaning. Until now. "Betsy, why didn't you mention this to me before?"

"Oh. She asked me not to."

I fight the urge to scream at her, but I remind myself that she's only fifteen years old. None of this is her fault, nor her responsibility.

"Did I do something wrong?" she asks.

I reassure her that no one did anything wrong. Then I stumble through something about Betsy perhaps misunderstanding Mrs. Hudson, and how none of it matters anyway, since she lost the baby.

Betsy agrees, but since we're on the phone and I can't see her face, I'm not sure if she agrees because she believes me or whether she just wants to stop talking about it. Either way, I'm fairly certain she has no idea what "getting rid of a pregnancy" even means. Regardless, we move on.

Betsy tells me not to rush, that she'll even give Jo-Jo her bath before bed. I'm about to remind Betsy that I bathed Jo-Jo this morning after her sleep poop, but decide that someone may as well have a good day, and why shouldn't that someone be Jo-Jo? Two baths in one day(!), making orange "dooce," and licking spoons covered in cake batter and frosting. What a life!

"Thanks, Betsy, that would be great. You're a lifesaver."

The fact that Betsy's parents made her leave home is increasingly upsetting; she's truly a delightful and helpful young lady, who, granted, made a mistake. But sending her away? I know in the long run they're saving her reputation and giving her a chance to complete her education and get on with her life, but it still doesn't sit quite right with me. Yet what other options are there? When Kathy, our first unwed mother, came to us, and again when Betsy arrived, their misfortunes were a benefit to me. Somehow I didn't allow myself to focus on that fact. But the flip side is that unwed mothers have nowhere else to go. Now Rose, who has done absolutely nothing wrong, is in the same situation. Yet she cannot stay here—that much is clear.

Miss Betsy Ann Eubanks

I always liked when my mother made a Whip 'n Chill cake for my birthday, but Lily said she needed to bake a cake that didn't require refrigeration so she could just leave it on the counter at Mrs. Seigel's house for her birthday surprise. Since Jo-Jo is napping, I decide to do Lily an extra favor by washing the spatula, bowl, and all the other stuff she left soaking in the sink. It's a small thing, but she seems to really appreciate it whenever I do something she hasn't asked me to do. And after Mrs. Bloom's baby slipping out during canasta—and Mrs. Hudson's miscarriage—I think Lily could use some cheering up.

Once I've done the dishes, I look for the box of mac and cheese in the cupboard and the pot Lily uses to make it, and I place both on the counter, just like Lily does when she's getting herself organized to prepare dinner. I remember that I'll also need a colander to catch the noodles after they've boiled, and I put it on the counter with the box and the pot. I grab the wooden spoon Lily uses to mix everything together, and then I check to make sure the casserole is in the freezer. Luckily, Lily has notes on everything that's covered in tinfoil. When I'm married, that's what I'm going to do, too, so it'll be easy to find whatever I'm looking for. I feel so grown up; this is the first time I've really been in charge of the whole house. When I write to my mom about it, I know she's going to be bursting with pride.

Mrs. David Berg

(Lily)

I help Rose get dressed and clean her face as much as I can without hurting her. Even dabbing her lip with warm water elicits an involuntary jerk, as she pulls back her head, away from the washcloth. I manage to remove the dried blood from her hairline, and once we finish in the bathroom, I help ease my sister onto the stool that's in front of the vanity table in her bedroom. "Where do you keep your ice bag?"

"Hall closet, with the towels," she says.

I find it, exactly where Rose said it would be, and grab it on my way down the stairs to the kitchen. As I head toward the freezer, I notice the cake and the balloon floating aimlessly over the counter, just where I left them—was it just a half hour ago? I was so excited and happy to surprise my sister. *Sur-prise, sur-prise, sur-prise.* Guess the surprise was on me.

I grab a metal tray from the freezer, pull back on the handle to release the ice cubes, and drop them, one by one, into the insulated bag. I screw on the cap, and as I head back up the stairs, I feel the weight of my baby deep in my abdomen. Once I get to Rose, I hand her the ice bag, which she holds against the right side of her face, covering both her eye and her lip.

"What do you want to do?" I ask my sister as I strip the bed of the bloodstained sheets. I leave the pile of linens on the floor and pull the bedspread over the mattress before I sit on the edge of the bed.

Rose begins to think out loud, making it plain that she wants to be out of the house by the time Marty returns from the office or wherever he went. The question is: Where can she go? Of course my first instinct is to bring her to our house. She counters with a very valid point: Where would we put her? I assure her that she could stay in the big-girl room we're working on for Jo-Jo, realizing that since Betsy's arrival, I've done precious little to get the room ready. In fact, aside from buying pink sheets and a pink polka-dot bedspread, I've done nothing. But Rose keeps saying how embarrassing this is. She doesn't want David, Betsy, or even Jo-Jo to see her in this condition. She also doesn't want our neighbors, specifically my canasta group, to see her, which would force her to explain her bruises or why she's staying with us. No matter how often I tell her this is not her fault, no matter how often she repeats that she knows it's not her fault, I can tell she thinks this is her fault. Maybe not her fault that she was beaten, but her fault for marrying Marty—a man she dated for one year, but trusted to be honorable and loving because that was how he came across. But there's more to it than that.

Marty's mother and our mother were best friends. Didn't that mean something about their kids, how they were raised and the people they'd become? "It's *bershert,*" Rose had said on more than one occasion, using the Yiddish expression when something is meant to be. I cannot fault her logic because I felt the same way. Worse, I think I encouraged her, or at least reinforced her thinking. People, Jewish people, with an education and careers, who come from good families, have traditional, happy marriages. They have unions where the man goes off to work and supports the household and the woman stays home and keeps the house, cooks, and raises the children. At least that's how it's supposed to be.

When Mrs. Seigel offered to plan the wedding, stepping into what would have been our mother's shoes, Rose and I were giddy, sharing our belief that somehow Mom's best friend was channeling our own mother. More than once, Rose said it was like Mom herself was planning the wedding. Looking at Rose's face now, obliterated by an ice bag, it seems we were both suffering from a fantasy that was too good to be true. And I, the older sister, who on more than one occasion took on the mothering role, never encouraged Rose to slow down. How could I, when I married David right after high school? Rose was a grown woman who had already graduated from college! It was time for her to settle down and start a family, and Marty seemed like the perfect choice.

But even if Rose had taken more time, would we have known? When I question her, Rose assures me that Marty never even raised his voice to her before they married. "And he's never done anything like *this*," she says. "A few months after we married, there were some harsh words and then a slap." She removes the ice bag from her face, not that it matters; her face is so swollen she doesn't even resemble her real self. "Then there were a few other things, but he always felt horrible and apologized, telling me he was under a lot of pressure at work and how much he loved me. It hardly ever happened. Maybe four or five times total."

I remember Marty asking us whether Rose was always clumsy, and how she tripped over her own feet. "What about that?"

Rose returns the ice bag to her face. Whether the cold feels good or whether she's using the bag as a shield to hide behind is unclear. "He almost had me believing that backing into the dresser *was* my fault," she says. "I thought, 'Well, I guess that's how it could have happened.' Do you think I'm crazy for believing him?"

I don't think she's crazy, but I also don't understand how she could mix up being shoved with tripping. But I also know this isn't the time for that conversation.

AFTER MUCH BACK AND FORTH, we are left with two options: We agree that, for the time being, Rose can live either with Dad or with Grandma Mollie. We are both fairly certain Marty will show up, demanding she return home, and Dad, being a man, would be able to provide her with physical protection. "Well, I sure can't tell Dad that Marty raped me," she says.

"Oh, goodness gracious, Rose! Of course you can't say that to Dad." Not for the first time I bristle over Rose's word choice. From watching *General Hospital*, I know it's not really even considered rape if the two people are married, like Dr. Tom Baldwin and Audrey were when he forced himself on her. But even if it was against the law, what then? It's not like Rose can have Marty arrested. That's when I realize the sad truth: It doesn't matter what it's called or whether it's a crime. All I know is that what happened to my sister should not happen to her or to any woman, ever. But I also know how Dad is. If we weren't Jewish, I'd say that Dad thinks Jo-Jo happened by immaculate conception, rather than believe his daughter had relations with her husband.

"So, what would I tell him?"

I shrug my shoulders. "Maybe don't use the word 'rape' and just tell Dad that Marty hit you. I mean, it's the truth."

Again, Rose moves the ice bag away from her face. "I don't know if I'm ready for everyone to know."

"It's not everyone, Rose. It's Dad."

Rose doesn't respond right away. I have a million other things I want to stay, starting with *You shouldn't be protecting Marty*, but I force myself to remain silent, giving her the time she needs. After all, this is her life and her reputation at stake, not mine.

"I don't want anyone to know, at least not yet." Rose removes the ice bag from her face and places it in her lap. I can hear sloshing, letting me know the ice is already starting to melt. I tip my head toward the ice bag. "Is it still cold enough?"

Rose nods and sits up a bit straighter, using her body language to let me know she's made a decision. "We're going to tell people that when I did the laundry, a ball of socks fell out of the laundry basket and landed on the stairs. I didn't see it, and after I put away the clean clothes, I was carrying the basket back down the stairs and I tripped on the socks and fell down the stairs, and that's why I'm so banged up."

The ease with which my sister has created this fabrication is horrifying. The fact it's plausible makes me wonder when Rose became such a good liar, and how many other times I've taken her words at face value when, perhaps, I shouldn't have. And then I wonder whether she's being honest now. Was Marty perfect when they were dating? Was he violent toward her only a handful of times before last night?

"Grandma Mollie," Rose says, interrupting my thoughts about my sister's honesty. "If she'll have me, I want to go there. Marty has always been a little scared of her, I think. He'll never just show up at her house, and if he does, I'm betting on her to win whatever showdown he has in mind."

She not only has a point, but I like the idea of her staying with Grandma. Once Rose is feeling better, she can help Grandma prepare Shabbat dinners, do household chores, and just keep an eye on her.

"Will you tell her the truth about Marty and what happened?"

Rose takes a moment to consider my question. "Yes. I think she needs to know. I'm going to have to talk to Marty at some point, and she'll overhear me on the phone, at the very least. I don't want to have to sneak around her house."

I can't argue with her logic. I ask her where she keeps her suitcase and pull it out from under the bed. I pack up everything she tells me to take from her closet and drawers. "My eyes won't be swollen shut forever, so toss this in there, too." She hands me a book from her nightstand. It's *The Feminine Mystique*, by Betty Friedan.

"Robin gave me that book for our Secret Santa exchange."

"Figures. It's such a Robin-type book. I'm almost done with it and was going to give it to you when I finished. Have you read it yet?"

Does reading only the first paragraph count? "Just started," I say.

"There's a lot of good, thought-provoking stuff in it," Rose says. "When you're done, we should talk about it."

"Sure. Why not?"

Rose then delivers her favorite line of "Not to change the subject, but to change the subject," and asks me to please not tell David. She's caught me completely off guard. David is my husband; how do I keep something this big from him?

"I'm just not ready yet. This all happened so fast, I need some time to sort out some things. So, just tell him about the socks and the stairs, at least for now. Okay?"

I don't think about the fact that telling this lie will be the biggest deception I've ever committed in my marriage. I don't think about how lying to my husband might impact my own marriage. Instead, I think about staircases. I think about how Betsy, that cheerleader from her high school, and now my sister have all turned flights of stairs into a solution for their problems.

Mrs. Marty Seigel

(Rose)

Even though Lily called Grandma Mollie, first asking if it was okay if I stayed with her for a while, but also telling her I'd been hurt and needed some of her chicken soup to make me feel better—"She'll tell you all about it after I drive her over"—Grandma wasn't prepared. When she opened her front door, her hand flew to her mouth and she started talking in Yiddish, clearly upset. Most of what she said was beyond my limited understanding of her native tongue, but I'm fairly certain that even someone born Catholic, who'd never even met someone Jewish before, could figure out what she meant when she called Marty a "no-goodnik."

It was hard to admit the truth about my marriage. But telling Grandma was strangely illuminating for me. Hearing my story, in my own words, not only gave me clarity, but also helped me understand that I had some options I'd not previously recognized. I told Grandma I wanted a divorce. It wasn't just me talking out of anger. I absolutely, positively knew I wanted a divorce, in spite of whatever shame or disgrace went with that choice. I also understood that, although times were changing and the hippies and their free love were altering people's ideas about relationships in general, I wasn't a hippie, and neither were my friends, family, or the other teachers at my school. Getting a divorce would be hard. Marty would try to stop me; he definitely wouldn't want the stigma. But I've seen *Divorce Court* on television, and I know from Judge Voltaire that I can't get a divorce just because I'm unhappy. I have to be able to prove—in a courtroom—that Marty was cruel and violent toward me. That's when the penny drops. Lily. Took. Pictures.

I know Marty. He would do anything to prevent anyone he knows, particularly his parents, his brothers, and people at his office, from finding out what he did. So it's possible, I realize, that I won't even need to fight him in court. I could simply threaten to, and rely on the fact he won't want our dirty laundry blowin' in the wind, as Bob Dylan would say.

I understand that, for the first time, I have power over Marty. After devouring some chicken soup with matzoh balls, I ask Grandma if I can use her phone.

Mrs. David Berg

(Lily)

Once Rose was settled in at Grandma's, both women gave me directives to go home to my family. "But you are my family." Still, I knew what they meant, and besides, I was exhausted. Since learning about Becca last night—was it only last night?—I got maybe four hours of sleep. Then this day . . . even if I were well rested, this day would have been too much. Yet during my drive home, I felt surprisingly grateful. Grateful that David is David and he'd never think of laying a hand on me. But the truth is, when I married David, I didn't know that. I didn't date him for much longer than Rose dated Marty before their marriage. The same thing could have happened to me. David is a good provider and a kind and gentle husband. He would never force himself on me, and he sure would not hurt me the way Marty hurt Rose. I feel guilty for ever asking *Is this all?* when I'm so fortunate. So very, very lucky.

I beat David home. Betsy is playing with Jo-Jo in the basement, and I ask if she minds entertaining my little girl a while longer so I can have dinner with David when he arrives. As usual, Betsy is agreeable.

Almost on cue, David walks through the front door. While he washes his hands, I turn on the radio in the kitchen, assuring he and I won't be overheard. As I put the tuna-and-noodle casserole on the table, I ask David about his day.

"The good news is that both of my patients in the septic abortion ward are doing well. Becca should be discharged tomorrow, and the fifteen-year-old won't be having babies, but she'll survive."

"Why were you gone all day? It's Saturday."

"I traded 'on call' days with another doctor who had a big family reunion or something. And just as I was getting ready to leave, one of my patients had an emergency. A woman who was seven months pregnant went into early labor."

I instinctively touch my own belly. "Oh, no. Why did that happen?"

"No idea." David places his thumb and middle finger against his closed eyelids. It's his new "tell" when he's trying to remain composed. By the time he resumes talking, it's clear he is choking back tears. He's been so much more emotional about his work these last couple days. I think he needs a vacation. I make a mental note to see if we can go somewhere with Jo-Jo before the baby comes. At least tomorrow is Sunday. I'm going to insist he sleep in and do next to nothing all day.

"Her water broke, and a few hours later she delivered a stillborn baby." He inhales deeply and shakes his head. "No matter how often it happens, I never get used to it."

I reach across the table and put my hand over his. "I certainly hope not. That's what makes you such a great doctor. You care." David offers a smile, but even if you didn't know him the way I do, you could tell it's not sincere.

"Does it happen often that a woman has a baby too soon? It's not something I've heard you mention before, is it?"

"Things go wrong," David says. "You know that. That's why every birth is a miracle, and we should thank God every day for Jo-Jo, and for that little guy you're carrying."

Now the smile on David's face is real.

"Oh, he's a little guy is he?"

"I'm sure of it," he says. "Unless it's a girl."

I feel bad knowing I'm about to ruin this light and rather playful moment, so I begin with an apology. "I'm sorry to add to what has already been such a trying day, on top of last night, which was also horrible, but I need to tell you about Marty and Rose, and it can't wait."

By the time I finish, I've never seen David so angry and upset. If I didn't know him better, I'd worry that he might drive over to their house and kill Marty with his bare hands. But David swears he'll stay out of it. At least for now. "Remember, Rose made me promise to tell you the cockamamie story about her falling down the stairs because of the ball of socks," I say. "So she can't know that you know the truth. Promise me. And not the kind of promise I made Rose that I just broke. But a real one."

He promises.

"Do you think I'm a terrible sister for betraying Rose and telling you?"

He smiles and shakes his head. "No, honey. I think you're the very best kind of sister who wants to protect Rose and the very best kind of wife who doesn't want to keep secrets from her husband."

I get up from the table to clear our plates and give David a peck on the cheek. "Thank you for that. I just couldn't keep something this big from you. That's not the kind of marriage I want." I think about Becca and how I kept her desire to end her pregnancy from David. Would it have made a difference if he knew? It's not like David could have done anything about it. Still, from now on, no secrets. At least not big ones.

I send David upstairs to relax while I do the dishes. As I wait for the sink to fill, my mind drifts again to last night. I keep going back to David saying that women aren't called for jury duty because our society thinks we're too delicate to hear about bad things. At the time, it seemed like nothing more than a random thought or a stall tactic David was using to put off telling me about Becca. But now I wonder: Is it true? Are we really so delicate we can't hear certain things, or are we just told that, and after hearing something over and over again, we begin to believe it?

Mrs. Marty Seigel

(Rose)

Thankfully, the aspirin I took has started to work, although Grandma would say it's the medicinal powers of her chicken soup. Maybe we're both right. But for whatever reason, though my body still hurts, I'm no longer in the agony I was earlier today; at least I'm able to sit upright. My right eye is still swollen completely shut, but I can see out of my other eye, and if I turn my head and center my left eye over what I want to look at, well, I can actually see.

I know if I don't reach Marty before he arrives home, he'll start searching for me, and that means calling around, starting with my family. The last thing I need is Dad worrying about me. Fortunately, when he left the house this morning, Marty told me he was going to his office. Working on Saturday is one of the "must-dos" if you want to make partner, at least according to my husband.

Before I phone Marty's office, I jot down a list of what I want to say to him, which isn't easy considering my eyesight. Then I change my mind about the order of what I plan to tell him, and by the time I'm done, the paper in front of me looks like the board game from Chutes and Ladders, without the spaces.

A woman, whose voice I don't recognize, answers and asks me to hold while she transfers the call. She must have told him I was on the phone because he answers with "Hi, Rose." Then he says, "What's up?" He sounds so casual, which must mean his office door is still open, allowing the woman to hear him. I spontaneously suggest he get up and close the door. "I'll wait."

He takes my advice and returns to the phone. "Okay. But before you say anything, please believe me. I know I messed up. I love you, Rose. I love you so, so much. I don't really know—"

I cut him off. "Marty, I have some things to say and I want you to listen."

"Of course. Of course. I'll do whatever you say. Anything."

I look down at my crib sheet and tilt my head, making it easier to see out of my left eye. My hand, not surprisingly, is shaking. "I'm going to talk and I want you to listen and not interrupt me until I'm done. Agreed?"

"Anything. Yes. Rose, whatever you say."

"This has to stop," I say. And because he cannot control himself verbally any more than he can control himself physically, Marty interrupts.

"I agree," he says. "And I promise, I'll make it up to you."

"There is nothing you're going to do to make this or anything else up to me. Marty, I want a divorce."

Again, he interrupts me. "No, Rose. We can work this out. I promise I'll do better. I love you. You're my whole life." I let him talk. He offers more promises of change. More declarations of love.

Finally, I've had enough. "Marty, you need to listen to me." I can hear how much my voice is shaking, and I'm certain he does, too. I take a deep breath, telling myself to be strong and to speak with conviction. "Number one: I do not want to work this out. Number two: I want a divorce. And number three: You're going to grant me one."

"Why would I do that?" Just from the tone of his voice, I know that, at least from Marty's point of view, I've gone too far. It's like I've flipped a switch in him and—*click!*—just like that, he's gone from contrite to being on the attack. He no longer tries to convince me that he loves me or how sorry he is and how this will never happen again. He only wants what he wants, which is to control me and to make me understand that he is in charge, and he will make any and all decisions regarding our marriage. He, like me, doesn't want the stigma of divorce. But unlike me, he's convinced the answer is to stay married.

"If you don't agree to a divorce, I will tell people what you've done to me. Your parents, your brothers, everyone in your office, everyone at my school, and every single person I run into at the grocery store, including the checkout girls."

"Like anyone would believe you," he says. "What makes you think I can't do the same? I can tell all those people how you're suffering from hysteria and how unfortunate it is that I may even have to get you locked up in the loony bin."

If, moments ago, I flipped a switch in him, he's just done the same in me. If there was even the slightest doubt, nagging in the back of my brain, that divorce wasn't the answer and perhaps marriage counseling could help us, it's gone.

"I have pictures." My voice, for the first time, is steady, albeit barely above a whisper.

"What did you say?"

"I have pictures of what you did to me. And I will share them with everyone, starting with your parents." *Friends, Romans, countrymen, lend me your ears.*

For once, he doesn't respond. I know that at this moment, Marty truly hates me and would kill me, if only I was in striking distance.

I break the silence. "However, if you grant me a divorce, no one will ever see those pictures." I feel strong, or at least stronger than when this phone call began. "You will tell everyone we 'had differences and couldn't live together' and just leave it at that. If anyone asks what that means, or wants details, you will simply say, 'It's a private matter.'" I sound more matter-of-fact than emotional. "And, Marty, if I get word that you've said anything more or anything different, to even one person, I will make sure those pictures are seen by anyone and everyone. Do you understand?"

He is silent.

"I can't imagine you want to be the talk of the town or suffer that kind of embarrassment. Do you? Might make getting the promotion you've been counting on a lot more complicated, don't you think?"

Marty still doesn't answer. It's only when I hear a click that I realize he's hung up the phone.

After I end my call with Marty or, more accurately, after he ends the call with me, I phone my dad and tell him the story about tripping on the socks on the stairs. "I got banged up pretty badly." I don't even give my dad time to express concern. "Marty and I agreed I shouldn't be home alone until I'm feeling better, so I'm staying with Grandma for the time being." I hate making Marty sound like a concerned and loving husband, but if this whole ruse is going to work, I expect there will be a lot of times I'm going to hate the words that come out of my mouth. "We had differences and couldn't live together"? What a grotesque understatement.

I hate lying to my dad; I actually hate lying to anyone. Period. Mom was right when she said that lying never amounts to any good. Actually, her exact words were *"Oh, what a tangled web we weave when first we practice to deceive."*

Oh, Mom. What a mess I've made of my life.

Just as I'm about to end my call with Dad, Grandma appears in the hallway and motions for me to hand her the receiver. "Avrum," she says, calling my dad by his Yiddish name, rather than his English name of Arthur. "Did Rose tell you she has a cold coming on? I can hear the sniffles, and I'm giving her my chicken soup, but no Shabbat dinner on Friday. I don't vant to hear nothing about it from Lily if Jo-Jo gets sick from my house."

When Grandma hangs up the phone, she looks at me. "What?" she says, only it comes out "Vat?" because she can't say *W*s. "You vant to have to tell him vhy that no-goodnik isn't here for dinner? You vant your pa to see all the colors of the rainbow on your face?"

I suddenly see a new side of my grandma. I realize that, probably because of her age and her accent, I've made assumptions about her that I now question. That, for instance, because she never had formal schooling, and because she uses broken, accented English, she's not very smart. That since she never worked, she's naive about the ways of the world.

I look at the short woman in front of me, who came here speaking not a word of English, who married an older man who was a stranger to her, but whom she says she loved and who treated her with tenderness. If this woman who gave birth to my dad when she was little more than a child herself could carve out a life for herself, then certainly I can, too.

"Grandma, while I'm here, I'd love to hear even more of your stories," I say. "You can tell me about your life in the old country, before you came to the United States, and how you met Grandpa Max and all about your marriage. I'm going to write everything down, so when Jo-Jo grows up, she'll know all about you. What do you think?"

"Ve'll see," she says. "Ve'll see if there's time."

"We can make time. Even though a voman's vork is never done."

That makes her smile.

ON MONDAY MORNING, THE ALARM clock Grandma's given me wakes me, and I slap at it, trying to make it stop. I reach for the phone on the nightstand. I tilt my head, trying to make out the numbers. Everything is still blurry, so I use my hands, as if I'm reading braille, to locate the last circle on the rotary dial. "Operator, do you have the number of Barber Elementary School?"

"Please hold for the number."

"Actually, could you dial it for me?"

"Dialing now."

The office secretary, Bonnie, is a friend of mine. I feel bad lying to her, but it's not like I have a lot of options. I tell her I won't be in today. "I'm fairly sure I've got the Hong Kong flu."

"Oh, no. Rose, you sound just awful. So many of our teachers have gotten it. But you just take care of yourself and I'll line up a substitute. Shall I get her for the rest of the week?"

"Thanks, Bon. That sounds about right. If it turns out not to be the flu and I can come in sooner, I'll let you know."

When I hang up, I'm struck with how exhausted I feel, and I lie back down and drift off to sleep.

When I wake again, a little more than an hour later, I wish I'd been more clearheaded when I called the school this morning. Telling Bonnie I have the Hong Kong flu could turn out to be a huge mistake. What happens if, like so many people not just in America but all over the world, I actually get the flu? Then what will I tell them at work?

That tangled web I've woven is getting more twisted with every passing day.

Mrs. David Berg

(Lily)

Once I finish the dishes and spend some time playing with Jo-Jo before putting her in her crib, I go into our room and find David in his pajama bottoms, relaxing on the bed. "Can I get you anything?"

He pats my side of the bed. "Nope. Just join me."

While I undress, I think again about how incredibly tired I am. Maybe it's exhaustion because of my pregnancy, or more likely the accumulation of everything that's happened in the last few days. Still, whatever the reason, I don't feel at all like myself, which may be why I was able to come to this realization: I am the mother of one little girl and have another baby growing inside me, and yet, after David told me about the fifteen-year-old who gave herself that procedure with a hanger, it struck me that I know next to nothing about my own body and how it works. When I say this to my husband, he lifts his eyebrows. "What, my dear wife, do you want to know?"

Even before he asks, I can tell my face has already turned every imaginable shade of red, and I feel a droplet of perspiration dripping down my neck.

"You're going to make me say the words, aren't you?"

"Yes indeedy," David says, and when he smiles, I can barely make out the dimple in his left cheek, hiding under the scruff of his five-o'clock shadow.

"Well . . ." I take a deep breath, trying to remember the words I practiced at least a dozen times while I was washing the dishes. "Remember back when we were dating and I asked you whether you were attracted to the naked women who were your patients?"

"Vaguely," he says.

"You said your patients were just body parts, which I know now can't possibly be true because you care so much about them. If they were just body parts, you wouldn't be so upset when things go wrong with them or their babies."

"You're right," he says. "I do care about them. But when I'm examining a woman, there's a professional detachment that makes the exam, well, clinical. There's nothing erotic or sensual about it."

I just know I'm turning red all over again. Rose is right. I am such a prude.

"I want you to teach me," I say.

"Teach you what?"

David seems genuinely confused. This flowed so well when I rehearsed what I was going to say in the kitchen, but now I sound like Elmer Fudd, from Looney Tunes.

"I want you to pretend I'm your patient. And I want you to do an exam on me, and when you do, I want you to tell me the names of all the body parts, what they're for, and how they work."

David laughs. "So, what you're telling me is that you want to play doctor with me. Is that right?"

"Stop it," I say. I hit him over the head with one of my bed pillows. "This is really hard and now you're making fun of me. If you keep laughing, I'll never ask you anything again."

He immediately wipes the smile off his face. "Oh, Lily. I'm only laughing because, well, because I thought you'd never ask. And it would be my pleasure. Truly, dear. My pleasure." He gives me that smile again, and I tell him that now would be a fine time for my first lesson.

February
1966

Mrs. David Berg

(Lily)

Ever since Rose's birthday, when I discovered her beaten in bed, I've wondered whether she had a *pushke*. Things were so chaotic when I packed her bag to get her out of the house, I forgot to ask.

I remember when Rose and I initially learned about a *pushke* from Mom.

At the start of every month, Dad handed Mom an envelope that was filled with cash; it was her pay packet, not unlike the pay packet David gives me every month. The money was intended to cover groceries and other household expenses, and it was up to Mom to make it last. I think he must have included more when we neared Chanukah so she could buy us gifts, but I don't know that for a fact. I add it to my mental list of things to ask him the next time I see him.

Since Dad is an accountant, everyone thinks I get my math skills from him, but Mom was a real wiz with numbers. I don't think I ever once heard her tell Dad she ran short or needed extra cash to get us to the end of the month. One of my favorite Mom memories is a game we played when we were in the car. Mom would say, "Six plus four." She waited for me to answer "Ten" and then she'd say something like "Plus twenty-three," and I'd give her the new total. "Minus four." It went on and on like that, with Mom adding or subtracting numbers while I supplied the new total, always doing the arithmetic in my head. The game was over when we arrived at our destination. My "win-loss status" was determined by whether I had the correct number by the time we got to wherever we were going. I cannot wait to play with Jo-Jo when she gets older; continuing the tradition is such a great way to keep Mom's memory alive.

Anyway, Mom was great with numbers, and every month, she removed what she called a "little extra" from the pay packet Dad handed her. When I was around twelve, which would mean Rose was ten, I distinctly remember Mom opening the envelope after Dad left for work. She took out a single dollar. "Follow me, my petite fleurs," she said as Rose and I walked behind her, like marching ants, into her bedroom. Mom passed the bureau that held Dad's clothes and stopped in front of her dresser. She opened the top drawer where she kept her brassieres, reached into the back and removed a cigar box, opened it, and deposited the dollar. "This is where I keep my *pushke*."

I was glad Rose asked what a *pushke* was because I was wondering the same thing.

"It's getaway money." Mom smiled and lifted her brows, like it was our special secret. "A *pushke* is Yiddish."

"What are you getting away from?" Rose asked.

Mom bent down and gave both of us big hugs before kissing the top of my head. "Just teasing. But you girls are getting older, and one day, before you know it, you'll both be married."

I always feel a mixture of joy and melancholy when I have vivid memories of my mom, and the pay packet Dad handed her on the first of every month is a recollection that's burnished into my memory.

"As a wife, it will be your job to keep the house and raise your children," my mom used to remind us from time to time. "Unless you want to be a teacher"—*yes, Mom, Rose became a teacher, and I know you would have been so proud of her!*—"or a nurse, but even then, once you get married, you'll probably stop. So, my petite fleurs, it's always a good idea to keep a little cash on hand for a rainy day. Understand?"

Not only didn't I understand, but I was terribly confused. Getting away on a rainy day? Why would you need a cigar box rather than an umbrella? But that's the thing about being young. You start to learn when to ask questions and when to remain silent. I instinctively knew this was a case of the latter. Only recently, more than a decade after Mom has passed away, do I recall her words and understand the subtext.

Since I was only fourteen when she died, I find it increasingly hard to remember details about my mom, like the sound of her voice. Yet whenever Rose drums her fingers on the table, I'm flooded with memories of the clickity-clack of my mom's pointy red nails rhythmically hitting the counter when she asked us each morning at breakfast if we had any preferences for dinner. I barely waited for her to finish her sentence before trying to beat Rose's typical request of meat loaf by yelling out, "Macaroni and cheese." I also have a crystal clear memory of Mom taking me shopping for my first garter belt and nylons to wear for Rosh Hashanah services when I finally turned thirteen. Those are the memories I try to hold onto. And, of course, the *pushke*.

Miss Betsy Ann Eubanks

Last night, Lily reminded me that today I have my doctor's appointment at Raven House and to please be ready at eleven a.m. She seemed a little short with me, but when I asked her if anything was wrong, she said she has a busy day, that's all.

The plan is for her to drop me off at Raven House, where the doctor comes every month to examine all the girls. It's not a big deal; he takes my temperature and blood pressure and feels around my belly and listens with his stethoscope and has me go to the bathroom in a cup. Lily usually comes back for me two hours after she drops me off, unless Jo-Jo is napping. Then she returns whenever Jo-Jo wakes up, or when it's a good time for Lily to wake her, if Jo-Jo's napped long enough.

After I finish with the doctor, I usually kill the time while I'm waiting for Lily by talking to some of the girls. Since I'm only at Raven House once a month, each time I come, there are new people. Since last month when I was here, some of the girls have already left to go to the hospital to have their babies. Some of the other new faces are the girls who've just moved back into Raven House for their last month of being preggers, and of course there are the brand-new girls. They're easy to spot because they don't have enormous bellies yet. I have to admit, the housemother was right about my being fortunate to live with a family like the Bergs.

Today, after I finish with the doctor, the housemother says she wants to see me. This is the first time she's done that, so I figure I've done something wrong. She stands behind her desk and tells me to take a seat and then asks how things are going with the Bergs.

"It's groovy. They're both very nice, even though Dr. Berg isn't around a lot. And Jo-Jo is a dreamboat and calls me Bessy."

"That's nice, dear. The Bergs seem like a lovely couple and I'm glad it's working out so well for you. Not everyone is generous enough to open their home to a wayward girl." She straightens the corners of a stack of papers on her desk that already looked pretty straight to me. "I asked to speak to you so I can make sure you're clear about what comes next."

"Groovy."

"On March 15, one month before your due date, Mrs. Berg will bring you here. That will be the last time you see her, so you should say your goodbyes before she drops you off. Of course we cannot control your behavior, but Mrs. Berg knows that we strongly discourage any contact between the unwed mother and the host family once you return to Raven House. It's best for everyone if, when you leave their house, you close the door on that chapter of your life. Literally and figuratively. It may not seem best to you right now, but you're only sixteen, so you have to trust us."

"I'm fifteen," I say.

The housemother squints her eyes at me, and I can tell she doesn't appreciate my setting her straight about my age.

"Of course, if something unforeseen happens, the doctor may have you return to Raven House earlier, but for the sake of this conversation, let's just assume all goes according to plan.

"During the time you're at Raven House, you will be assigned a job, depending on what's vacant and what needs doing when you come back to us. It could be laundry or cooking or dishes. Nothing too taxing.

"You will also be assigned a bed, and you will stay with us until your labor starts, when you'll be taken to the hospital."

"Is it Heatherview Hospital where Dr. Berg works?"

"No, dear, it is not. Which is just as well." She gives me her squinty eyes again. "Did you not just hear me when I told you that when you leave the Bergs' house for your last month of confinement at Raven House, it will be the last time you see them?"

I nod, because I can tell she doesn't want to hear any more from me.

"Again. Once your labor starts, you'll be taken to the hospital where you will have your baby. We will call your mother and let her know that she is to come to get you in three days. During that time, you may see your baby if you so wish, but it is not recommended. Girls who see their babies have more difficulty when it's time to sign the adoption papers.

"When your mother arrives, you will sign the papers, as will she, since you are only . . . fifteen." She pauses before saying "fifteen," making a big deal about remembering I'm not sixteen.

"Once the papers are signed, it clears the way for a nice *married* couple to adopt your baby, and then you can return home and act like none of this ever happened. Do you understand everything I've told you?"

I tell her I do. "But I have a question. Can I pick who gets to adopt my baby?"

The housemother gets a wrinkle that looks like a number 11 between her bushy eyebrows. "What?"

"Can I decide which nice married couple gets my baby? Because I know one."

The housemother smiles and then uses her hand to cover her mouth. "I'm sorry, dear. But that's not the way it's done."

"Well, there's this really groovy lady who lives next door to the Bergs," I say, trying to make her understand. "And she's married.

And she really, really wants a baby and can't make it stick." I tell the housemother about the blood on the chair during the canasta game and how Mrs. Berg couldn't get out the stain, no matter what, and how she used her S&H green stamps to get some new chairs, just so Mrs. Bloom wouldn't see the stain on the old chair and feel bad.

"That's lovely," the housemother says.

That is the exact minute when I know the housemother isn't listening to a word I'm saying because there isn't one thing that is lovely about any of what I just told her.

Talking to her, I know, is a waste of my breath. I decide I'll tell Mrs. Berg about my great idea; I'm pretty sure she and Mrs. Bloom will agree that it's groovy.

Mrs. David Berg

(Lily)

A little more than a week after being discharged from the hospital, Becca finally called me. I asked her if she wanted to talk in person, but she said the phone might be easier.

"I saw the psychiatrists. I even went in wearing a sweater with the sleeves pushed back to my elbows, and I didn't wear a single bracelet. Everything went exactly as I planned because both doctors agreed that having the baby would be dangerous to my mental health. The problem was my OB-GYN. He got very high and mighty, telling me that unless I'd been seeing a shrink for some time, those reports meant nothing to him; he called it a scam and told me he wanted nothing to do with it. I freaked out, but decided he wasn't going to stop me. I found another doctor. At the new doctor's hospital, they have a policy where all therapeutic abortions need approval from some board or another, and when this new doctor gave them my paperwork, they turned me down for I don't even know what reason."

"Oh, Becca, I'm so sorry. I'm sorry I was such a horrible friend and you didn't feel like you could talk to me about this when it was happening. But I understand why you didn't." I've done my best to stay strong, but I can't help myself; I start to cry. "I promise you, Becca. I'll do better. I really will."

There's silence at the other end of the phone. "Becca?"

Still silence.

"Becca? Becca, are you there?"

Just when I think we've been disconnected—or has she hung up on me deliberately?—my front door swings open, and Becca comes flying through the entry hall. "I've missed you so much," she says, rushing toward me, her bracelets tinkling, as she takes the receiver from my hand and rehangs it on the base of the phone, which is attached to the wall. Then she takes me into her arms and gives me a huge hug. "Can we just put all this behind us and never mention it again?"

I realize she still hasn't told me what, exactly, happened. I have no idea how or where she got the procedure—the *abortion*—that landed her in the hospital. But I am trying to respect her wishes, and if she doesn't want to mention it again, if she is choosing not to tell me, then I'm determined to do whatever she wants. But I can't help but wonder: Is it *me* she doesn't want to tell, because I'm so straitlaced, or does she just not want to talk about it at all? With anyone? Ever?

I push away from Becca's arms so I can see her face, hoping to get some answers to my unasked questions. "We can do whatever you decide. I want to do whatever you're comfortable with. But please don't think you can't tell me because you think I'm too fragile to hear it or that I'm going to judge you, because I promise you, I won't."

Becca cocks her head. "Are you crazy? Neither is true. First of all, you're not fragile. You're one of the strongest women I know. You lost your mom when you were barely a teenager, and you all but raised Rose, and look at you! You're a wonderful mother, married to a man who adores you but who works insane hours, and somehow you make it all look effortless. Fragile, you are definitely not."

I'm stunned. This is not at all what I was expecting. No one has ever told me I am strong, not even Rose. Or David.

That's when I feel it. It starts with a sharp buzzing in my nose and then the tears seem to explode from my eyes. I locate the Kleenex box and grab one, two tissues, only to realize the box is now empty. *Another thing to add to the grocery list.* I wipe my eyes and then give my nose a good strong blow.

"And second," Becca says, "as far as judging me? Well, if you were judging me, you were doing a mighty fine job of keeping your judgment to yourself, because I sure didn't feel that way. Yes, I know you wanted me to be happy about the baby, but when I explained why I couldn't handle another pregnancy, you kept your lips zipped, even though I know you don't believe in abortion. And that, my friend, is not being judgmental. It's being a friend. A good, kind, best type of friend."

She extends her arms and motions with her hands for me to come toward her. Then she reaches out and hugs me again. Even harder this time.

"You know how they encourage the unwed mothers not to contact us once they leave to have their babies?"

I nod my head, which is still against Becca's shoulder, thanks to the never-ending hug.

"That's what I'd like to happen here. I don't want to ever speak about it again. It's behind me. Can you be okay with that?"

"To quote Betsy, I think it's 'groovy.'"

I ASKED SARAH IF SHE wanted help setting up before canasta today, and she said it wasn't necessary.

We skipped cards the last few weeks, first because of Sarah—we wanted to give her some time after she lost the baby—and then because of Becca, who, as far as the canasta group is concerned, had a miscarriage, but was bleeding so much she had to be admitted into the hospital.

It feels wonderful to be all together again. And I'm not the only one who feels that way, because, for once, not one of us tells any one of the others how she could have played a hand differently or, worse, complains that someone screwed up her signaling.

We are adding up the points from the final hand when Robin stands and stretches out her arms while rolling her neck. "I know the answer even before I ask, so I don't know why I even bother. I must be a glutton for punishment," she says. "But the ASA—the Association for the Study of Abortion—is leading a protest march to change abortion laws and to make it safer and easier for women to get them if they're medically necessary."

"When is it?" I blurt out, startling myself with a question that completely bypassed my brain.

I'm not the only one who's surprised. All eyes are on me.

"Of course it's not something I would ever choose for myself," I say. "But we don't know everyone's circumstances. I'm starting to think that every woman should be able to decide for herself what's best for her and for her family. But even more important, it should be safe."

"Oh. My. God," Robin says, emphasizing every word. "You've read the book, haven't you? You've read *The Feminine Mystique*!"

I confess that I'm a little past the halfway point. "And you were right, Robin. There's a lot in it I can relate to. That said, what makes you think it's the book and not Joe South who is my inspiration?"

"Who's Joe South?" Sarah asks.

"A singer. He's the one who wrote the hit song 'Walk a Mile in My Shoes.'" I quietly sing the chorus: *"And before you abuse, criticize, and accuse, just walk a mile in my shoes."*

Robin claps. "Well done."

"When is the march?" Becca asks. "Depending on my work schedule, I might also want to go."

Just as all eyes were once on me, now they shift to Sarah, the only one who hasn't weighed in. She shakes her head. "Please don't be mad at me. I'm sorry. But I . . . I just can't." She looks down at the cigarette between her fingers, and I notice a single tear falling down her cheek.

Mrs. Marty Seigel

(Rose)

I missed a week of school before I returned to the classroom. I still had bruises on my arms and legs, but they were easily covered by my dress and my fishnet pantyhose. I had some faint yellowing around one eye, but when my friend Bonnie asked about it, I told her I was so out of it because of the Hong Kong flu that I left open a cupboard and then walked right into it. "You're lucky you didn't lose your eye," Bon said.

"Don't I know it."

Thanks to President Johnson and the Elementary and Secondary Education Act, our district now has funding to have staff development days at my school. Today is our first gathering, and I, like most of my fellow teachers, am intrigued about how—and whether—presentations like this, along with Johnson's "War on Poverty," would affect us. Not very much, is my guess.

The speaker talks about new educational practices that some schools are starting to implement. Instead of our usual rows of desks, facing front, where teachers write on the blackboard and the students take notes, she explains that in some schools, there's already more emphasis on freedom and creativity in the classroom, as opposed to learning by rote. "Much of what's happening is mimicking what we're seeing in the world," she says. If that's true, and there is no reason to doubt her—she is the expert, after all—I wonder why all the hippies and the civil rights protests, especially those in the South, are something we want to bring into the classroom. Another teacher raises her hand and asks that very question. The woman explains that is absolutely not what she was insinuating. "I think we can all agree that all that talk about feminism and civil rights and people taking drugs does not belong anywhere near our schools," she says. "Let me give you some concrete examples, though, of how we, as teachers, can be more creative and engaging in the classroom."

She explains that while there is no substitute for memorizing addition and multiplication tables, allowing children to see how arithmetic works can also be beneficial. When she suggests using Sugar Smacks cereal, she gets a laugh from the entire auditorium, where we're meeting. "Here's an example of what I'm talking about," she says. "You walk around the room, giving each child a handful of cereal. You tell them to count out two pieces. Then you have them add three more pieces and ask them to find the total number of cereal bits." I immediately know this is an approach my students would love, especially those who are easily bored and act out when I turn my back to write on the chalkboard. "Then, when you're done with all the mathematics exercises you have planned for that day, you allow the children to eat the cereal." I notice lots of heads nodding and murmurs of approval. "Now don't you think," the woman asks, "that your students will be downright eager to do their addition again the next day?" The room erupts in applause.

The staff development meeting ends at eleven, which means I still have plenty of time to look at an apartment I saw advertised in yesterday's newspaper.

It's dead-of-winter cold, but I'm bundled in my coat and the sun is out, which not only helps take the edge off the chill but actually feels good on my face, so I decide to walk, leaving my car in the school parking lot. I like that the apartment is walking distance from school, since I have no idea whether I'll be able to keep my car after the divorce. I only have my car now because, once I could finally see well enough to get safely behind the wheel, Lily drove me by the house to get it. Naturally, she took me when we knew Marty was at work. Also naturally, when he arrived home that night and discovered the empty garage, he called me at Grandma's house and pitched a fit. Once he finally took a breath, I reminded him I needed to be able to get to work, and that meant I needed wheels. He countered by reminding *me* that he owned that car and made the monthly payments, and if I insisted on going through with the divorce, I could kiss the car goodbye.

That was my wake-up moment, the instant it became clear to me that I needed a lawyer. There was no way I could use anyone at Marty's firm, so I was relieved when Lily reminded me that Robin's husband, Harry, was in private practice, and she thought he could handle my divorce, or at least give me the name of someone who could. In my initial meeting with Harry Thompson, who, yes, could represent me in a divorce, I made it clear to him I didn't want him to breathe a single word about my case to Robin, as I did not want my sister's canasta group gossiping about me and my poor choice of husband. He assured me that discretion was the better part of valor. That's when I knew I was in good hands. A man who could quote Shakespeare was a man I could trust.

Harry insisted I tell him *everything*, and then he sat patiently and listened as I recounted the entire sordid affair known as my marriage. When I was done, he said that under normal circumstances, I wasn't entitled to alimony because I hadn't been married long enough. Still, he was convinced he could likely get it for me anyway since Lily was brilliant enough to take pictures of my injuries, but—and here's the rub (more Shakespeare! I love this man; too bad he's married)—I'd have to tell the judge what happened and present the photographs as evidence *in open court*. Harry said I could forget about accusing Marty of rape because, according to the law, a man can't rape his own wife, for the very reason that she's his wife. Harry suggested I simply say that Marty beat me, show the pictures, and leave it at that.

I didn't even have to think about it. I'd rather live in a hovel, ride a bus everywhere, and eat macaroni and cheese for the rest of my life than take alimony from Marty. I didn't want him to have any power over me ever again. And once we divorced, I never wanted to see or talk to him again, and I knew, I just knew, in the same way I know my very name (*A Rose by any other name would smell as sweet*), that if I took a single penny from Marty, he'd make me see him to get my check. I didn't ever want to look at him again; I needed to be done with him. So, no alimony. Period. Yes, Harry. I'm sure.

AS MUCH AS I ENJOY living with Grandma, and I especially love that I haven't had to prepare a single meal, I know I need to get on with my life, and that means finding a place to live. Since, postdivorce, my car status will be a big unknown, I've concentrated my hunt on housing that's walking distance from school. The apartment I'm seeing today was advertised at $71 a month. I double-check the address, and in less than ten minutes I'm there.

The man who shows me the apartment is probably close to my dad's age. He's friendly and well-groomed, which makes the idea of my living in his building less scary. Strange as it seems, I find inspiration in that new show *That Girl*. A single girl lives alone and seems happy. Why can't I be her? She wants to be an actress and has to support herself with temp jobs. I have a real job. My job is steady and pays me almost $6,000 a year. If she can do it, why can't I? She also has a boyfriend, and who knows, maybe someday I'll have one, too. Maybe I'll even get married again, but lately I'm wondering if marriage is for me. I hate to cook, and cleaning definitely isn't my bag. But I would like to have a baby one day.

The apartment itself is clean, with large rooms that don't feel es-pecially large because the ceiling is lower than in our house, or what used to be our house. The walls are all painted white, which the man says I can paint any color I want, as long as I paint them white again when I decide to move out. The bathroom has the basics: a toilet, sink, and a stall shower—which will do—even though I enjoy taking a bath from time to time. I double-check that the monthly rent is $71, and when he verifies the price, I tell him I'd like to take it.

Mrs. David Berg

(Lily)

I try to make a game out of the housework, just to make it, what? More interesting? Fun? Or maybe just to help pass the time. Here's how it works: I pretend I'm on *Candid Camera* and Allen Funt is spying on me. Only, unlike the people on his show, I actually know there's a hidden camera on me, watching my every move.

I turn on the radio and find a music station without too much static. Then, with my feather duster in hand, I dance through the room, making sure to dust every surface, all the while keeping to the beat of the music, and—here's the challenge—I cannot pause or stop because I must, at all times, keep the duster touching some surface. The question is: How long can I sustain everything?

Today when I start, Stevie Wonder's "Uptight (Everything's Alright)" is playing on the radio. I begin with dusting the lamp and the end table on one side of the living room couch. Once I complete that, I drag the feather duster over the top of the sofa, which has a plastic slipcover on it to help keep it clean, before I make contact with the side table at the other end of the couch. Stevie's singing *Baby, everything is alright, uptight, clean out of sight* by the time I move up from the base of the lamp to the shade. When there's no remaining surface, I pivot to run the feather duster along the wall and head over to the love seat. Finally, I exit the living room, and as I turn toward the hall, I raise the feather duster over my head as I pirouette into the hallway and begin dusting the wrought iron room divider.

This is when I realize it's not the hidden camera watching me; it's Betsy.

Of course I stop dancing and dusting. "Color me embarrassed," I say.

"Why? Because whatever you're doing, it looks like way more fun than my mom ever had when she was dusting."

I start to laugh. At first, it's just a small sound, a tiny snort of sorts. But then it grows and becomes more of a giggle. Within seconds, it takes on its own life and escalates into more of a belly laugh. I place my hands over my stomach to steady myself as I laugh harder and harder. Betsy, at some point, joins in. She, too, puts her hands around her tummy to brace herself and her baby.

Jo-Jo emerges from the basement, where she was playing with her choo-choo, which I only know because it's still in her hands.

"Mommy laughing," she says. "Betsy laughing"—only it comes out "Bessy."

"Yes," I say as I bend over, literally, with laughter. I try to get ahold of myself, but it doesn't work. The harder I try, the more gloriously I fail. I use my fingers to wipe the tears from my eyes.

"Mommy crying?" Jo-Jo asks, looking concerned.

I reassure my precious angel that I'm not the least bit sad, but I do it while laughing. Betsy, too, shows no sign of slowing down. So, not wanting to be left out, Jo-Jo starts to laugh. At first, it's forced, a mere imitation of what she sees from Betsy and me. But before long, Jo-Jo clearly discovers something that tickles her, even if it's just the sight of our roly-poly bodies, because suddenly her laugh becomes sincere.

When we finally all calm down, a thought strikes me: How very, very lucky I am to be a housewife and mother and able to experience moments like these.

Miss Betsy Ann Eubanks

I'm excited to tell Lily about my idea to give my baby to Mrs. Bloom, but Lily hasn't been around very much this week. Instead, she's been spending a lot of time at her grandma's house. I know it's her grandma's because she always leaves the number where she can be reached under a magnet on the refrigerator door, even when she takes Jo-Jo with her. So, this morning, as we're making the beds together, I tell her I've got an idea and it's really far-out. (I didn't say "groovy" because Lily says I use it too much and if everything is groovy, then nothing is.)

"Betsy, you can ask me anything. You know that." She walks across the room and picks up the flat sheet. She squats by one side of the bed and I do the same on the other, and we tuck in the top sheet using hospital corners, just like she taught me. Next she picks up the bedspread from the floor, and hands me a corner.

"When I was at Raven House to see the doctor, the housemother called me into her office."

"Really? What did she want?" Lily folds back the top of the bedspread. She places the feather pillows over the fold, then drags the spread over the pillows to cover them. Finally, she uses the side of her hand to give the bedspread a karate chop, which makes a perfect crease under the pillows. It looks so pretty. I only ever had a blanket on my bed, like I still do on my cot in the basement. But when I get married, I already know I'm going to get a bedspread and make the bed just like Lily does, with hospital corners and all.

I explain about how the housemother wanted me to know what happens after I move back into Raven House. "And that's when I got my great idea to see if Mr. and Mrs. Bloom want my baby when I have it."

Lily, who's been gathering up the old sheets to throw down the laundry chute, stops moving. "Whoa. I don't understand. Why would Mr. and Mrs. Bloom want your baby?"

"Because it's like Mrs. Bloom said. She can't get a baby to stick. And I can't keep my baby. Well, I guess I could, but my mom's always writing to me about how it would be selfish to keep this baby when I can't afford to take care of it and how it would be an illegitimate bastard, anyway, and everyone would know."

Lily opens her mouth like she's about to say something, but then she changes her mind and snaps it shut, just like a turtle. Then she opens it again. "What did the housemother say?"

I imitate her, putting my hand on my hip, even though that's not what she actually did. I make my voice sound very stuck-up, though, which is exactly how she sounded to me. "'That's not how things are done, dear.'"

Lily laughs. "Come with me. I can't hold these sheets a minute longer." She turns her back on me and I follow behind her. When we're in front of the laundry chute, I open the door as Lily bunches up the sheets and shoves them inside.

"It's a lovely thought, Betsy. Very generous of you to be thinking of others. But I'm not sure Mrs. Bloom is ready to give up on having her own babies." Lily heads back into the hall bathroom, and again, I follow her. We gather all the towels and replace them with clean ones. "I'm sure it will all work out for Mrs. Bloom. She said the doctor is giving her a new medicine to help the next baby stick. But even if she did want to adopt a baby, well, she knows you and you know her, so it wouldn't work."

"That's exactly why it's such a good plan. I know my baby would be wanted and they'd take such good care of it." Lily has started down the stairs, and I follow her into my bedroom, where the sheets and towels are heaped in the laundry basket that catches everything we throw down the chute. Lily and I take turns placing the sheets into the washing machine, making sure to wrap them around the agitator in the center so they won't get all tangled up and make the machine stop. Lily grabs the sheets from one side of my cot, and I do the same on the other side. We add my sheets to hers, wrapping them around the agitator in the exact same way as before. I add a scoop of Cheer, close the lid and turn the dial to "heavy load."

We head upstairs just as the train whistle sounds. I call "green" at the same time Lily says "red." We wait to see who's right.

"Betsy, there's a reason adoptions are secret and the unwed mother and the adoptive parents don't ever know each other," Lily says. She tells me that some married couples don't even tell their children they're adopted because they want to protect their child from ever knowing it was an unwanted baby which was why it was given up for adoption in the first place.

I'd never even considered the fact that my baby will know I didn't want it.

"The reason adoption works is because it's all anonymous," Lily says. "Married people sometimes even move to a new state because no one knows them there—so no one has any idea the baby isn't really theirs."

"If the Blooms moved, then I'd never be able to check on my baby to see how it's doing."

"Betsy, you've just demonstrated my point. The couple who adopts an unwanted baby needs to know the unwed mother could never show up and say she's the 'real' mother. Imagine how confusing that would be for the child and for the parents who've raised that child. Some strange woman shows up one day and says, 'You're mine.' It would be just terrible for everyone."

"I guess. But I would never do that."

Lily sighs, and we watch the train, which must be close to the caboose by now. "Oh, sweet, sweet Betsy. That's how you feel now, but you may have a change of heart five, ten, even fifteen years from now. I don't think that's a risk the Blooms would be willing to take."

I consider everything Lily's said and figure she's right. But that doesn't stop me from asking whether she will just ask Mrs. Bloom anyway.

The caboose is green. "You win," Lily says, and I'm unsure if she's talking about the train or whether she's going to ask Mrs. Bloom if she wants to adopt my baby. But I don't ask, because if I don't ask, I don't know, as my dad used to say to my mom. And when you don't know, you can always hope.

Mrs. Marty Seigel

(Rose)

After I say I want to rent the apartment near the school, the manager asks me if there's a man who can cosign the lease. "I'll be living here alone and I'll be the one paying the rent," I say. "I work at the elementary school around the block on Beech Street."

"I can't make any promises. I need this month's rent and one month's security. You got that?"

I take the lease from him and tell him I'll return it tomorrow with a check. Fortunately, that's not an empty promise. I have a checking account in my own name, but only because the bank let me open it without Marty cosigning. I think about my mom and her pay packets, squirrelling away a dollar here, fifty cents there. I thank my lucky stars that Lily all but forced me to go to college and earn my degree. "Do as I say, not as I do," she said when I pointed out that she got married right after high school.

I walk back toward the school and stop at a pay phone on the corner. Oh, Lady Macbeth, how very right you were. *If it were done when 'tis done, then 'twere well it were done quickly.* I've put this off longer than I should.

I drop a dime into the phone and dial my dad at his office. After his secretary and I exchange some pleasantries, she puts me through.

"Hello, hello," my dad says, offering his standard greeting of a double hello. "To what do I owe this pleasure?"

I explain that I got out of school early because of a staff development day and thought I'd check with him to see if he's available for lunch.

"I can always make time for one of my petite fleurs," he says. Dad seems particularly happy to hear from me, and I feel a pang of guilt knowing that after seeing me, he'll be considerably more somber.

On the drive across town, I begin to mentally catalogue what I need to tell him. Do I start with the smaller thing? *Dad, you know when Marty wasn't at Grandma's the last few Friday nights for Shabbat dinner? He wasn't working late; I told him not to come.* Or do I start with the elephant in the room? *You know when Lily told you I tripped on a rolled ball of socks and fell down the stairs and how I was staying at Grandma's until I felt better? That's not exactly what happened.*

I choose option B and stick with the version of events Harry Thompson suggested I recount for the judge. In other words, I tell my dad what happened, but I do not say, nor even do I even hint at, the word "rape." I also tell him about the photographs. As I watch the color drain from my father's face, he threatens to kill Marty, and then he switches gears, apologizing to me for not knowing what was going on in my marriage and asking why I didn't come to him sooner, only to wind up back at his desire to see Marty dead. He repeats this cycle a few times before he seems to tire out himself. Once I know he's able to listen to me and to truly hear me, I begin again.

"I got Marty to agree to grant me a divorce," I say. I go on to stress the importance of keeping the truth of what happened quiet and keeping the pictures to myself. "If other people know about the photographs, I lose my leverage over him, and Dad, I get that you don't believe in divorce, but I need this."

My dad clenches his jaw, and once more, he threatens to kill

Marty. "It's true. I don't believe in divorce," he says. He lowers his voice. "But you know what I believe in even less?"

I shake my head.

"Men who raise a hand to a woman." My dad's eyes fill with tears, and I feel guilty knowing I'm the cause.

"There is something you can do for me," I say, wondering if offering him an opportunity to help me—to *do* something—will make him feel any better.

"Anything. Just tell me what you need, Rose."

I pull out the lease from my purse. "The building manager is sort of old-fashioned. I think he'll rent me the apartment, but it would be a whole lot easier with a man to cosign."

Dad smiles and takes the paper from my hand. "You got a pen?"

Miss Betsy Ann Eubanks

We are in what will be Jo-Jo's big-girl room. Lily bought pink sheets and a pink polka-dot bedspread, which we've just put on the bed. "We can wait to put on the guardrails until Jo-Jo's ready to switch rooms," Lily says before asking me if I'll help her hang the drapes. She points to the tiny desk and chair against the far corner of the room. "Can you bring me the chair?"

I've got to be honest, when I see Lily step on the chair, I am more than a little worried it will break. Lily is pregnant, after all, and that chair is meant for someone Jo-Jo's size. But it all works out. I hold the drapes and hand Lily the metal hooks, section by section, until, bingo, the pink polka-dot drapes that match the bedspread are up. "It looks so pretty," I say. "Like from a magazine."

Lily walks over to me, arches her back, and bumps her belly against mine. "Another job well done."

I look at her stomach and realize we are about the same size, which is pretty huge, even though I'm more than a month ahead of her.

"It's my second time," she says, like she's reading my mind. "So my body got bigger faster than it did when I was carrying Jo-Jo."

I remember she told me that once before, but now I think about what it means. "So one day, when I'm married, my husband will know that I already had a baby because I'll get bigger faster?"

Lily takes all the packaging from the bedding and the drapes and puts it in the pink polka-dot wastebasket. "Let's get Jo-Jo up from her nap and take her out for a walk," she says. "We can talk and she can get some fresh air."

"Groov—" I stop myself, remembering Lily's advice to not say "groovy" all the time. Once Jo-Jo is changed and has some apple-sauce, Lily asks if I'll put her in her snowsuit.

"Even though it's warmer today and most of the snow has melted, we don't want Jo-Jo catching a cold," she says. While I beg Jo-Jo to cooperate with me, Lily excuses herself to pee, only she calls it "use the bathroom." The snowsuit is stiff, and by the time I've finished, Jo-Jo is crying, and her arms are extended outward, like she's a tiny robot.

"She'll calm down once we're outside and she has something interesting to look at," Lily says. She pushes the stroller down the sidewalk, and I have to walk behind her because whoever shoveled the sidewalk didn't make the path very wide and there's a lot of snow and slush on the sides. But even if the shoveler did a better job, I'm not so sure we could walk side by side on account of our bellies being so big.

"What you said earlier, Betsy, about whether your husband will know about this, um, pregnancy . . ."

She doesn't finish her sentence, but she doesn't need to. "Yeah. My mom said when I go back home, we're all going to just forget this happened. She said no one ever needs to know."

Lily assures me that's true. "It's also up to you about what you tell your husband when you get married. Dr. Berg has told me that unless a woman has recently had a baby and still hasn't fully healed down there, it's all but impossible to tell whether or not she's had a baby before, and if he can't tell, then your husband won't be able to tell, either."

"Well, that's certainly good news. Because Mom told me I shouldn't tell anyone, ever. Not even my future husband, on account of no man wants damaged goods."

Lily stops walking and turns toward me. "'Damaged goods'? She said that to you?"

"No. She wrote it in one of her letters."

Lily asks if I'd mind pushing the stroller for a while. She moves aside so we can switch places. "There was a time, not that long ago, when I felt the way your mom does," she says. "But I've been rethinking a lot of things lately, and that's one of them."

I'm not sure I know what Lily means, but I don't question her, mostly because she's so busy questioning me. And what's really far-out is that she doesn't even wait for me; she answers her questions by herself.

"Did anyone ever tell you about how babies are made? No. Did you understand the link between your monthly and how it's related to getting pregnant? No. And even if you did know, did you know that birth control isn't even legal for girls who aren't married? No."

But the one question that I never even thought about before is when she asks me why I think they have maternity homes like Raven House.

The answer is obvious. "Because when girls who aren't married get pregnant, they need someplace to go."

"That's exactly right. Rose would give you a gold star," she says. Then she goes on to tell me there are places like Raven House all over the country. "What happened to you isn't unique to girls in Ohio or, in your case, Michigan. It happens to girls all over the entire country. And that means a lot of girls wind up in trouble."

"Like me."

"Exactly like you. And remember, a lot of girls go all the way with their boyfriends and never wind up with a bun in the . . . never wind up pregnant. But that doesn't make them any better than you. They are just luckier."

What she's saying makes sense, but so does what my mom said. Why would someone want me when I've been with someone already and even had a baby, when he could have someone who is not damaged?

"Times are different than they were in the '50s," Lily says. "I may not agree with the hippies and their lifestyle of taking drugs and that horrible music, but they have a point about some things."

"Like what?"

"'Make love, not war,' for one thing. That war in Vietnam is killing a lot of our boys, and for what? Who even knows where Vietnam is?"

I sure don't. But I didn't know where Akron was, and how close it was to my house in Michigan, until I looked at the map in the back of my social studies book.

"My point, Betsy, is, well, I'm not sure what my point is. Except you are a good person. You have a gentle nature; I picked up on that the moment you arrived at our house. And Jo-Jo, who is an excellent judge of character, liked you immediately. You made a mistake. People make mistakes. If you decide to share that fact with your future husband and he finds it disqualifying, then maybe he's not the right husband for you. People make mistakes all the time. Sisters make mistakes. Friends make mistakes. And sometimes the best answer to a mistake is correcting it by doing something that maybe you thought you disagreed with but then you realize it's the best solution. Like getting a divorce. Or putting your baby up for adoption."

"Whoa. Man, I'm not getting a divorce. I'm not even married."

Lily touches her belly. "Of course you're not. I don't even know what I was thinking. I'm just not feeling great. I'm a little crampy or gassy or something. Let's head back home."

Mrs. David Berg

(Lily)

When we return from our walk, Betsy insists I rest. "I can see by the way you're grabbing your belly that you're not feeling good."

"I don't ever remember this feeling when I was pregnant with Jo-Jo. Does it ever happen to you? A pulling and crampiness?"

Betsy says it happens all the time. "But maybe you should call Dr. Berg and ask him."

Out of the mouths of babes. I do just that. David asks me to recount my day. Then he says I might have pulled a muscle while I was hanging the drapes, or when I carried Jo-Jo downstairs after her nap, or when I was out for our walk. "Then, too, the baby might just be in an awkward position. Are you bleeding at all?"

I haven't used the bathroom since we got home, so I reach up under my tent dress and wriggle out of my maternity underwear. Nothing.

"I wouldn't worry," he says. "But since you've got Betsy, why don't you stay in bed until I get home. I'm not on call tonight, so I should be back around 5:30 or 6:00, assuming no one goes into labor this afternoon."

I yell for Betsy and ask her to bring Jo-Jo into my bedroom. "I'm going to lie low until David gets home. Will you get me some of

Jo-Jo's books and toys?" I pat the blue blanket on David's side of the bed. "We can play together right here." I turn my attention toward my daughter and give her one, two, three smooches. I count the kisses before I plant each one on her cheek, and she does her best to count along with me. Next I nuzzle my nose into Jo-Jo's cheek, right where her dimple is. You can certainly tell she's David's daughter.

Betsy returns with *The Giving Tree* and *Where the Wild Things Are*, along with the See 'n Say toy. Jo-Jo hasn't yet learned how to pull the string to hear the cow moo or the sheep baa, so after I do it a dozen or so times, I ask her if she'd like a story. She nods her head. I nod my head right back at her. "And what does that mean? Yes or no?"

She says "yes," and I'm happy that I've gotten her to speak. She often uses gestures instead of words, which Dr. Spock says is totally normal, but he says that moms need to talk to their babies a lot. I wonder whether I'm not doing it enough and that's why Jo-Jo nods her head instead of saying "yes." Not for the first time, I worry that I'm not a good enough mother. Maybe it's because I don't enjoy it as much as I should, or at least not as much as other women. It's hard to know for sure because the women closest to me, like Becca and Robin, have kids who are older than Jo-Jo. And of course Sarah and Rose don't have any kids at all.

Maybe that's why I'm having these cramps and something bad is probably happening to the baby inside me: because I'm not a good enough mom. I know if I said this to David, he would reassure me and tell me I'm a great mother, but it's not like he's around to see me in action. Even Becca, who, ever since her abortion, makes an obvious point of complimenting me more often, usually sees me when Jo-Jo is napping. How does she know what kind of mother I am?

And here's a skeleton in my closet that only I know: Between our first unwed mother, Kathy, and now Betsy, if I'm being honest, I've turned over more and more of my mothering duties to them. What kind of mother does that? What kind of mother doesn't want to spend every waking moment with her perfect child?

While Jo-Jo turns pages and pretends to read *Where the Wild Things Are*, I glance at *The Feminine Mystique*, which is still on my nightstand, even though I finished it a while ago. I blame this on the author. Betty Friedan put these ideas in my head. There's a big part of me that wishes I'd never read her silly book. But then there's an even bigger part of me that's glad to know I'm not alone. That my feelings are the same as a lot of moms and housewives.

I open *The Giving Tree*, and as I read it to Jo-Jo, it isn't lost on me that the little boy is incredibly selfish. He just takes and takes until that tree has no more left to give. I say a silent prayer that if God just makes this pregnancy okay, I will not be selfish, but instead, I'll spend more time enjoying my babies and will not bring any more unwed mothers into the house under the guise of "help," when really, I'm just using them to shirk my responsibilities to my family.

Miss Betsy Ann Eubanks

I'm so glad Lily is feeling better. She said Dr. Berg thinks it must have been something she ate, but I don't care what it was that caused her to stay in bed all afternoon last week. I'm just glad she's all better and we don't have to worry about another problem like the one with Mrs. Bloom and her baby getting unstuck and sliding out.

This morning, Lily and I are remaking her bed together, just like we do every Thursday after Dr. Berg leaves for work and when Jo-Jo goes down for her morning nap. While we're doing the bedspread, Lily says she wants to be the one to put Jo-Jo in her crib for her afternoon nap. I ask her if it's because I'm doing anything wrong, but she says it's just something she wants to start doing again. "Soon, you're going to be leaving us, so I have to begin getting used to doing more by my lonesome, right?"

I give her that salute they use on the TV show *McHale's Navy* and agree.

I can't say I really understand what one thing has to do with the other, but I usually just agree with Lily unless it's something I really want to know more about.

Mrs. Marty Seigel

(Rose)

I don't have much to unpack, so moving into my new apartment doesn't take long. Lily gave me an old card table she wasn't using, along with a set of four chairs. "I'm sorry that one is a bit stained," she said, pointing to a chair that had the faint remnants of what looked like spaghetti sauce. That's when she told me about Sarah and her multiple miscarriages.

"So, you'd actually be doing me a favor if you take the chairs. You could even put the stained one in the rubbish," she said. "I just didn't want it in the house where Sarah would have to see it and be reminded of that horrible day."

I completely understood.

Since it's only me living in the apartment, I don't really even need four chairs. Dad insisted on giving me the mattress, box spring, and headboard from my childhood bedroom, "just until you can afford to replace it." He also offered to buy me a new couch, but I told him I'd only accept it if I could pay him back. Granted, it may take a while, but it'll make me feel better to know that I'm capable of making my own way, if not entirely alone, then with some help from my family—help, not charity.

I have a box of toiletries that I take into the bathroom. I unpack my toothbrush, toothpaste and deodorant, hairspray, toilet paper, razor, and razor blades and place them on the lazy Susan I've already put in the cupboard under the sink. I grab a bottle of Tylenol and one of aspirin and place those on a shelf in the medicine cabinet. I put bandages, Mercurochrome, a thermometer, and Vicks VapoRub on another shelf. At the bottom of the box is my diaphragm. Obviously, I don't need it, but I also don't want to throw it away, since only married women are allowed to get fitted with a birth control device like a diaphragm or IUD or get a prescription for the Pill. Even though I can't imagine being with another man after my divorce, at least not anytime soon, it's not like I don't have room for the diaphragm and the jelly. I look for a discreet place to hide them both.

Mrs. David Berg

(Lily)

When David examined me after I felt the strange pulling and crampiness, he told me not to worry. He said that during the last third of a pregnancy, the uterus and abdomen are expanding, and that can create discomfort exactly like the kind I described. When I reminded him I never felt that way with Jo-Jo, he just shrugged and said that every pregnancy was different. It was weird talking to David like that—more like a doctor than like a husband.

Since I'm past the midpoint of my pregnancy, at least there's no more queasiness, thank goodness. This is when I felt my best when I was expecting Jo-Jo, so I should be enjoying myself before I get even bigger and before the baby kicks at my bladder all night long. Soon I'll have this baby and I'll be up all hours of the night to feed it and rock it back to sleep. And, oh my gosh, the diapers! And catching spit-up with burp cloths! Right now, I remind myself, is as good as it gets, at least for the foreseeable future.

I wouldn't say I'm unhappy with my life. In fact, I'm grateful. I'm married to a man who loves me and provides for me and for Jo-Jo. We live in a lovely neighborhood in a split-level house and have two televisions and two telephones. We even have two cars, a luxury by the standards of so many women who have to drop off their husbands at the office if they need the car that day. Yet I keep coming back to *Is this all?*

I feel ridiculous sharing these feelings with Rose, especially since she has enough problems of her own, but she is a good listener, and if I can't talk to my sister, then who can I talk to?

"Sounds to me like you're suffering from 'the problem that has no name,'" she said yesterday when I stopped by to see her new apartment.

"It pains me to admit it, but I think I am."

"What?" I can see the surprise on her face. "Wait. You actually know what I'm talking about? You've read the book?" She walks to a bookshelf, which she's made from some cinder blocks and a piece of wood. She pulls *The Feminine Mystique* from the makeshift shelf. "I was going to loan you mine."

"No need. Didn't I tell you that Robin gave me her copy when we did our Secret Santa gift exchange? Anyway, it was fully anno-tated with 'Yes!' and 'Right on, sister' and lots of exclamation points adorning the margins." I settle myself onto Rose's new couch. "Nice. Comfortable."

"Thanks, I'm glad you like it. Not to change the subject, but to change the subject, do you want to talk about it?" Rose waves her copy of the book in the air.

I tell Rose about the days before Betsy, even before I had Jo-Jo. "I'd make David breakfast, and then what? I'd do the dishes, make the bed, do the laundry, iron, vacuum, dust, take out the trash, listen to the radio, read a magazine. There were entire days when I didn't see another person unless I went to the supermarket or had an appoint-ment at the beauty shop or with the dentist or some other doctor. I understand why Sarah spends so much time sewing. There were days where, I swear, I only heard my own voice, and that was only if I was singing along to the radio. So, what's a housewife to do?"

"That, my dear sister, is the $64,000 question! But isn't it at least good to know there are a lot of other women who feel exactly the way you do, who aren't excited by the turn their lives have taken and who want more?"

"You might be right, Rose-Petal. It is good to know I'm not alone, even though it doesn't change things. But it's good to talk about it with you. Believe it or not, I feel better. I really do, I'm not kidding. I think I just needed to say how I was feeling out loud. And I wanted someone I trust to hear me. Because, as much as I love David, he's not that person. At least not for this. Not now anyway. Listen to me, rambling on."

Rose smiles at me and then gives me a wink. "Ramble away, dear sister. Seriously."

"I just don't know what's happening or what's going to happen. What I do know is that I want to have this baby and get it sleeping through the night in record time. Then I want to see how it feels to be a mother of two. And then? I don't know what comes next, but I want to talk about it once I'm there. Does that make any sense?"

"It does. And when you're ready to talk, I'll be here to listen. Because you're so smart, Lily. The only reason you didn't go to college is because you got married. But look how capable you are! You've always been great with numbers, but in high school, you got As in every subject, not just math. And you did it all while you were taking care of me after Mom died." Rose hangs her head, examining her go-go boots. "And you were the one who knew to take pictures after, well, after what happened with Marty."

"That's only because I watch *General Hospital*." We both laugh about that. "You would have thought of it, too, I'm sure. You were just in shock."

"Maybe. But probably not. The point I'm trying to make is that you shouldn't sell yourself short. Promise me that when you're ready, we'll pick up this conversation again?" Rose extends her pinky finger.

"Swear," I say, entwining my finger with my sister's.

Mrs. Marty Seigel

(Rose)

There are so many perks of living by myself in my own apartment. A big one that is really a small thing, but makes me almost giddy, is knowing I will never again walk into the bathroom and see an empty cardboard tube hanging on the spindle where there should be a roll of toilet paper. That bit of silliness is on my mind when I toss the empty tube and look under the sink for a fresh roll. It's tucked in the back, behind my monthly supplies. That's when it hits me. I haven't had my period since I moved into Grandma's house and certainly not since I moved into my apartment.

I sit on the floor in my tiny new bathroom and cry. I sob so hard and for so long that when I finally stand up and get a glimpse of my face in the mirror on the medicine cabinet, my eyes are almost as swollen as when Marty first beat me.

If you have tears, prepare to shed them now. I'm so upset I can't even recall whether that line is from *Julius Caesar* or *King Lear*. I turn on the faucet, allow the water to run until it gets cold, saturate a washcloth, and hold it over my face. Then I sink back down to the floor and cry some more.

I can't tell if twenty minutes have passed or two hours, but finally, I'm convinced I have no tears left to cry, and I relocate back to the bedroom, where I flop down on my bed and stare at the ceiling. My tears are replaced with rage, and I kick my legs up and down against the mattress. I'm ticked off that I married a man who beat me, but mostly, I'm filled with anger that, apparently, that wasn't enough. Oh, no. For some reason I need to be further punished. He has to rape me and then I have to wind up pregnant. *Why, God? Why are you doing this to me? What have I done that's so terrible?*

I knew that night was a dangerous time for sex, which was why I asked Marty to wear the damn rubber, which is probably what set him off and caused him to rape me in the first place. 'Round and 'round I go, reworking everything in my mind, always winding up right where I started, in the same god-awful predicament. It's all just so horribly unfair. I'm finally all healed; there isn't a black-and-blue mark anywhere on my body. I got Marty to agree to a divorce. I've got my own place to live, and I've got the support of everyone in my family. So why is this happening to me?

When I was a young girl, my mom was the one I turned to when I thought I was getting a bum deal. Sometimes I'd cry, but mostly, I just complained about how unfair my life was. I remember once wailing on and on about how I wasn't invited to Mary Kate's slumber party and the injustice of it all. Mom let me vent, and then she finally said, "Rose, when you've finished your pity party, let me know, and we can do something constructive to solve your problem." I was probably nine or ten and firmly believed there was no solution. But after talking it over with Mom (while baking cookies), she helped me realize that Mary Kate wasn't my friend; in fact, she was a bully who often picked on me at recess. Her friends typically followed her lead. "Imagine," Mom said. "You're at her slumber party, and she decides your pj's aren't cool enough or your sleeping bag isn't fancy enough and she starts teasing you. And maybe her friends join in. Or maybe they don't. Either way, why would you even want to put yourself in that situation?"

Of course Mom was right. I didn't want to spend even a single second with Mary Kate. Mom helped me understand I was just upset because I was left out. Mom asked if there was another little girl in the class who I liked. "You could invite her to sleep over here that same night. And I will make Jiffy Pop and you can watch TV."

There was another girl in my class, but it turned out that she was invited to Mary Kate's party, too. But even before I could start round two of my pity party, Mom came up with the perfect solution. "A sister is the best friend a girl could ever have. I always wanted one, but I wasn't as lucky as you. Why don't you ask Lily if she'd like to come to your bedroom for a sleepover?"

After reassurances that Lily wouldn't think it was a dumb idea, and a promise from Mom that she'd still make popcorn *and* let us watch television *and* let us stay up late, I invited Lily into my bedroom for a sleepover. That was the first of what, over the years, we called our sister-sleeps. When Mom died, our nights became one never-ending sister-sleep. We decided we wanted to share a room, and we did just that until Lily moved out to marry David.

"That's it," I say aloud as I swing my legs off my bed. "This pity party is over." I walk into the kitchen and start opening drawers, trying to remember where I put my address book when I unpacked. When I find it, I call my gynecologist and make an appointment to go in for a pregnancy test. Before I completely freak out, before I freak out my sister, best to know for sure whether the rabbit lives or dies.

March
1966

Mrs. Marty Seigel

(Rose)

I typically like this time of year, when the worst part of winter is behind us and spring is around the corner. But this morning, it's still bitterly cold, and as I walk to school, there's nothing I can focus on to cheer me up.

Unfortunately, I'm pretty transparent. So much so that one of my students asks me why I look sad and whether I want a hug. I give her a big, wide, toothy smile and tell her I'm not sad at all; I was just thinking hard. That prompts me to ask all my students to take turns showing what their thinking-faces look like. But that student was correct. *Now is the winter of* my *discontent.*

I am sad, and I've been feeling sorry for myself ever since my doctor confirmed my pregnancy. It was torture, waiting almost two weeks for the results of my urine test to come back. When I saw my doctor, I immediately told him that I'm getting a divorce and I even shared the horror about how I was raped by my husband. I made it quite clear that I didn't want to keep this baby—well, as clear as a person can be without using the word "abortion." I told him I understood that *he* couldn't help me, but didn't he know someone who could? He told me he had no intention of risking his license by breaking the law and suggested I leave his office. He didn't add . . . *and never come back*, but he didn't have to. Message sent and message received.

I've debated with myself the best way to handle this. Should I just tell Lily and ask her not to mention it to David, knowing full well she probably will anyway? That's what she did when I asked her to simply tell David I tripped on the socks and fell down the stairs. At least that's what I think happened because when I finally told him the truth, I had a strong sense he already knew. But I understand why she tells him everything. He and Jo-Jo are her entire world. Why would she *not* share everything with him? But the truth is, I want David to know; after all, he's much more likely to be able to help me than Lily.

Even though I'll see my sister and David on Friday night, I called Lily yesterday and told her that I needed to speak to her and David, privately, before Shabbat dinner. She told me I could swing by tonight, since David isn't on call.

It was sweet of them to keep Jo-Jo awake long enough for me to give her some kisses and hugs before Betsy took her upstairs for bedtime. We wait for Betsy to come down and retreat to the basement before getting serious.

I thank them both for seeing me.

"Why so formal?" Lily asks. Before I can answer, she works to lighten the mood. "I'm Lily and this is David. You know us, remember?"

That helps me feel more comfortable, but I am still not looking forward to this conversation, even though I've rehearsed what I am going to say. How do I tell them that I've been living in my own version of *The Tempest*? *I have been in such a pickle since I saw you last.*

David clearly senses my anxiety and asks if I want a glass of wine.

So, with a wineglass in my visibly shaking hand, I begin. "Lily, remember when we were kids and whenever I had a bandage on I'd try to peel it off slowly?"

"Do I ever. You'd be sighing and *ouch-ouch-ouching* and after five minutes you'd only have a teeny-tiny section of the bandage unstuck."

"David, what Lily isn't telling you is that her solution was to let me try to handle things myself before she'd just walk by and rip it off."

"Quick is best, hurts less," Lily and I say at the same time, chanting one of our many sisterly sayings.

"Well, I'm going to take a page out of Lily's book and just spit it out." Then I tell them I'm pregnant.

We sit in silence. I don't know how long we stare at one another, but it feels interminable. "Just in case anyone is too embarrassed to ask, it's Marty's. From the night he raped me."

When I said this to my doctor, I was upset and had trouble talking through my tears. Maybe I'm all cried out, but I no longer feel like crying. Now I'm just angry.

David, ever the professional, asks whether I'm certain.

"I had a urine test and got the results from my doctor a couple days ago.

"I've been thinking about it for the last two weeks, while I was waiting for the test to come back. I do not want to have this baby."

Lily hops up from the couch and squats down next to my chair. I worry she will topple over any second; her tent dress looks like she's got a beach ball under it. She grabs hold of my hand—the one not draining the glass of wine. David also gets up from the couch and approaches me. But he's coming to retrieve my empty wineglass so he can refill it.

"Are you sure you don't want the baby?" she asks. "I mean, the baby is an innocent in all this. And you'd be such a good mother."

I love my sister. Sometimes I think I love her even more than I loved our mom, maybe because there's no generation gap between us, but right now, I do not feel love toward Lily. I cannot believe I have to explain to my sister why I don't want to keep a baby that was conceived not out of love, but out of violence and hate. I do not want to have to explain that once my divorce from Marty goes through, I don't want to see him or talk to him ever again. Does Lily not understand that if I have this baby, Marty's baby, we will be tied together for the rest of our lives? He will want to see this baby; he will use it to control me. That means I will never, ever be free of him. And what if the baby resembles Marty? Every time I look at my child, I will see the face of the man who beat me. Who raped me. This should not be a difficult concept for Lily to understand. Fortunately, when I tell her all of this, she does.

"Don't cry, Lily. He is not worth your tears. Trust me."

"I know," she says. "It's just that I hate that you have to go through this."

I look at David, who's been mostly silent this whole time. "Can you help me?"

Mrs. Marty Seigel

(Rose)

When I ask David if he can help me, you can hear the proverbial pin drop. To an outsider peering in, we could be mistaken as doing a Jack Benny comedy routine. David looks at Lily, who looks at me, who looks at David, who looks at his wife, who looks back at her husband.

"David, can you help me get rid of it?" I gesture toward my stomach.

Lily's mouth falls open. "Rose, I can't believe you'd ask him to do such a thing."

"Lily, he's an OB-GYN. He's the perfect person to ask."

We both stare at David.

"You could try for a therapeutic abortion," he says. "They are sometimes granted if the life of the mother is at stake. If you have a physical condition that would be exacerbated by a pregnancy. A heart condition, for example. But that's not the case here, is it?"

I mumble my acknowledgment that no, it is not.

"The law defines 'the life of the mother' as mental wellness, too. If you saw two psychiatrists and they said it was their finding that you were suicidal and if you were forced into having this baby, you might take your own life, that also qualifies. But I have to warn you, gynecologists and hospital boards are getting stingier with granting therapeutic abortions based on the say-so of psychiatrists you've only just seen now. You haven't been seeing a psychiatrist for any period of time, have you?"

Again, I mumble my acknowledgment that no, I have not.

"Rubella is another possibility."

"What?" Lily and I say simultaneously.

"Rubella. The German measles. Since the epidemic began in 1963, they've found that women who contract rubella while they're pregnant often give birth to infants with deformities. They're allowing those women to have therapeutic abortions. So, maybe you could find a reason to visit a child in your school who's out with rubella and you can catch it from them."

Lily informs David that she and I both had the measles when we were kids. In fact, I was the culprit who brought it home from school and gave it to her.

"Not regular measles, rubella, which is a different virus from your garden-variety measles." He lifts his eyebrows, thinking he's on to something.

I shake my head. "Since I work in a school, I got the vaccine last year, along with all the other new teachers."

"Well then, I guess the only thing left for you to try is to get those letters from psychiatrists."

"It's not the only thing," I say. "What about a non-therapeutic abortion?"

Lily's voice is shrill when she asks what in the world I could possibly be thinking. "Don't you know what you're asking for is illegal?"

Once my sister calms down, no thanks to me, I tell her that I'm not asking David to do anything illegal. I'm simply asking him for the name of someone *else* or someplace where I could go to have a safe, albeit illegal, abortion.

He hangs his head. When he looks up, I see his eyes are moist with tears. "I'm sorry, Rose. I really am. But if I'm caught assisting in any way, even just giving you a name or a phone number, I could lose my medical license."

I know what that means, yet Lily says the words out loud anyway. "If David loses his license, what would we do? He couldn't practice medicine. We'd lose the house along with everything we've worked so hard for."

I surprise myself by thinking, *Everything* we've *worked so hard for?*

Do I resent my sister for staying home and allowing a man to take care of her? Or am I jealous because I'm living in a tiny apartment, counting every penny I spend, because I, too, once had a dream about a man taking care of me?

On the car ride home, I decide it doesn't matter why I resent my sister's words. It's only because of her that I got the education that allowed me to have my job. A job that has become my safety net, ever since my choice of husband exploded all over me.

Mrs. Marty Seigel

(Rose)

By this time next month, my divorce should be final, but until it actually happens, I remain wary. Every day, I worry about whether today might be the day when Marty telephones and announces that he's changed his mind. He calls incessantly, asking me to please give him another chance, promising to do better. My instinct is to just slam down the phone as soon as I hear his voice, but I know better than to do something that will surely set him off. *Talkers are no good doers.*

At first, when his calls started, I sat there listening to him plead his case. When he finally finished, I always said the same thing: "I'll think about it." Nowadays, as soon as I answer the phone and hear his voice, I rest the receiver on my shoulder with the earpiece facing away from me so even though I can hear the sound of his argument, I cannot distinguish the words. Once I can tell he's stopped talking, I reiterate my promise to think it over. In truth, there's nothing to consider. Still, I don't want to upset him any more than he is already, partly because I don't completely trust he wouldn't find me and hurt me, but mostly because I don't want him to back out of his promise not to fight me on the divorce. I've got the pictures and duplicates of the pictures safely tucked away. Because he's my attorney, Harry also insisted on having a copy, and he told me to make sure Marty knows that he has duplicates, "just in case he gets any crazy ideas." But I don't want to threaten him so many times that he becomes immune, which I could definitely see happening. It's strange and sad that I seem to have a better understanding of my husband and his behavior now than when I lived with him.

On my drive to Grandma's, I wonder whether, by this time next month, I'll be taking the bus to Shabbat dinner. Harry says whether I get to keep the car is completely out of our hands. The judge could give the car to Marty since he bought it or, more likely, the judge could insist we sell it and split the proceeds. Harry says that's what will happen with the house. In lawyer-speak, Harry explained that since our house was acquired during our marriage, half of it is legally mine. So if Marty wants to keep the house, he can buy me out of my half, but if he doesn't want it (or can't afford it without my salary), he will have to sell it and split the proceeds evenly with me; that's the law.

Harry thinks my chances of keeping my car would improve dramatically if I showed the judge the pictures Lily took, but for all I know, Marty and the judge have a professional (or personal?) relationship, so showing the judge the pictures might even backfire. One thing I do know: if those pictures are made public—even just to the judge—Marty could renege on his agreement to grant me a divorce in the first place. It still seems crazy to me that we can't get a divorce just because we want one, but again, Harry says that's the law.

My choice was to sue either for "gross negligence of duty" or "extreme cruelty." Marty wasn't happy with either option, but I got him to agree to the latter. Who am I kidding? I basically blackmailed him into giving me a divorce, telling him that if he fought me, I'd plaster those pictures everywhere. Harry understands my reluctance to use what he calls my ace in the hole, and he continues to remind me that I'm not entitled to any alimony, since the standard is one year of support for every three years of marriage, and we didn't make it that long. It's all so horribly sad, but I'm no longer blaming myself for marrying in haste. Marty presented a false front; he was not the man he professed to be. Once again, Shakespeare had it right in that antisemitic play *The Merchant of Venice*: *All that glisters is* most definitely *not gold*.

Mrs. David Berg

(Lily)

We're not technically late, but tonight we are the last to arrive at Grandma's. As soon as we walk through the door, Grandma takes Jo-Jo by the hand and walks her into the living room, where she removes my daughter's coat. Then, before Jo-Jo can react, Grandma swoops up her great-granddaughter and carries her over to the side table in the dining room where the candlesticks, kiddish cup, and challah have already been placed. All the while, Grandma, still holding Jo-Jo, plants one noisy smooch after another on my daughter's cheek. Once Jo-Jo understands the rhythm of the kisses, she begins to pull away from Grandma's lips, just as Grandma is moving in for the kiss. This game of bobbing and weaving to avoid being smooched is a new one between them. I look around at all the smiling adults, and when I catch Rose's eye, I'm relieved to see that even she, with everything going on in her life, is charmed by this spontaneous display of love and affection. She winks at me, which is the real relief.

That meeting with David and me about her pregnancy last night was tense, and I know she wasn't happy with me when she left. I knew I had not done anything wrong, but that didn't stop me from feeling guilty. I just couldn't put my finger on what, exactly, I'd done. Voicing my objection to putting David in a position to not just do something illegal but to risk losing his license? *What was she thinking?*

Rose's wink lets me know that maybe I misread the situation last night. Or maybe I didn't misread it at all, but whatever she blamed me for, she now understands is not my fault.

Finally, we get down to business. Candles are lit, wine, which was already poured, is sipped, challah is ripped, and everyone takes a small bite as all appropriate prayers are uttered. Finally, everyone takes a seat at the table. Grandma no longer even puts out a chair for Marty.

Dinner is uneventful, unless you count Grandma forgetting to serve the pickles until the meal is almost over. But this isn't a sign of her aging; she almost always forgets something. Since she doesn't know how to write, she can't make a list for herself, so her throwing her arms in the air and saying "Oy, I forgot the [fill in the blank]" is an almost weekly occurrence.

Everyone in the family knows I like to get Jo-Jo home and into her crib as close to her bedtime as possible, so Rose is usually the one to usher us out of the house, volunteering to help Grandma with cleanup. But tonight, probably because my heart is just breaking for Rose, I tell her I'm going to do the dishes. As expected, she insists that she doesn't mind.

"Neither do I." I grab my sister's hand and pull her toward the bedroom where our coats, purses, hats, and scarves are piled on the bed. I pick up her coat and hand it to her. "Now go," I say loud enough for everyone who has moved from the dining room into the living room to hear.

Then I reach for my purse, which I put on the nightstand when I took off my coat. "I don't know how you're going to do it," I tell Rose in a hushed voice, so I won't be overheard, "but I know you and I know you'll find a way. I just want you to be safe about it." I release the clasp on my handbag and remove an envelope. "Here." I push the packet into her hand. "Getaway money."

"Your *pushke*?" Rose's eyes immediately fill with tears, and then she throws her arms around me and just squeezes.

Mrs. Marty Seigel

(Rose)

Grandma, your number two helper is on her way to assist with cleanup," Lily says as she leaves me in the bedroom and heads toward the kitchen.

I take a deep breath to steady myself. A quick look in the envelope convinces me it contains hundreds of dollars. I can't believe Lily's generosity, especially since it's coming on the heels of that very difficult exchange last night. In retrospect, I can't decide whether Lily was more upset that I want an abortion or that I asked David for the name of someone who could give me one. Is she opposed to abortion no matter what, or is she just opposed to my having an abortion because, in her mind, it's already her niece or nephew growing inside me? Or maybe it's none of those things, and it's simply a case of her wanting me to become a mother so we can raise children together. It could be all of those things or none of them, and maybe one day, when I'm not in the thick of this crisis, I'll sit down with my sister and ask her outright. For now, I'm just grateful to have her support, because I know, as sure I know my own name—that giving me her *pushke* was Lily's way of reminding me that she is, as has always been the case, in my corner. This, coupled with my own *pushke*, which I retrieved when I went back to the house to get my car, should be enough. I, of course, have no idea how much an abortion costs, but from the magazine and newspaper articles I've read about illegal abortions, I know it's something in the hundreds. No, it wasn't an article. It was in a documentary special about abortion that Walter Cronkite did on CBS. That's got to be it. Regardless, I pray that between Lily's *pushke* and mine and what (very) little I've managed to put away from my job, it will be enough. *Amen.*

I button my coat, leave the bedroom, and enter the kitchen. "I'm so sorry, Grandma. It looks like you're stuck with the number two helper because your number one helper has been given the night off." I give Grandma a kiss, thank her for dinner, and tell her I'll call her during the week, which is not news to her. I always call her at least once between dinners. Then I give Lily a kiss on her cheek. "Thank you." Grandma thinks I'm thanking Lily for taking over the kitchen cleanup. I'm glad she doesn't know any better. I give my sister a knowing look and mouth the words "for everything."

I stop in the living room, where Dad and David are watching TV. Jo-Jo is leaning against Pa, her name for Dad. Jo-Jo's eyes are at half-mast; she looks so angelic. "Say bye-bye to Auntie Rose-Petal," David says.

"Bye-bye," Jo-Jo says, opening and closing her little hand, because she hasn't yet learned how to properly wave.

"Dad, you've got her?" David asks, gesturing toward Jo-Jo. After Dad nods, David tells me he'll walk me to my car.

"Totally unnecessary."

"I know, but I want to."

"Again, totally unnecessary."

"Then I'll see you to the door."

I'm tempted to remind David that on most Friday nights, he and his family eat and practically sprint out of the house to get Jo-Jo to bed, and yet somehow I manage not only to get to my car but actually find the front door all by myself. But before I can speak, David grabs my forearm and leads me from the living room to the front door. He moves forward to give me a peck on my cheek, at least that's what I'm expecting, except I don't get a kiss. Instead, he leans toward me and slips something into my coat pocket and, feigning a kiss, he whispers into my ear: "Do not mention this to anyone. Ever. Especially not to Lily."

I UNLOCK MY CAR DOOR and convince myself to exercise self-control and to wait to look at whatever David put into my pocket. If Lily glances out the window while she's washing dishes, I don't want her to see me sitting in my car with the overhead light on. That would be an invitation for her to come out to check on me. So, using all of my self-discipline, I force myself to drive home, and exercise even more discipline by staying within the speed limit. Once I get into my apartment, I put my hands into my coat pockets. In one pocket, I feel Lily's *pushke*. The other holds an envelope that is much thinner. I tear the short end and blow into it, just like Johnny Carson does when he's being Carnac the Magnificent. The envelope contains a small scrap of paper. I make a silent wish that whatever is on this paper is also magnificent, and then I unfold it. It simply says:

> *Monday morning, call 555-2160. Ask for an appt with Dr. Wingate, then destroy this paper.*

I exhale, not even aware I was holding my breath, and walk across my tiny apartment to the couch. Still wearing my coat, I allow my head to roll back, and without warning, I get a tickle in my nose and tears fill my eyes. *Oh, David. How can I ever repay you?* I decide I can do one better than what he's asked. I memorize the number I'm going to call after the weekend, and once I'm sure I won't forget it, I shred the slip of paper, wriggle out of my coat, and go into the bathroom where, for good measure, I flush Dr. Wingate's name and number down the toilet.

Mrs. David Berg

(Lily)

David was called into the hospital, and Jo-Jo is down for her afternoon nap, so this is my last, best opportunity. Normally, when you say goodbye to someone, it doesn't mean it's forever, unless, of course, they die. But in so many ways, in all the ways that count, that's what I know my goodbye to Betsy will be. It's a death. A death of us, our relationship, actually our friendship. When I drop her off at Raven House tomorrow morning, that will be it. Forever. We will never see each other or talk to each other again. I know it's up to me to make sure that "never" is, in fact, the case. If, just for a moment, I let down my guard and tell Betsy that it would be nice to get a letter from her from time to time (and oh, how it would be!), she'd sharpen her pencils and begin writing that minute. Except that defeats the purpose of sending her here in the first place, and yet I don't know how to say goodbye.

Betsy's parents—well, at least her mother—and the staff at Raven House have continued to stress the importance that this chapter of Betsy's life end once she has her baby and gives it up for adoption. It would be selfish of me to encourage her to keep the door between us even slightly ajar. I owe it to her to make sure she understands that goodbye means goodbye *forever*, but just thinking about it has me in tears. I take a few deep breaths and remind myself that I can't fall apart. I'm the grown-up, and she is, if not exactly a child, still not an adult. So, I need to be the strong one and upbeat enough for both of us.

I imagine myself saying something like *Once you're back home and with your friends, I hope you'll forget all about us.* No. That's almost mean, and besides, I don't want her to forget me any more than I want to forget her. Maybe I'll say, *You've got so many great things ahead of you, Betsy. Never forget what a lovely, smart, and kind young lady you are.* No. That would make me cry for sure. Oh, to hell with it all. I take a deep breath and go into the basement. The moment I lay eyes on that young girl, bopping her head along to the radio, I burst into tears. She rushes into my arms and we hug. And we cry. A long, long, hard *I'll never see you again* cry.

Miss Betsy Ann Eubanks

When Lily puts the car into park in front of Raven House, we both start crying all over again, which is wild because I can't believe I've got any more tears left to come out.

Yesterday, after I hugged Jo-Jo goodbye, I (of course) started crying (again), and I got this horrible headache. Lily gave me an aspirin, and even took some herself in between wiping her own eyes. It seemed to make it better, but now that we're in front of Raven House and I'm crying again, my headache is back, worse than ever.

"I don't think there's anything left to say that we didn't say yesterday or again this morning," Lily says. "So it's probably easier if you just leave and don't even look back. What do you think?"

I nod and grab the Kleenex box on the seat between us and take out a few more tissues. "Can I just ask you one more question?"

"That would be . . . well, groovy," Lily says. She smiles, but it's the fakest smile I've ever seen.

I try to play along, but I'm a pretty terrible actress, and I have to give my drippy nose a big blow, like Jo-Jo does whenever I hold a tissue against her face. Like Jo-Jo *did*.

Yesterday, when Lily and I said our for-real goodbye, we talked all about how much we were going to miss to each other, and how we had become such good friends. Lily told me she's going to think of me whenever she watches *General Hospital* and she's going to start saying "groovy" from time to time, just as a way to remember me. I told her I thought that was . . . cool.

"So, what's your question?" she asks me now.

I blow my nose one more time. "How does the baby get out of me?"

Mrs. Marty Seigel

(Rose)

The weekend lasts forever, but finally, mercifully, it's Monday. I have no idea whether I'll need to miss school after the abortion, so I decide I'd best go in today. The question is, how do I place a phone call sometime this morning when I'll already be in the classroom? Better question, how do I place a phone call somewhere other than the school office, where I would have no privacy? I have no idea what they'll ask me when I call Dr. Wingate's number, but my guess is I won't want any eavesdroppers.

Even though my apartment is near the school, it's still too far for me to get home, make a call, and get back to my class in the same amount of time it would take me to use the restroom, which is the only type of break I get in the morning.

Once I arrive at school, I head immediately to the office. "Good morning, Bonnie." This is the third time I'm about to lie to my friend. The first time was when I called in sick with the Hong Kong flu after Marty beat and raped me. Then I lied again when I had to explain why I had yellow bruising around my eye when I came back to school. And now I'm doing it again—because he didn't just beat and rape me; he left me pregnant. I feel my stomach twist, and I'm unsure whether it's thinking about Marty that's upsetting my tummy or if it's morning sickness. "Listen, Bon. Something came up Friday with my divorce."

Bonnie drops her head, a gesture meant to signal that she understands this is still just between us. When I told her about my divorce, I simply said that Marty and I never really saw eye to eye on anything and had agreed to just move on—"Still, until the divorce is final, I prefer that no one at school know about it." She assured me she wouldn't say anything to anyone. There's no question that she's kept her word, which makes me feel even worse over what I'm about to do.

"My lawyer told me the judge wants to talk to me later this morning around 9:15 a.m. before he heads into court for the day. I told my attorney that I'm in class then, but he said it's important and it would only take a few minutes. Five at the most."

Both because Bonnie is a friend, but also because she's not an idiot, she doesn't need it all spelled out. "No problem. Since it'll be quick, I can step in to cover your class." She glances down at the scheduler on her desk. "How about if I set you up with the phone in Old Man Winter's office so you can close the door and talk about whatever it is you need to discuss in private?"

"Old Man Winter" is what most of the teachers call the assistant principal, though never to his face. "That would be great. But won't he need his office?"

"Not today." She taps at the scheduler with the eraser end of the pencil she's removed from behind her ear. "He'll be auditing one of the fifth-grade student teachers then." She writes something on the scheduler. "At least he will be now."

AT 9:10 A.M., BONNIE KNOCKS and simultaneously opens the door to my classroom. I introduce her and tell my students that I'll be stepping out for a few minutes and expect them to be on their very best behavior for Miss Kaufman.

I cannot only feel, but I think I can actually hear, my heart beating. I stop at the drinking fountain on my way to the office, scared but surprisingly excited by the phone call that I hope will be the beginning of the end of this nightmare.

I go into Old Man Winter's office, close the door behind me, and call the number I've memorized. I give my name and ask for an appointment with Dr. Wingate. The woman who answers the phone says the doctor will see me on Thursday at ten a.m. and gives me an address. "Do not eat breakfast that morning and bring five hundred dollars cash with you to the appointment." Before I can agree, she hangs up the phone.

Mrs. Marty Seigel

(Rose)

When I return to my classroom, Bonnie asks how the call went. "A tiny wrinkle," I say. "I'll explain over lunch. Meet me in the teacher's lounge at noon?" Bonnie nods, and I ask the class to thank Miss Kaufman before she leaves. Is there anything more precious than a group of second graders saying "Thank you, Miss Kaufman" in unison? Or maybe it's not as cute as I think it is and it's just that my mood has improved a million percent. Thursday, at ten a.m., this will all be behind me.

Over lunch, I tell Bonnie my fourth lie—the matter was not as easily solved as my lawyer led me to believe and I'm going to need to see the judge in his chambers on Thursday morning, so she'll need to line up a sub. I feel bad lying to her yet again, but having an illegal abortion is not something I'm about to share. Besides, David passed me the phone number for Dr. Wingate; I owe it to him to keep all of this a secret.

"But you'll be back in the afternoon, right?" Bon asks.

"Good question. I think just to be on the safe side, you should get a sub for the whole day. If the judge is anything like my lawyer, he could be long-winded." I know I might have to miss Friday, too, but if my cover story is that I'm meeting with the judge on Thursday, I can't very well tell Bonnie to also get a sub for Friday.

I have no idea what to expect. I don't know anyone who has had an abortion. Actually, that's probably not true. According to the Cronkite documentary on TV, the odds are pretty great that I do know women who've had abortions; I just don't know I do because it's not something women talk about. On the other hand, I, like every adult, am all too aware of the articles in the *Cleveland Plain Dealer* about arrests leading to the dismantling of abortion rings, and filthy motel rooms where women get their abortions and wind up with infections or bleeding to death. Before I found out I was pregnant, Lily told me stories about David sometimes seeing patients whom he had to put on a separate floor at the hospital that's just for women whose abortions went south. Lily says these women either tried to do it themselves or developed complications from bad ones. David wouldn't give me the name of a shady doctor, though. This is what I try to convince myself, while at the same time acknowledging that abortion is shady, by definition, because it's illegal. So, David gave me the name of a doctor who will be breaking the law on Thursday. If that's not shady, what is? I'm scared, and not for the first time I wonder about the very tangled web I'm weaving.

"I'll be back Friday, though." I smile, even though the lightheartedness and relief I felt immediately after making the appointment has completely evaporated.

When I get home, I unfold the map and look for the street where I'm expected at ten a.m. on Thursday. I'm surprised to discover it's in a busy section of town, not terribly far from the hospital, in fact. I guess I was expecting a literal back alley.

Mrs. Marty Seigel

(Rose)

I had trouble sleeping last night because I was so nervous about today, but when my alarm clock goes off, I am startled, so I know I must have nodded off at some point. When I get out of bed, I'm immediately struck with a bout of nausea and barely make it to the bathroom before I vomit. I brush my teeth to get the horrible taste out of my mouth, but before I can rinse my mouth, the toothpaste makes me gag and I vomit again. It's almost like my body knows what's going to happen today and it's rebelling. Or, I tell myself, I could look at it another way: This pregnancy is making me sick, and I'm going to see Dr. Wingate to get well.

I shower and dress and look longingly at the coffeepot. When I made my appointment, the woman said I should skip breakfast this morning. Does that mean I can't have anything to drink, or did she just mean solid food? I decide to pass on the coffee, just in case.

I make it all the way to my car and put the key in the ignition before it hits me: I left the money in my apartment. Back up the stairs I go, silently encouraging myself to calm down. When I reenter my apartment, I go right to the dresser in my bedroom. I grab the envelope that I assembled last night. It contains $250 from Lily's *pushke* along with $250 of my own money, that came from my *pushke* as well as my bank account. When I counted it, I discovered that Lily actually gave me $325, but I didn't want to wipe her out, so I split the cost for the abortion in half, which would still allow me to stay somewhat solvent. I put the envelope into my purse and head for my car a second time.

I turn on the radio, hoping it will help calm my nerves or at least help me pass the time. From what I figured, based on the map, the office is roughly a half hour away. I find a station that plays all the current hits. When I locate the building, the DJ announces the latest Beatles hit, "Help!" I sing along, and by the time I'm parking the car, the Beatles are asking, *Won't you please, please help me? Help me. Help me.* I take that as a good omen.

Dr. Wingate's office is not at all what I expected. It's in a regular building, and it looks exactly like a regular office, with a regular waiting room. I look around and see another woman reading a *Ladies' Home Journal* magazine. She's visibly pregnant and looks like if she sneezes her baby will just fall out of her. There's another woman who also looks ready to pop. And then there's a woman who looks like me. I'm suddenly worried that David has merely sent me to a regular OB-GYN who he thinks might be able to help me because there's no way Dr. Wingate is an abortionist. But then why would his nurse tell me not to eat breakfast? And why would she ask me to bring $500 cash?

"Can I help you?" the woman behind a desk asks.

"I'm Rose Seigel." I don't exactly whisper it, but I don't broadcast it, either.

"Nice to meet you, Rose. It says here that you're a new patient. I have some paperwork for you to fill out." She hands me a clipboard with a sheet of paper attached. She uses her pen to point to a section of the waiting room. "Why don't you take a seat over there and return this to me when you're done?"

Frankly, I'm confused. This all seems on the up-and-up, and yet I'm here for an illegal abortion. "Illegal" being the operative word.

Literally. But I don't ask questions; I do as I'm told. I fill in the blanks for my name, address, phone, social security number, ethnicity, the date of my last menstrual cycle, and a couple other things. The form also has a line for an emergency contact. My first impulse is to write down Lily's name, but I remember David's words when he slipped me Dr. Wingate's phone number: "Don't tell anyone. Especially Lily." I leave the space blank and return the clipboard to the woman behind the desk.

"The doctor is running a bit late." She again uses her pen to point to the very pregnant women in the waiting room. "There are a few patients in front of you, but it shouldn't be long. Just take a seat."

I return to the same chair, and again, I do as I'm told and I wait.

Another woman, dressed in a nurse's uniform, appears from a door that I assume separates the waiting area from the exam rooms. She calls a name, and I watch the first woman, the one who is not noticeably pregnant, disappear. A few minutes later, one of the pregnant women is called. I wait some more. When she reappears, she has one hand resting on her belly. We make eye contact and she smiles at me. "He said it won't be long now. I told him I'm holding him to his word." She pats her stomach and exits the office. A moment later, the second pregnant woman is called back to the exam room.

Finally, it's my turn.

I don't know what I was expecting, but Dr. Wingate isn't it. He is young and looks alarmingly like Darrin from *Bewitched*. Oh, if only I had the power to twitch my nose and make this all go away.

Dr. Wingate tells me to climb up onto the exam table. "What brings you in today, Mrs. . . ." He looks at the clipboard in his hands. "Seigel?"

I gesture at my stomach. "I want to get rid of it."

He nods his head. "I just wanted to make sure I have the right person. Dr. Berg told me to expect you and that I should take extra good care of you."

For the first time since I found out I was pregnant, I actually believe everything will be okay.

Dr. Wingate tells me to remove all my clothes except for my bra. He hands me a cloth gown and steps out of the room.

I've just snapped up the gown when I hear a light knock on the door and Dr. Wingate reenters the room. He washes his hands and opens some drawers and cupboards and removes various items. He places everything he's assembled on a tray and puts the tray on a small table near me. He washes his hands again, but this time he puts on a pair of rubber gloves when he's done. "First, I need to draw some blood."

I straighten my left arm as he ties a rubber hose above my elbow. He wipes the area with alcohol, inserts a needle, pulls back on the syringe, and fills a few test tubes with blood.

"Mrs. Seigel, I want you to lie back and put your feet into the stirrups."

I use my elbows to lower myself down onto the table, but before I'm able to lift up my legs, he tells me I need to scoot farther down. "I won't bite."

Dr. Wingate adjusts the sheet across my knees, and because my feet are in the stirrups, I can't see anything, which, frankly, is more than fine with me.

"Mrs. Seigel. That blood I just drew?"

"Uh-huh."

"I'm going to put it back into you, but it's not going into your arm; I'm going to insert it through your vagina. But to get to where I need it to be, I need to go through your cervix. I'm not going to lie to you, it's going to hurt in a pinchy, cramping sort of way, but it's only going to last a couple minutes."

My legs are shaking, and I feel his hand on my thigh. "You need to try to relax, because the more relaxed you are, the easier this will be."

"Got it." I feel my legs continue to shake. "I'm trying."

Finally, he tells me he's going to insert a catheter into my cervix—
and man, was he right! It hurts. A lot. "You're doing great. I'm almost
done injecting the blood. Keep breathing."

Eventually, he reaches for my elbow and helps me to sit up.

"Is it over?" I ask.

"No. But the worst part is over. Now let me tell you what happens next."

Dr. Wingate explains that in forty-five minutes or so, the blood
he just put in will start to leak out of my cervix. "When it does, you're
to call me. Got it?"

I nod. "Then what happens?"

"When you telephone me, I will give you the next steps. We've
found it's better for everyone's safety if things are portioned out on an
as-needed basis. Besides, that way you don't have to worry your pretty
little head about anything." He winks at me.

He looks at his watch. "I'd tell you to grab an early lunch, but I
don't want you eating anything." He snaps off his gloves and tosses
them in the wastebasket. "I'll leave you alone to get dressed."

No sooner does he leave than another woman, who I haven't seen
before, enters the room. "You have the money?" she asks. I'm fairly
sure this was the same woman I talked to on the phone when I called
the office. Both have deep, gruff voices.

"Yes."

She extends her hand, waiting. Still in the cloth gown, I step
down from the table and reach for my purse. I hand her the envelope
with the money, and just as quickly as she appeared in the exam room,
she disappears.

On my way out of the office, the woman at the reception desk
yells after me to take good care.

Dr. Wingate said it would take about three-quarters of an hour
for the blood to start seeping out of me, so I decide to go home, as I
don't want it to happen while I'm in the middle of a store or another

public place. Then again, maybe that wouldn't be so bad. At least it would look like a real miscarriage. I decide my first instinct was best and get in my car to go home.

The radio is still turned to the popular music station, but this time it's not the Beatles who serenade me home, but Gary Lewis and the Playboys. They want to know who wants to buy this diamond ring, because she took it off her finger and it doesn't mean a thing.

I cry for the rest of the drive.

UNFORTUNATELY, THE DOCTOR WASN'T EXACTLY accurate with his estimate about when the blood would start leaving my body. Even more unfortunate is that I'm in my car when it happens, and by the time I feel it leaking out, it's already on the upholstery. Now, even if I get to keep the car after my divorce, every time I get into it, I'll have to see this permanent reminder of what I've done.

I get to my apartment and I call Dr. Wingate and tell him I've started to bleed.

"It sounds like you're having a miscarriage, Mrs. Seigel."

I wonder if someone is near Dr. Wingate and he's concerned about being overheard, but I don't say anything.

"I will call the hospital immediately and arrange to have you admitted," he says. "When you arrive, there is no need to go to the ER. Go right to admitting. When you get there, tell them you're my patient and that we've talked by phone. Tell them you're bleeding and having some cramping and that I told you to go right to the hospital and to ask for Dr. Berg, who is expecting you. Do you understand?"

Although I say yes, I do not understand. I don't understand at all.

Mrs. Marty Seigel

(Rose)

At admitting, I repeat the script supplied to me by Dr. Wingate. Before long, I'm checked in and taken to a room.

When David walks in, he is void of all color. For the benefit of the patient in the bed next to me, or the nurse in the room, who is getting me into a gown and filling the water bottle, David pretends not to know me. At least I assume that's the reason for the ruse, when he introduces himself and says it's nice to meet me.

"I'm sorry it's under these circumstances," he says. "I've talked to Dr. Wingate and I know all about your miscarriage." He reaches out and covers my hand with his. "Since I was already here and just finished a delivery, he asked me to take care of you. We're going to do a D&C," he says, "just to make sure you've expelled everything and there's nothing left behind."

I REMEMBER BEING WHEELED INTO the operating room and I remember waking up again in my hospital room. About an hour later, David reappears and pulls the curtain closed, providing a modicum of privacy from my roommate. He picks up the chart attached to the foot of my bed. "All went well," he says. "But because you had anesthesia, I'd like you to stay overnight, just to be safe."

"If you think it's necessary." I nod toward the phone. "I'll just call my school and tell them I'll be out another day."

David bends down toward me. "I'm going to let Lily know that you were admitted to the hospital while experiencing a miscarriage, and I was on call and did the D&C," he whispers.

I nod.

"That's all she needs to know."

I nod again. "I just have one question," I say. "Is this something you've done before?"

David turns and leaves without answering.

Mrs. David Berg

(Lily)

The house has been quiet since Betsy left. I cannot tell a lie; I miss her even more than I thought I would. Even tonight, when I'm in the family room, watching the Barbra Streisand special *Color Me Barbra*, I sometimes feel the urge to yell toward the utility room and tell Betsy to come watch with me.

Halfway through the show, David comes home and tells me that Rose had a miscarriage. Of course I'm worried about Rose; she is in the hospital, after all. But David assures me that she'll be discharged tomorrow and be back at school on Monday morning. "Like nothing ever happened," he says as he pulls me up from the couch and into his arms for a hug. He rubs my back in small circles, and we stay that way for a few minutes before he finally signals, with a few pats, that he's about to pull away. I sit back on the couch, grab the clicker, and shut off the television.

Part of me is so relieved that Rose didn't have to go through with an abortion and that her body just took care of things by itself. Or maybe it was an act of God. His gift to her, after all she's suffered through, after everything Marty did to her. She shouldn't also have to make the agonizing decision to have an abortion on top of every-thing else. Someone was clearly looking out for her, because I know my sister. Even though she was hell-bent against having this baby, she would've regretted her decision. Perhaps "regret" isn't the right word, but she'd have felt guilty. Maybe not right away, but eventually.

I think that one day Rose would look at Jo-Jo, or the baby I'm carrying now, or maybe she'd remarry and have a child of her own, but one day, she'd realize what a miracle it is to be able to grow a baby inside her and she'd wonder about the one she got rid of. Or maybe that's just me projecting my feelings on my sister. Rose has insisted, at every turn, that it's not a baby: "It's just gobbledygook." I would definitely feel guilty. But then again, I wasn't raped. Honestly, sometimes I think I could give myself whiplash because of the frequency with which I change my mind. How is it possible to know abortion is illegal and to feel it's wrong, and yet look at Becca and Rose and not understand why they made their decisions?

But Becca wasn't raped. Still, she had some pretty compelling reasons for not wanting to have another child. Her desperation almost cost Becca her life. And if she died, her three boys would have been motherless. How could that possibly be right? But as tragic as it was that Becca almost died, it was because of her that I knew I had to help Rose with whatever she wanted. It wasn't my place to judge her or to make her do what I would do. It was about allowing Rose to make her own choice, about her own body, about her own life. That's ultimately why I gave her my *pushke*.

That's when it hits me: the upside to this miscarriage. Since Rose didn't need to pay for an abortion, she can give me back my *pushke*. Then I feel guilty because that is probably the most selfish thing I could ever think at a time like this!

"David, am I just a horrible sister for thinking that, since Rose had a miscarriage, she can give me back my *pushke*?"

"Your what?"

That's when I realize I never told David I gave Rose my *pushke*. In fact, I've never explicitly told David about my *pushke*. But he had to know. Isn't it something all wives do?

"You know about my *pushke*. I'm sure I've told you. It's the left-over money from here and there that I put aside for a rainy day. It's how I was able to buy you the watch last year for your birthday."

David looks at his wrist. "How much did you give her?"

"Everything I had. A little more than three hundred dollars."

David shakes his head.

"I know, I know. It's a lot of money. That's why I want to know if you think it's terrible of me to be happy that I'll get it back."

David puts his hands on top of his head and blows air out of his mouth. Then he runs his hands through his hair.

"What? What's wrong?"

"I'm going to tell you something, Lily. And I want you to listen to everything before you say anything. I don't even want you to ask any questions until I'm done. Okay?"

I nod because I want him to know I'm taking his request seriously; I will not speak until he's finished with whatever it is he's going to tell me.

"This is the first time I've ever done anything like what I'm going to tell you. That's the most important thing that I want you to remember . . ."

Mid-November
1985

Dr. Elizabeth Perry

This Planned Parenthood clinic is close to the Ohio State University, so it's not unusual for us to see undergrads or even grad students. The young women who populate our waiting room typically choose to come here versus the student health center on campus either because (A) their health center visits would be billed to their parents or to their parents' health insurance and they don't want their parents' involvement or (B) they're looking for services the university doesn't offer.

We see a lot of female students who want to be tested for an STD (although we also test men), and girls who need a prescription for the Pill, one of the new copper IUDs, or another form of birth control. We also see our fair share of students seeking an abortion, something student health doesn't offer, making us their best option.

"Hi, I'm Dr. Perry," I say to the girl with the cornflower blue eyes wearing a paper gown and sitting atop my exam table, which is also covered with paper. "What brings you in today?"

"I just went through it with the nurse. Do I have to repeat it all over?"

She has a point, and not for the first time, I find myself admiring the spunk of young girls today. When I was her age, I never had the guts to question people in authority, especially doctors.

"I want you to tell me why you're here in your own words. Just so there are no misunderstandings. It's also our way of making sure no one is pressuring you to do something you don't want to do."

Her eyes fill with tears, and I realize what I interpreted as spunk is more likely her reluctance to repeat why she's here. Again. She probably doesn't want to have to verbalize it any more than necessary because it only makes it more real.

"Well, first off, I get a lot of bladder infections," she says. "I don't have one now, but I get a lot of them, and I was wondering if there's anything I can do."

I wait, but when it's clear she's not going to say any more, I offer a gentle prod. "And second? You said 'first off.'" I wait again, knowing how hard it often is for girls to say the words.

"I need an abortion," she finally says and gives a loud sniffle. I hand her a tissue from the box we keep in every exam room, precisely for this purpose. "The date of my last period was seven weeks ago. And I know I'm pregnant because I'm never late and my boobs are killing me." She crosses her arms around her body, covering her chest, as if supporting them in such a manner will stop the ache. "I also peed on a stick at my dorm yesterday morning and it turned pink."

"Whoa," I say. "Let's slow down a bit." We had a new office manager start a few weeks ago and she's changing up our recordkeeping, so, as has been the case entirely too often, I've got a patient before me and I don't even know her name. "Did you complete the paperwork? Because it wasn't in the pocket on the outside of the door. And I'm embarrassed to admit that I don't even know your name."

"I did the paperwork. And my name is Joan. Joan Berg. But everyone calls me Jo-Jo."

My mouth is suddenly dry and I sit down on the rolling stool. I look at those blue eyes, and now that I know it's Jo-Jo, I immediately see Lily's face gazing back at me.

She's staring at me, waiting for me to say or do something, but my mouth is so dry I don't know if I can speak. I take in a deep breath and force myself to exhale slowly. I take in another breath. In, then out. I've seen gunshot wounds during my rotations; I can handle this. I am the doctor here, I remind myself. In, then out.

"Well, it's nice to meet you, Jo-Jo. I'm Dr. Elizabeth Perry, but everyone calls me Betsy." Everyone most certainly does *not* call me Betsy; I became Elizabeth when I went off to college. That doesn't matter, though. I have no idea if Lily ever mentioned me to Jo-Jo, but if she had, it would have been as Betsy. I look at Jo-Jo's face and those beautiful blue eyes and wait for some indication that she recognizes my name. Nothing. Of course not. Perry is my married name.

"Well, my patients call me Dr. Perry, but I've only been Dr. Perry for a few years—well, I've been a doctor longer than a few years, but I've only been Dr. Perry since I've been married, and that's only been a few years." Oh good Lord, I'm rambling and I sound like an idiot. "I was Betsy Eubanks before I became Dr. Perry."

Jo-Jo opens her eyes wide. "Wait," she whispers. "You're Betsy? The pregnant girl who lived with us when I was a baby?"

Oh God. What Pandora's box did I just open?

Ms. Jo-Jo Berg

I leave Planned Parenthood with my abortion scheduled for Friday. Now, for the first time in weeks, I feel relaxed, or at least a lot less panicky.

Before I left the clinic, Dr. Perry handed me some pamphlets along with her card and told me to call her if I had any questions. "Really, anything. I'm going to take good care of you," she said; then she gave me a hug. It was a little awkward, the way she acted like she knew me, which I suppose she does. But I have absolutely no memory of her—not that I should; I wasn't even two years old when she lived with us. Still, I feel like I should know her, at least a little bit, based on some of the stories my mom used to tell. But those stories were about a young pregnant girl who was pretty clueless. Dr. Perry is a doctor, and she is definitely not clueless.

When I get back to my dorm, I call my sister. "Listen, I want your opinion about something."

"Well, hello to you, too. Long time, no talk. What's up?"

"First off, it's only been a little more than a week, and I told you, I had to take a makeup midterm, so I was busy studying." What I don't tell her is that I was so completely stressed out about probably being pregnant that I was afraid she'd figure it out, just from the sound of my voice.

"Okay, okay. I'm just messing with you. What's going on?"

I tell Jenny that I just came back from Planned Parenthood. "And no, it's not what you're thinking." Not technically a lie—at least it won't be after Friday. "I went because I've got another bladder infection"—definitely a lie—"and the idiots at student health keep writing me prescriptions and telling me to drink more cranberry juice. I figured I'd try Planned Parenthood and see if they had any other ideas."

"Did they?"

"Yeah. The doctor thinks I'm not getting new infections, it's all the same one. And she says I need to stay on the antibiotic longer to really knock it out of my system."

"Hmm, sounds like a good idea."

"But the doctor . . . she's the reason I'm calling." I tell my sister about Betsy Eubanks, also known as the unwed mother who lived with us when Mom was pregnant with Jenny, also known as Dr. Elizabeth Perry, the doctor I just saw. "You know how much I love hearing stories about Mom when she was young, right?"

"Really? Why would I know that? Let me introduce myself. I'm your sister. Of course I know!" Jen's humor has always leaned toward sarcastic, something Mom didn't appreciate when Jenny was growing up. I can almost hear Mom's voice right now saying, *Watch your mouth, young lady!*

"Sorry," I say. "I know you know. It's just that Dr. Perry lived with us when Mom—even according to Mom—was at the height of her prim-and-properness, if that's even a word. And I think it would be so cool to hear what Dr. Perry has to say about her."

"You might want to get back, Jo-Jo."

This isn't the first time Jenny's made that Beatles joke. "Why do you think I should back off?"

"She was an unwed mother, that's why. She might not want to talk about it."

"I already brought it up and she . . ."

"Jo-Jo, tell me you didn't!"

"I know, I know. But once it dawned on me who she was, it just slipped out."

Jenny exhales, loudly. "And? How did she react?"

"She seemed perfectly fine. In fact, she seemed sort of excited that I even knew about her."

Jenny clicks her tongue a few times, which tells me she's thinking. Then, sounding quite confident, she says, "Well, if that's the case, I think it's an okay idea to ask her about how Mom was in the olden days."

"You do? You don't think it's weird?"

"Of course I do. But Jo-Jo, you're weird."

"Point taken. But what do I do?" I'm a little embarrassed to admit that I'm holding a pen so I can jot down notes about anything Jenny suggests as a way to approach this. "Dr. Perry gave me her number at the clinic, but she's a busy doctor. It's not like I can just call her and ask her if she has time to shoot the breeze about when she lived with us. Can I?"

Jenny's tongue is clicking away. Finally, she offers the advice I was so hoping to hear: "Call her."

Dr. Elizabeth Perry

The day after seeing Jo-Jo, I find a pink "While You Were Out" slip on my desk with her name and number. When I return the call, I get her answering machine, so I leave a message letting her know the best time to reach me is later that day, between 4:30 p.m. and 6:00 p.m.

When we finally connect, Jo-Jo sounds nervous, but I'm used to skittish girls in their teens and early twenties, so I give her the time she needs. Turns out, it isn't her upcoming abortion she has questions about, but Lily. "I love stories about my mom, from when I was too young to remember," she says. "Especially the ones about her being all prim and proper. Once Aunt Rose told me how Mom always said 'in the family way' instead of 'pregnant,' and I teased Mom about that for years!"

This is the moment where I must quickly decide whether to open Pandora's box. My head says to keep that lid sealed tight, but my heart wants a teeny-tiny little peek inside. I feel my stomach twist and decide just to go for it. "Then you're in luck," I say. "Because I've got more than a few good stories about your mom. But Jo-Jo, this has to be a two-way street."

When she asks what I mean, I tell her that I expect her to reciprocate with updates about her family and everyone in the neighborhood.

"Deal!"

"Look, instead of doing this over the phone, why don't we get together?"

"Deal again," she says, sounding almost giddy.

We make plans to meet at a nearby diner on Thursday once I'm off work.

Ms. Jo-Jo Berg

I get to the diner first, and before I know it, I've shredded my paper napkin into strips. I guess it's safe to say I'm nervous, although I'm not sure why, exactly.

When Dr. Perry arrives, she's not in scrubs like she was when I saw her on Monday; she's wearing a pair of black pants and a pretty silk floral blouse. She's also wearing lipstick. There's no question about it, she's beautiful.

"I want to hear all about your family, and you need to catch me up on the neighbors who played canasta," she says as she slides into the booth across from me. "Oh, and your aunt Rose and, well . . . Oh, listen to me jabbering on. I guess I'm just excited to hear about everyone," she says. "And oh my God, I don't even know if your mom had a boy or girl. We were pregnant at the same time, you know?"

She's talking so much and super fast, too. If I didn't know better, I'd think she was the one who's nervous, not me. But I do know better: She's a doctor and I'm just a college student.

I tell Dr. Perry that my mom had a girl, whom she named Jennifer, also after her mom. "Sometimes, just to be annoying, when we were little girls she called her Jen-Jen and me Jo-Jo. But mostly, she called her Jenny. As far as everyone else goes, where should I start?"

"How about with canasta?" Dr. Perry says. She puts her napkin in her lap. I look at my shredded one and ball it up, hoping she didn't notice. "And then I'll tell you some stories about your mom," she says. "I've been remembering some good ones over the last couple days. Sound like a plan?"

"Perfect." I can't believe I was worried about calling Dr. Perry. She's being so nice and not acting like she's doing me a favor at all. In fact, she sounds really excited.

"I'll start with Robin," I say, "who wound up becoming a big women's libber. And I mean *big*. They say she burned her bra and everything. And get this—after Jane Fonda got arrested in Cleveland, Robin even went out and got a haircut to match Jane's. But here's the best part: Robin got Mom involved in the movement!"

Dr. Perry slaps the table. "No way."

"Yes way!"

A waitress appears and asks if we know what we're having. Dr. Perry says we haven't looked at the menus yet, but asks if she'll bring her a cup of coffee, black, while we're deciding. I ask for a Diet Coke. Before she walks away, Dr. Perry looks up at the waitress again. "Oh, and can you bring her"—she nods her head toward me—"an extra napkin when you get a chance?" So much for her not noticing the one I shredded.

I redirect the conversation back to Robin. "She even got Mom to go to some protest marches and they both wound up volunteering with NOW. I've seen pictures of Mom with one hand holding a sign that says 'Judge Women as People, Not as Wives' and her other hand is on the stroller holding Jenny, with me standing next to them.

"Robin, her husband, and the twins moved out of the neighborhood a while back, though. He became a partner at some big law firm in downtown Cleveland, and they wanted a house closer to his office."

"You don't understand," Dr. Perry says, "when I knew your mom, she was uber-conservative. She didn't even use the word 'pee.' She'd say she had to use the *bathroom* or excuse herself to go to the *restroom*. And what your aunt Rose said was right. When I first arrived, your mom didn't ever say 'pregnant.' Instead, she said 'with child' or 'in the family way' or 'expecting,' or, in my case, 'in trouble.'"

We both laugh. "I know Mom used to be pretty straitlaced," I say.

"That's putting it mildly. She was the epitome of a '50s housewife." Dr. Perry makes air quotes with her fingers when she says the word "housewife."

"Well, the '60s finally caught up with her because, for as far back as I can remember, Mom was always about rolling up her sleeves and working hard for causes she believed in. And if she felt there were injustices or laws that needed changing—watch out! She was a woman on a mission."

Dr. Perry laughs again. "I always had a sneaky suspicion your mom would do great things. Not that being a housewife"—she again makes air quotes—"and mother to you and your sister wasn't great."

I assure her that I'm not offended. "I knew what you meant."

"Your mom was always so good with people. She would have been a terrific social worker. Believe it or not, although the circumstances were less than ideal, your mom changed the trajectory of my entire life. She talked openly to me about, well, everything, which is something my own mom didn't do. When I showed up at your house, I was this lost fifteen-year-old pregnant girl who didn't even understand the mechanics of how I got pregnant."

I'm stunned. "How is that even possible?"

She smiles. "That's a conversation for another day."

It isn't lost on me that Dr. Perry's just implied this isn't a one-off—and we should meet up again. Just knowing that makes me feel a lot less nervous.

Dr. Perry looks over her shoulder, no doubt wondering about our drinks. She points toward the ceiling. "Oh my God, do you hear that?"

I hadn't noticed until she mentioned it, but Madonna's "Like a Virgin" is playing through the overhead speakers. "Talk about timing and irony," Dr. Perry says as she reaches for her purse, which is hobo style, a throwback to the '60s. She rummages through her bag and finally pulls out a small photo album, about the size of a wallet. "I have a picture I keep with me." She pushes back a lock of hair that's escaped from her blond ponytail and tucks it behind her ear. "It's there to remind me who I used to be and where I came from." She turns to the first pages. "That's my mom and my dad," she says, flipping through so fast I can't see them. Then she stops. "That's me." And she points to a little girl next to her, sitting in a stroller. "And that, Jo-Jo, is you."

It's not a picture I've seen before. Dr. Perry is very young and very pregnant, and me? I've got extremely pudgy cheeks.

"Whenever I'm having a tough day, or I see a young girl who is pregnant, I take a look at this picture. It's a reminder that we never know how things will turn out, and that sometimes things become possible even before they're imagined."

The waitress arrives and deposits the mug of coffee, my pop, and my new napkin. She puts a straw next to my glass and, without being told, walks away, clearly getting the message that we're still not ready to order.

Dr. Perry picks up her coffee and a bit sloshes onto the paper tablecloth. I'm about to ask if I can see the pictures that come after the photo of Dr. Perry and me, whether there's a picture of Mr. Perry or if she has any kids, but she puts away the photo album. "Tell me about your aunt Rose."

"That's another amazing story and another one of my mom's causes. You know Aunt Rose's husband abused her, right?"

She gasps and puts a hand over her mouth. "No. I knew they were going to get a divorce, but I never knew why."

"Well, that's why. Anyway, she wound up meeting this great guy and married him a few years later. He was a widower and already had a six-year-old boy, and then they had two more kids together. That six-year-old was my age and he's also a student here, so whenever Aunt Rose visits him, I always get a visit, too, and a care package of my favorite treats."

Dr. Perry has a huge grin on her face. "I'm so glad things worked out for her. I always liked her. When I first met your aunt, she flashed me the peace sign, and I knew right away she was one of the good guys. There was just something about her. You know what I mean?"

The waitress arrives and pulls out her notepad. "I'm sorry," Dr. Perry says. "We have a lot of catching up to do. Can you come back later for our order?"

The waitress shrugs. "No problem. It's not busy, so take your time."

I didn't realize how dry my mouth was from doing so much talking until I take a couple sips of my Diet Coke. "The man Aunt Rose married was a bit of a muckety-muck, and he introduced Aunt Rose to some big donors," I say, taking another drink from my pop. "She got them to contribute to a charity she set up. Aunt Rose wound up opening a place called Shelter from the Storm, which was a temporary home for abused women. When I was in high school, I started volunteering there. Well, not *there*, exactly. The location was always a secret, even from me, but I helped get donations of clothes and toys and stuff. Then I'd give everything to Aunt Rose or to my mom, who took it to the shelter so women who had to leave their homes in the middle of the night had something to wear, and some toys, if they brought children with them."

"That's amazing, Jo-Jo."

"Totally. Shelter from the Storm was a huge part of my mom's life. She did all their bookkeeping, but she also worked there, part-time, doing other things. During the day, when Jenny and I were in school, Mom sometimes just went there to talk to the women. She said that even though it was sad to see how scared some of them were and how upended their lives were, it made her feel good to be doing something to help make the world a better place. Mom used to say it was a Jewish thing, called *t'kun olam*. But I think it was a Lily and Rose thing, trying to do good things and setting an example for their kids."

"I'm so glad your mom was able to figure out a way to make her life so meaningful, in addition to being a wonderful mom and housewife, of course." This time she skips the air quotes.

I wonder if she's *jujjing* me. Mom would never, ever have been happy being only a housewife and mother. But I guess that's exactly what she was when Dr. Perry knew her. I just can't imagine my mom not having her own interests and her own projects—and being a sort of activist—but that's probably because I don't think about my mom as having a life before my childhood memories begin.

"So, we're on to Becca," Dr. Perry says.

I ask her if she knew Becca's mantra about her boys being juvenile delinquents.

She laughs and says she can't remember Becca ever *not* saying exactly that.

When I tell her all three of Becca's boys are in medicine, Dr. Perry almost falls out of the booth.

"No way," she says again. "Decidedly not juvenile delinquents."

"Not in the least. One is a researcher; one is an OB-GYN, like my dad. Oh, and like you." I point to Dr. Perry. "And one is just finishing up medical school. Isn't that groovy?"

"'Groovy'? Yes, it is, but what decade are you living in, Jo-Jo?"

"Ah. It's just something silly I picked up from my mom. She used to say it from time to time, and I guess it just rubbed off on me. People comment about it all the time. 'Groovy' and '*jujje*.' I use both words a lot."

"That's cool," Dr. Perry says, and I'm unsure whether she's mocking me. She picks up the menu. "Shall we have a look?"

"Aren't you going to ask about the Blooms?"

Dr. Perry smacks her head, "I coulda had a V8" style, and puts down her menu.

I really like Dr. Perry. I thought it would be weird, talking to a doctor who's so much older than me, but she's almost like a much (much) older sister.

"I don't know how I could have forgotten about the Blooms," she says. "Yes, tell me, whatever happened to them?"

"I'm glad you're sitting down because, get this, they had two babies—you'll never believe it—ten months apart."

"How is that even possible?" Dr. Perry asks.

"You're the doctor and you're asking me?" I laugh and tell her to take a guess. She declines, insisting she hasn't a clue.

Before I answer the riddle of how it's possible to have children so close together, I remind her that my knowledge about the Blooms is all secondhand, since they moved away when I was three-ish. "He was an engineer at Goodyear and got some new job or transfer or something out to Silicon Valley, I think." Then I paraphrase what my mom told me:

Sarah Bloom had a history of miscarriages. She had a bunch of them, maybe five or six. They'd all but given up trying for their own baby and decided it was time to look into adoption. Well, on a Tuesday—Mom remembered that because it was her canasta day—when Sarah opened the door to go to Becca's house (it was her turn to host), there was a baby all wrapped up in blankets on Sarah's doorstep. There was a note that said something like "Please take care of her. If you do, I swear, you'll never hear from me."

"That's it?" Dr. Perry says. "No one knew whose baby it was or where it came from?"

"Mom said no one had a clue, and if they did, they didn't say."

Dr. Perry exhales, like she'd been holding her breath. "Wow. That's quite a story. What did Sarah do?"

"She kept her, of course. Obviously I don't know any of the details, but I have a feeling something a little shady happened. Robin's husband—remember, he's an attorney—took care of all the paperwork and made it all legal, at least according to Mom. I didn't give it much thought for the longest time, but as I got older, I realized it was strange that they didn't call the police and instead just kept the baby. I mean, that's weird, right?"

Dr. Perry nods. "Then again, things were different back then."

"Anyway, that's how Sarah wound up with two babies ten months apart, because a couple months after she found the baby by her door, she discovered she was pregnant again and this time, everything worked out."

"The baby stuck," Dr. Perry says.

"Huh?"

"I remember Sarah saying she couldn't get a baby to stick. But that one stuck."

"Exactly. Mom used to say that the baby on the doorstep must have brought the Blooms good luck. They named her Elizabeth." I gesture toward Dr. Perry, since that's her name, too.

"Elizabeth was a popular name back then," Dr. Perry says. "Still is."

I notice that Dr. Perry is tearing up. She immediately grabs her napkin to wipe her eyes. "I'm sorry," she says. "I'm just a sucker for a happy ending."

The waitress, who has started in our direction again, sees Dr. Perry crying and just turns around and goes back in the direction she came from.

Dr. Elizabeth Perry

I was surprised Jo-Jo didn't ask me why I never got in touch with her mom after I had my baby, especially since I asked so many questions about what happened to everyone. I had a prepared answer, all ready to go, about how Raven House discouraged contact—which was the truth—and how I had a lot of pressure from my parents to just put everything behind me and to move on. Again, completely true. I was also prepared to tell Jo-Jo that her mom and I agreed that's what we'd do when we said our final goodbye. But Jo-Jo didn't ask. Maybe she assumed that I wanted to just pretend those months with her family and my pregnancy never happened. But the real truth is, I wanted to make sure that Sarah and Joel Bloom knew I was completely out of the picture. Exactly as I'd promised. If I sent so much as a single letter or even a Christmas card (or Chanukah card), that could have been all it took to create doubt about whether I planned to live up to my promise to never, ever contact them again, or whether some day, I might just show up at their house.

However, the Blooms apparently worried about me reappearing anyway, which is probably why they relocated to the West Coast. But who knows? Maybe Joel really did get a legitimate job transfer and their leaving town so quickly was just a coincidence and had nothing to do with me.

She named her Elizabeth. So, she knew. Then again, how could she not? They all knew, yet they chose to keep my secret.

Ms. Jo-Jo Berg

Dr. Perry asks if I have everyone's phone numbers and addresses. "They were all so nice to me. I'd love to drop each of them a note or send each family a holiday card and let them know what became of me and how to get in touch, in case they're interested."

I tell Dr. Perry that I've got everything in my address book back at my dorm and I'll write down all the contact info and bring it with me when I come in tomorrow for my procedure. "I don't know if I've got a phone number for the Blooms, though. But I definitely have their address from our holiday card list."

"Thanks, Jo-Jo. Whatever you've got, I'll take. Another thing," she says, "after your procedure, would you like to come spend the weekend with me? You should be fine, but I'd love to be able to keep an eye on you, and if you're with me, you wouldn't have to worry about meals or anything."

I tell her that sounds good, but wonder what she'll say to her husband. "I mean, does he know about, well, you know?"

"That I was an unwed mother who lived with a family when I was fifteen?" She nods. "Yes. He knows. He knows everything. But as far as you're concerned, we don't need to tell him"—she lowers her voice—"about your procedure. I can just tell him you're Lily's daughter and you came into the office to have some polyps removed. It's totally up to you."

I pick the second option.

She gives me a huge smile. I don't tell her she has lipstick on her front teeth because soon our food will arrive and it'll probably just come off once she bites into her burger.

"Before our food comes, there's something else . . ." I reach into my purse to grab the paper I put into the inside pocket before I left my dorm. "I figured it would be easier than my trying to summarize it," I say. But the truth is, it'll be easier if I don't have to worry about losing my shit in the middle of a restaurant. I extend my hand, which I'm surprised to see is shaking, and give her the letter.

Dear Jo-Jo and Jenny,

If you've found this, it means you girls or your dad have cleaned through my dresser. And if you're cleaning through my drawers, that can only mean one thing.

As you know, my mom, your grandma Joan, died when I was 14 and Aunt Rose was 12, so I am all too aware of how history is repeating itself. That's the bad news. The fact that it was breast cancer in both my mom and me is scary, and it means you two need to make sure to find doctors who will keep an extra close eye on you both! That said, I really believe that by the time you're old enough to have to worry about it, they'll have found a cure. Amen. The good news is that now, while I'm writing this, you girls are 17 and 19, so we got to spend so much more time together than I had with my own mom. I got to raise you both into adulthood, and for that, I thank God every single day. And who knows, just because I'm writing this letter to you now doesn't mean I won't make it another year or two. You never know for sure.

I loved my life as your mom, never forget that. But my life started out so very "small," and I want yours to be much bigger. It is my dying wish—it is literally my dying wish— hey, ya gotta laugh, or at least put up with your mom making bad jokes . . .

Anyway, it is my dying wish that both of you girls graduate from college. Hell, go to grad school (if you want) but get an education. I want you to have all options available to you. Options I didn't have. And even options Aunt Rose didn't have, because of societal norms and laws written by men. Grrrr. Did you know that in 1965 women were typically fired from their jobs when they became pregnant? That women couldn't get prescriptions for birth control pills or get a diaphragm from their doctor unless they were married? Many banks also wouldn't let a woman get a credit card unless her husband co-signed. If you were unmarried, you were shit outta luck, as you like to say, Jo-Jo. And forget about trying to get a mortgage. Women couldn't even serve on juries because they were deemed too fragile. (I only did jury duty once, and maybe that last thing wasn't so terrible.)

Okay, I'll stop with the wisecracks.

Here's the bottom line: These days women can have it all and that's what I want for you. I want you capable of supporting yourselves so you can marry (if you want) for love and not because you need taking care of. I want you to be a mom (if you want) who also has options. I want you to have a job or a full-blown career (if you want), but to do any of these things, you need to get your degree. Do not, repeat, DO NOT let anyone or anything stop you or get in your way.

I started the journals that I've rubber-banded to this letter when you were 17 months, Jo-Jo. Your aunt Rose gave me the idea when she said she wished she knew more about our mom. So, here is the good, the bad, and the ugly. There are some things reported here that probably should have stayed private, or maybe I shouldn't have written about them at all, but I did. I wrote down things because sometimes, when I was confused, it helped give me clarity. Remember, I was young, so, so young when I got married and started our family. I not only didn't have all the answers, I sometimes didn't even know the right questions.

I debated going through these journals and ripping out some of the pages, particularly those that dealt with others, like Kathy and Betsy. They are the unwed mothers I write about in the early years, before you were even born, Jenny. Saying goodbye to Betsy really crushed me. Thank goodness for you, Jen-Jen, who came along soon after, so I couldn't dwell on how much I missed that girl. Even though she was only 15, she helped me to grow up in ways I didn't even realize at the time. I often wonder about her and what became of her life. ANYWAY: I decided to leave them in because, frankly, they're a big part of my story and an even bigger part of my growth. And that was the purpose of these journals. And by giving them to you now, I'm allowing you to know me, and who I was before your memories of me began. It's a side of me you didn't know, so please be forgiving and be discreet.

There are some ugly truths you'll find here, but mostly, I hope you see the beauty. I married as a naive young eighteen-year-old who was still more of a girl than a woman when I started my family, but somehow I grew up. We all did. Together.

Take good care of your dad, who was always a loving husband and was able to adapt and give me more freedom as I aged and helped me discover how to spread my wings. He married one woman, and over time, he found himself married to someone else. That's how much I changed. But that was also true for me. Your dad grew and I grew up—and we somehow managed to do it together. Having said that: If he finds love after I'm gone, don't you dare think you're being disloyal to me by welcoming whoever she is into our family. He deserves all the happiness he can grab onto. So do both of you!

I am so, so proud of the young women you've both become, and I just know you'll keep growing and blossoming. Just because you don't have flower names doesn't mean you aren't now, and won't forever be, my petite fleurs.

I love you, Jo-Jo.

I love you, Jen-Jen.

Go, do great things.

Be forever groovy and don't jujje each other. (At least not too much!)

Goodbye for now.

Love, love, love and smooches,

Mom

Author's Note

In 2022, when the US Supreme Court handed down the *Dobbs* decision, which took away the constitutional right to abortion, women began protesting. Many of their signs and chants contained variations of "We cannot go back!" While I agreed, I wondered, particularly about the young people. Did they even know what "going back" meant? That's when it hit me: During all the years when it mattered to me, *Roe* was the law of the land. Did *I* really understand what was at stake?

The penny dropped and it became part of the nexus for this novel.

When I was a young girl, probably under five years of age, we had an unwed mother living with us. We actually had a couple of them. Last year, when I asked my mom about the girl who made the most vivid impression on me, yet whom I barely remembered, my mom's memory wasn't much better than mine. Ah, but that's the joy of writing fiction.

In order to make the story flow in the way I desired—and in some cases, the way I needed it to—there are some things I deliberately altered or stretched:

- Joe South's amazing hit "Walk a Mile in My Shoes" didn't really come out until 1970. But come on! How perfect are those lyrics when you're writing about being judgmental?

- Similarly, Rose quotes from *The Tempest*: "I have been in such a pickle since I saw you last." In the play, being "in such a pickle" refers to a drunken (i.e., pickled) state, not to be in a bind, but it fit too well, so I used it anyway.
- The rubella outbreak was 1963–65. I moved it to 1966.
- *That Girl* first aired in September 1966; I moved it up so it could be on TV in February of that year.
- The Hong Kong flu hit the US in September of 1968, so I made that earlier, too.
- The Civil Rights Act of 1957 allowed women to serve on juries in federal courts, but it wasn't until 1973 that all states passed similar legislation. However, in Ohio, where *In the Family Way* takes place, women could serve during the '60s.
- The Voting Rights Act was signed into law in August 1965. In December, Robin is still encouraging people to come out and protest in support of the measure.

If you find other discrepancies, they were not intentional. Please know I tried my best, and I take full responsibility for any screwups. Here are some things about the 1960s that I didn't have to fudge:

- In the 1960s, there were more than two hundred homes for unwed mothers across forty-four states.
- During the "Baby Scoop" era (1945 to 1973), more than 1.5 million pregnant girls and women in the US were sent to maternity homes, where their children were put up for adoption.
- Many large hospitals created septic abortion wards to handle the number of women who had botched abortions.
- 80 percent of the women seeking abortions were married.
- Betty Friedan's *The Feminine Mystique* was published in 1963. It spurred the feminist awakening, which evolved into the "women's movement" and the National Organization for Women

(NOW). According to journalist and author Gail Collins, a conservative magazine put Friedan's book in their roundup of the "'ten most harmful books of the 19th and 20th centuries,' which if not flattering is at least testimony to the wallop it packed."

- Domestic abuse and rape by one's spouse were typically just swept under the rug.
- California was the first state to offer no-fault divorce, where you could just claim irreconcilable differences. That didn't occur until 1969.
- DES was given to women like Sarah. It was discontinued in 1971, when researchers discovered it increased some women's chances of developing cancer. Daughters who were exposed to DES in utero often struggled with specific cancers and/or infertility when they were older.
- In the 1960s, a bank could refuse to issue a credit card to an unmarried woman. Even if she was married, her husband was usually required to cosign. In 1974, the Equal Credit Opportunity Act allowed women to get credit cards separate from their husbands. It also allowed women to open their own bank accounts. (Technically, they could do this in the 1960s, but many banks still didn't allow it without a husband's signature.)
- 1974 is when women could (finally) get a mortgage. Before then, it was legal for banks to refuse loans to single women, or to require them to have a male cosigner.

HERE ARE SOME OTHER THINGS mentioned in *In the Family Way* that you might want to explore on your own:

- The 1965 Supreme Court case *Griswold v. Connecticut* (https:// www.thirteen.org/wnet/supremecourt/rights/landmark _griswold.html) allowed for married people to legally use

contraception. (Note the important word here is "married.")
If you were unmarried, you were out of luck.

- In 1965, CBS aired "Abortion and the Law" (https://
danratherjournalist.org/investigative-journalist/early
-reporting-cbs/abortion-and-law). This documentary was
hosted by Walter Cronkite. (Dan Rather was one of a handful
of other correspondents.) As you might guess, there was a
lot of backlash when the doc first aired, but there was also
enough praise (or CBS wanted to keep Uncle Walter happy)
that CBS aired it again a month and a half later.

Acknowledgments

It's not exactly news to acknowledge that writing is a solitary endeavor. By the time I've come up with an idea, developed it, written the first draft, revised it—again and again and again—it's easy to lose perspective. That's when it's especially valuable to have an experienced editor in your corner. Enter Sara Nelson (who, according to her, spells her name the right way, unlike my character of Sarah Bloom). Sara immediately understood what I was aiming for and suggested some subtle yet utterly brilliant ways to get there. Thank you, Sara, for your wisdom and for your gentle hand!

I am tremendously grateful to everyone at HarperCollins but most especially to: Edie Astley, for your help large and small; Joanne O'Neill, for such a stunning cover; my publicist, Rachel Elinsky; Katie O'Callaghan and Zaynah Amed, marketing gurus; Mary Beth Constant, my fastidious copyeditor; and Cathy Barbosa-Ross, who is helping put *In the Family Way* into the hands of readers around the globe. I would be remiss if I didn't also give a special shout-out to Jolene McGowan of Matchstick Communications, who designed my lovely website.

I also owe special thanks to each of my early readers: Deenie Ruzow, Sydney Milgrom, Marci Ungar, and (the eagle-eyed) Jamie Radwan. It was invaluable to get feedback from women across such a wide age range. Be forewarned: I'm coming back to each of you again for the next one! (File that under "No good deed goes unpunished.")

I needed input about spousal abuse and the divorce laws in Ohio in the mid-sixties. For that I turned to Randal Lowry and Suzanne Carlson (of Randal Lowry & Associates in Akron, Ohio), who got back to me right away and were most generous with their time. Thank you, thank you! If there are any legal errors in my novel, they're not to blame; it's completely on me.

Similarly, if there are medical mistakes, it's not the fault of Doctors Tanya P. Hoke (OB/GYN Specialists of the Palm Beaches; West Palm Beach, Florida) or Michael E. Yaffe, (Columbus, Ohio), who both made the time and took care to answer my medical questions in astonishing detail. I appreciate you both.

Speaking of appreciation, huge thanks to Marly Rusoff, who has changed the trajectory of my career, not once, but twice. You are a legend and a precious gift to the publishing world.

I owe a gigantic thanks to my agent, Celeste Fine, and the rest of the amazing team at Park & Fine Literary and Media, including Charlotte Sunderland and Andrea Mai. Whether the issue was big or small, there was always someone who could lend her expertise and/or problem-solve.

Celeste is so much more than my scrupulous, hard-working, always-on-top-of-everything, exactly who-you-want-in-your-corner agent. Over a decade ago, we were colleagues at a literary agency. Because we were so different in age, experience, and background, management figured that by putting us together—in a shared office, no less—we wouldn't cause any trouble. (More than a slight miscalculation.) I owe them a huge thank-you for introducing me to one of my best friends and trusted confidantes. Celeste, over the years we have shared too many life-cycle events to count, but I am beyond thrilled that we were able to take this ride together. One thing I know for sure: My world is abundantly richer because of you.

My world is rich in other ways, too. My kids! Their spouses! My grandchildren! Whitney, Rome, Nathan, Leora, Mitchell, and Kristen fill me with so much joy—as does my husband, Harold, who partnered with me to create this life. None of this would be possible if you and I weren't such darn good pickers! Extra thanks to Harold for always supporting my writing, (even when he hasn't read it yet), for getting me food whenever I need to "write through," and for understanding that coming into my office just to say hello is never, ever a good idea.

Finally, thanks to you, the readers. As I mentioned in my opening sentence, writing is solitary business. Being able to share my work with you is a thrill. I know you have many books to choose from; thank you for selecting this one.

Additional Reading & Resources

Do you want to know more about the issues covered in *In the Family Way*? Here are some suggestions for starting your journey:

Feminism

The Feminine Mystique, by Betty Friedan.

Good and Mad, by Rebecca Traister, which looks at women's anger from the suffrage movement through #MeToo.

When Everything Changed, by Gail Collins, begins in 1960 and ends in 2008, and covers women's lives pertaining to politics, fashion, popular culture, economics, sex, families, and work.

Unwed Mothers

The Girls Who Went Away, by Ann Fessler, is an oral history containing one hundred first-person accounts of girls who became pregnant out of wedlock and were sent away. Ms. Fessler did an hour-long interview about the legacy of her book (https://www.youtube.com/watch?v=LtSMKzAZ4cE).

Abortion

When Abortion Was a Crime, by Leslie Reagan, traces the history of abortion beginning in the mid-nineteenth century and ending with *Roe*, in 1973. It is an opportunity to learn how abortion was policed and criminalized—and how women got abortions anyway, regardless of their illegality.

Madame Restell, by Jennifer Wright, is a story about New York's most (in)famous abortionist.

The Trials of Madame Restell, by Nicholas L. Syrett, is also about the brave/brazen woman who advertised her services in the newspapers in the nineteenth century.

Domestic Violence

I Closed My Eyes: Revelations of a Battered Woman, by Michele Weldon, is a memoir about her nine-year marriage to an abusive husband and provides tremendous insight into the cycle of domestic violence.

Black and Blue, by Anna Quindlen, is a novel about spousal abuse. Though a work of fiction, it is illuminating and thought-provoking.

Organizations for Women's Reproductive Health

Planned Parenthood (https://www.plannedparenthood.org/)
National Women's Health Network (https://nwhn.org/)
Center for Reproductive Rights (https://reproductiverights.org/)
Reproductive Freedom for All (formerly NARAL Pro-Choice America) (https://reproductivefreedomforall.org/)

About the Author

LANEY KATZ BECKER is an award-winning author and writer. Her debut novel, *Dear Stranger, Dearest Friend*, was a Literary Guild alternate selection, recommended by *Library Journal*, and featured on CBS's *Saturday Early Show*, among other media outlets.

Laney is also the author of the nonfiction anthology *Three Times Chai*, a collection of rabbis' favorite stories. Her writing career also includes working as an award-winning advertising copywriter, freelance journalist, and, most recently, for more than a decade, as a literary agent.

When she's not writing, Laney enjoys drawing, sewing, reading, playing tennis, long walks (while listening to podcasts or audiobooks), and playing canasta. A native Ohioan, Laney is a graduate of Northwestern University. Although she lived in Westchester County, New York, for most of her adult life, she currently resides on the east coast of South Florida, where she lives with her husband and their Havanese. She has two married children and two grandchildren.

You can reach Laney through her website: laneykatzbecker.net